SKY CHASE

THE FLIGHT OF SHIPS
BOOK ONE

LAUREN MASSUDA

In memory of my friend, Jillian Harper

ACKNOWLEDGEMENTS

I would like to thank my friends, mentors, and family, especially my parents, Giselle and Kamal Massuda, who've always been supportive in my writing career; my sister, Stacey Massuda, who got me into fantasy; and my boyfriend, Mike Munoz, who always pulled me out of slumps whenever I had doubts about my writing.

I'd also like to thank everyone at Water Dragon Publishing. Getting a book published has always been my dream, and I'm still processing the fact that it actually happened.

1

– CORDELIA –

T HE HORN'S BELLOW STARTLED ME AWAKE, and I snatched my boots at the foot of the bed. When I heard Flint yelling, "The Black Sting has arrived!" in a booming voice, adrenaline pulsed through me and I was out the door, but not before grabbing my crossbow. I swiftly loaded the arrows and kicked open the door that led to the upper deck. The morning sunlight blocked my vision momentarily, but, when everything cleared, I turned to the rouge-colored sky.

The Black Sting, a giant manta ray, soared about fifty feet above me and my crew, who had all spread out amongst the deck. The creature flew straight into the clouds and disappeared momentarily before engulfing the airborne ship in its shadow. Its fins slapped the wind currents and caused the white sails of *The Raging Storm* to tousle wildly.

The Black Sting's long, slender tail swished from side to side, cutting through a cloud that swiftly dispersed at its touch. I turned to my crew members who had all gathered at the lower deck. They carried weapons that ranged from crossbows to swords.

I raised a hand and yelled: "Get into your stations! Fire at my command!"

"Yes, Captain!" the crew cried in unison.

The young men and women carrying crossbows hurried to the upper deck with me, while the others stood below in defensive stances. They raised their bows on accord and pulled back their postures slightly, awaiting my signal.

"Steady, steady!" I exclaimed.

The Black Sting swooped down, its fins expanded, gliding with the quick wind currents. Flint took the helm and veered the ship away, dodging the attack. The Black Sting swirled in a hastier circle, swooping around the rotating ship in a flash of blue and black. It released a screeching wail as it widened its oval-shaped mouth.

The Black Sting swept upward, spiraling like a whirlpool, going fasting and faster until I finally yelled, "Attack!"

Arrows ripped through the air in streaks of silver, flickering in the morning light. The arrows pierced the creature's skin and threads of blood spewed out. The creature screeched, swerving to the left as more arrows whizzed like a rain of needles.

The Black Sting ducked under the ship and shoved its body into the keel, causing the ship to jolt and tilt sharply to one side. The crew skidded back, but held tight to the railing before they could topple out.

"Steer her straight!" I exclaimed, clenching a banister.

Flint maintained a tight grip on the wheel before steering the ship back into place. Everyone else, once taking a split second to get composed, rushed back into their positions just as the Black Sting flipped back towards the ship. It spiraled in at an incredible speed as its tail whipped into the deck, ripping out pieces of wood.

"Keep shooting!" I shouted, aiming my own crossbow at the Black Sting and firing.

The creature attempted to dodge, but arrows rained through the air in every direction. The Black Sting screeched and blindly soared forward into the ambush. The weight of its wings struck the men and women, knocking them down, but those who sustained balance inflicted more damage upon the creature as it dove in one last attack. It thrashed its wing into one crewmember and knocked him over the deck's baluster.

"Mark!"

I rushed forward and grabbed his shirt before yanking him back on the ship. He stumbled to the floor, breathing fast while clutching his chest. Mark threw his head up at me. Relief washed over his freckled face "Th–thank you, Captain," he breathed out.

"Save the compliments for later," I said, and helped him to his feet.

"Y–yes, sorry," Mark rubbed the back of his head.

"Get back to your —" I paused as my attention flew to the sky. My blood ran cold.

The wounded creature fled the ship with its fins flapping frantically away. It soon disappeared behind the clouds, leaving behind wails that echoed throughout the spacious sky.

"It got away ..." Mark huffed. "What now, Captain?"

"We're going after it," I stated firmly and faced Flint at the helm. "Turn the ship around, we're going after the Black Sting!"

"Wait, Captain!" Eamon marched over to me, his olive skin glistening with sweat and his copper hair bouncing in the unceasing breeze. His dark green eyes were sunken with exhaustion.

But I pressed on and demanded, "Are you questioning my order, Eamon?"

My crew surrounded us in a wide semi-circle. They whispered amongst themselves, but I shot them a glare which settled them into silence.

"It's too late to catch up to the Black Sting," Eamon replied. "Besides, it's wounded and probably won't be able

3

to attack for some time. Another ship should be able to kill it soon. We're not the only ones sailing the sky."

I grimaced and said, "We've been tasked to kill the Black Sting. No one else was asked to do so. If another ship gets all the glory, we'll lose credibility."

"Captain," Eamon said with composure, closing his eyes. "I assure you: we won't lose any credibility. But if you really want to catch it … why don't we take a break now and search later? We've been searching for three weeks and I'm sure you and the rest of the crew would like a rest."

I stared wordlessly at Eamon for several seconds with furrowed eyebrows. I didn't want to stop searching, but everyone was clearly exhausted from the fight, and it didn't help that it was the brink of morning. I, too, was exhausted, but I certainly would not show it to my crew. Plus, we had to fix the ship, and I didn't want to deal with any more damage if it got hit again.

As I huffed out a sigh and rubbed a temple, tension eased off my shoulders and I waved a hand dismissively. "Fine. We'll head back home, but it'll only be a short time until we return to our task."

"Thank you, Captain," Eamon said. "We're sorry we weren't able to kill the Black Sting."

"The next time we find it, we officially end it," I proclaimed, gritting my teeth. "That creature has been terrorizing islands and destroying ships. If we don't kill it next time, more lives will be lost and it'll be our fault." I turned on my heel and headed back toward my cabin. My buckled boots clinked into the floorboard. While I walked, I called to Flint, "Turn the ship west. We're heading home."

"Yes, Captain." Flint nodded and maneuvered the great vessel of *The Raging Storm* in the opposite direction.

Before I settled into my cabin, I turned back to my crew below. I noticed no one had taken any major blows; they were all able to stand on their feet despite having bruises and cuts. But just in case, I asked, "Did anyone get hit by the tail's tip?"

"I got hit by the tail, but not the tip. I'm good though," Bernard said, feebly rubbing his side and flinching at the pain.

"All right," I said, and then noted the broken pieces of wood scattered on some portions of the deck. "Those who aren't injured fix up the ship; those who are, rest up."

"Yes, Captain!" the crew exclaimed in unison.

I nodded and shut the doors of my cabin behind me. Stained glass decorated the slightly arched ceiling, giving the octagon shaped room a bright, vibrant touch. Morning sunlight streamed through the glass and highlighted the map that filled the back wall. An oil painting of the world, it depicted the plethora of islands called the Caelum Islands, suspended above a field of clouds. There was no land below the clouds. The world was made of islands in the sky, and my home was Domus, the largest island. It rested right in the center of the painted map, with its named displayed in fancy cursive above.

The job of *The Raging Storm*, and dozens of other ships, was to protect these islands from creatures like the Black Sting and from criminals. Every ship had a captain to command, and I was the youngest one. I started my training when I was eight and I learned much quicker than anyone one else.

I finally became captain at age thirteen, and this accomplishment made my crew and I fairly renowned across the world. But despite that, my father was never keen about the idea of me becoming a captain. My mother once was, but she was killed when protecting Domus from an invasion years ago.

When I told Father I wanted to become captain, he was wary about my decision, even before Mother was killed. The job of a captain was dangerous, after all, but I constantly assured him I could handle it.

I sat at my desk and collected some letters that I had purposely neglected to read. I didn't regret my decision when I finally got around to reading them. They were all from my father. He meant well, but he worried way too much about me. Before I could read them more in depth, a knock sounded at the door, followed by Eamon's voice.

"Can I come in, Captain Cordelia?"

"Yes," I beckoned, though my attention was on the letters. I heard Eamon entering the office and then the soft click of the door closing.

"What is it, Eamon?" I asked.

"Nothing. I was checking to see how things were going."

"Not too good." I inhaled sharply, slapping the letters onto the desk.

"What's wrong?"

"My father." I leaned back in the chair, rubbing a temple. "He sent me tons of letters asking about my well-being. Plus, he tells me that Caleb's birthday's coming up and doesn't want me to miss it this time."

"Well, this is your family — of course your father would be worried. After all, you've been gone for almost a month, and you have a little brother, too. How old is he? Four?"

"Five. He'll be six in a week," I said briefly, adding more pressure to the temple.

"Oh, that gives us plenty of time to return home by then."

I sighed and ran a hand through my hair. "Yeah, yeah ... might as well head back before Caleb throws another tantrum. Little brat ..." I muttered the last two words under my breath, but Eamon caught them.

"You shouldn't call your brother that, Captain. He's only a kid."

"An annoying one at that," I spat. "You don't have any siblings, so you don't know what it's like to have a brother who's ten years younger than you."

"I do have a few younger cousins though," Eamon noted. "Perhaps going back home will make you feel better. It doesn't hurt to visit family every once in a while. Even if you don't always get along with yours, they're always there for you."

"You're so sappy, Eamon." I rolled my eyes. "Never mind. We'll head back home, stay for a while, and finish our job afterward."

"And how long would a while be?"

"I don't know ... a day?"

"I think everyone would want more than a day — how about a week?"

"A week is too long. Three days tops."

Eamon sighed, defeated. "Fine. Three days."

"Good," I said. "Is there anything else you want?"

"No, nothing, Captain," Eamon said. "I only wanted to check if things were well with you."

"Everything will be well once that creature is dead," I exclaimed.

"It will be done soon, Captain," Eamon said. "Would it help if I make you some tea? It'll calm your nerves."

"Hmmm ... I'd like that, actually," I considered with a small smile, then I added: "Make it mint."

"Sure." Eamon nodded.

While he walked off to make the tea, I leaned into my chair and caused it to tilt back. I closed my eyes, trying not to concentrate on anything while my focus latched onto the darkness within my eyelids. I inhaled and exhaled softly, and my body gradually relaxed. In the close distance, the sound of tea pouring into a cup comforted me, unlike the constant noise of my crew talking from outside. They were so loud, but soon their voices became nothing more but buzzes in my ears.

Soon the fresh scent of mint glided to my nose, and I opened my eyes. Eamon settled the cup of tea in front of me before taking a few steps back. My face lit up, and I picked up the cup. I sniffed it once more before taking a delicate sip.

"It's good," I commented.

"I'm glad to hear, Captain."

Eamon started to leave, but then paused as he took notice of my desk. Letters and papers were strewn all over its cherry wood surface, and crumpled up pieces of paper lay abandoned on the carpet. Books stood piled on one side of the desk while maps lay sprawled on another. The actual surface of the desk was barely identifiable due to all the supplies swarmed across it in a huge collision. I've told myself that I needed to clean the desk, but I've never gotten around to it since I'm always occupied with more important matters.

"Can you promise me something, Captain?" Eamon asked. His tone had gotten unusually quiet.

"What?"

"Don't do any more work for a while and sleep," Eamon instructed calmly. "It's not good for your health if you keep working nonstop."

I pursed my lips and took another sip. The warm liquid flowed down my throat, leaving behind a minty-sweet aftertaste. I glanced down at the remaining liquid. I vaguely saw my reflection swaying in the subtle motion of my hand moving the cup.

"Fine."

"You should also clean your desk," Eamon also suggested. "I don't think I've ever seen the surface."

I huffed and set the cup down with a soft clink. "Anything else before I kick you out?"

"Nothing," Eamon said. "I just want you to keep your promise."

"I said that I'd keep it, didn't I?"

"Yes, but —"

"You worry too much, Eamon." I got up from the chair and went over to rest a hand on his shoulder. "I'll rest and I'll clean up the desk. You should also get some sleep; there are circles under your eyes."

Eamon smiled. "I'll do that."

I patted Eamon's shoulder before rounding back to my desk. "If no storms come our way, we should be back home within two days. I'll reply back to my father and tell him we're heading home. We'll rest for three days, gather up supplies, and then return to the ship. After we kill the Black Sting, we'll come back home until our next task."

"Alright, I'll go inform the crew," Eamon said.

"Thank you." I smiled subtly and then waved him off. "You're dismissed."

Eamon saluted me before heading out of the cabin. I gazed up at the stained-glass ceiling before my eyes fell to the mess that was unfortunately my desk. I sighed and closed my eyes.

"Falling asleep would be easier than cleaning that desk," I muttered to myself.

My body relaxed into the cushion and tension eased from my muscles once I felt fully adjusted. The noise outside appeared to lessen.

"Finally, peace and —"

A shrill squeak interrupted my moment of bliss and my eyelids flew open. Eamon's pet ferret, Amabel, pounced onto the desk, causing papers to fly and a quill to roll off. The ferret continued to pounce until I grabbed it by the scruff of its neck. I shot up from my desk.

"Eamon!"

The doors flew open. Eamon burst in with a hand clutching his sword, as if some real danger had arose. But there was no danger, just an annoyance.

"What in the world is your ferret doing here?" I demanded, shoving the squirming rodent forward.

"I'm terribly sorry, Captain." Eamon hurried over and took the ferret into his arms. "I don't know how Amabel got in here."

"You need to keep an eye out," I retorted, glaring at the ferret that currently cuddled under Eamon's chin.

"Sorry, Captain," Eamon said, holding Amabel close to him. "I'll make sure she stays in my cabin."

"Good. Get back to your station. Now," I ordered.

"Yes, Captain." Eamon saluted me once more and quickly exited the cabin.

I huffed and glanced out of one of the windows. A speck of black flew in the distance like a fly crawling on the window's glass. My eyes squinted. I wondered if it was the Black Sting ... or perhaps it was something else. Either way, I knew I shouldn't dwell too much on it. I didn't want to hear anymore of Eamon's lectures.

2

– CORDELIA –

T HE RAGING STORM DOCKED AT THE PIER OF DOMUS. As the largest of the Caelum Islands, it stretched hundreds of miles and, from a bird's-eye view, vaguely formed the shape of a turtle. Its inhabitants lived in a town where rows and rows of white buildings stood coupled together. They all sat on the ledges of rocky cliffs that hovered over a good portion of the island. The buildings faced the west, and, when the falling sun hit them just right, the white bricks and stones glowed like precious gems protruding from the ragged rocks of the cliffs.

A stone lighthouse stood on top of the cliff. Its bright, white light that never died out could be mistaken for a star in the distance. On another cliff stood windmills with their wide, blue and white blades spiraling in slow circles. Colorful kites frolicked together in the sky, toppling and spiraling with the wind. Children raced down the winding cobblestone streets with their kites fluttering behind. The strings of their kites got tangled together, but the children paid no heed as they rushed to the pier. A large crowd of eager people gathered around the docked ship, and more of them came to see.

Most of the port's inhabitants sported bi-colored hair that clashed with their casual attire. The women wore silver bracelets that jingled melodically whenever they waved their hands. The men wore patterned handkerchiefs or scarves that were always played with by the wind. The colorful crowd cheered and waved as my crew and I left *The Raging Storm*.

I was the last to get off the ship since I had to make sure everything was settled. As I walked away, my breath got caught in my throat when I saw the large crowd before me. I froze for a moment before continuing onward, although my footing slowed as I tried to keep myself composed.

I had hoped that Father wouldn't tell everyone we were coming home today. I clutched my hand into a fist, but then uncoiled it and forced on a smile when I finally set foot on the pier.

"Welcome home!" the crowd cheered.

"How was your trip?"

"You're back sooner than we thought! Just as expected from *The Raging Storm*!"

"Did you bring back the Black Sting's head? Are you going to use it as a trophy?"

"That would make an excellent trophy!"

I grimaced at the last two remarks. Oh, of course, they thought we destroyed the Black Sting. *Great. Just Great.* I needed to have a talk with Father. I politely excused myself — trying my hardest not to be rude — and pushed my way from the crowd that nearly squished me. I fled to a clearer area and straightened my overcoat.

"Ah, Captain!"

Eamon came jogging with a young boy on his back. The boy waved a toy sword in his hand while he clung to Eamon's hair in the other. The paper hat that adorned the boy's head struggled to stay in place. A huge smile brightened Eamon's face, despite the boy yanking his hair.

"Captain, this is my cousin, Diedrick," Eamon said. "He's a big fan of yours."

"Oh?" I raised an eyebrow and leaned forward, peering at the boy whose bright green eyes sparked enthusiasm. "Are you interested in becoming a captain when you grow up?" I asked.

"I wanna be part of your crew!" Diedrick exclaimed.

I smirked. "Maybe someday."

"I wanna be one now! I've been training!" Diedrick demonstrated by swinging his toy sword around, nearly hitting Eamon in the face.

"That's enough, Dee," Eamon insisted, getting the boy off his back. "There are years of training before you can be part of the crew."

"But I wanna fight!"

Eamon fixed the paper hat on Diedrick's head and kept a hand on it. "Now is not the right time — you still have a lot to learn. Even the captain and myself had a lot to learn when I was your age."

Diedrick glanced over to me, and then back to his cousin. He stuck out his bottom lip and tilted his head. "Really?"

"Yes," Eamon said.

Diedrick saluted me on his tippy toes, trying to make himself look tall. "I'll become part of your crew soon, Captain! It may not be now, but it will happen! And I'll be really strong by then!"

I smiled slightly. "I'll look forward to that."

Diedrick grinned fully, revealing two missing front teeth. "Great!" he exclaimed, and then took Eamon's hand, giving it a little tug. "Can you and the captain come for dinner? Mama is gonna make broccoli and cheese all stuffed in potatoes!"

"That sounds good," Eamon agreed. "How about you, Captain?"

"Father probably wants to see me tonight. It would have to be another time," I remarked. I also wasn't a fan of cheese.

"Oh, okay," Diedrick pouted, sticking out his lower lip again. "Maybe tomorrow?"

"I can't say," I said, and then paused, frowning. "Speaking of Fathers ... excuse me."

I walked through the crowds of people before I saw him.

"Father," I said briefly.

"Ah, Cordelia!" My father, Mayor Thomasthan, threw his pudgy arms around me and gave me a squeeze. "Oh, how I missed you! How was your trip?"

"Alright, can you let go?" I asked, trying to nudge myself out of his embrace.

"Certainly, certainly, ah-ha." Father chuckled and twirled his vibrant orange mustache with a finger.

"I see you decided to tell the entire town that we were coming back today," I muttered, crossing my arms.

"Of course, I had to tell everyone!" Father exclaimed. "We've all missed you!"

"It's only been three weeks."

"They were a long three weeks!"

"I'm sure you all could adjust for that long; you know we've been gone longer."

"Yes, but it's always good to see you all back safe and sound," Father stated.

"How has it been here, anyway?" I asked.

"Oh, same old, same old. Nothing much has happened since you left." Father's jolly voice blended well with the distant laughs and chatters from the crowd.

We walked down the pier, but Father paused, tapping his chin.

"Well, unless you count our neighbor, Earnest, losing his glasses again. Poor ol' chap, he always loses those. But I'm sure he'll find them, eventually. If not, I'll buy him another pair."

Father chuckled briefly, but I just shook my head.

"At least the island's safe, that's all that matters," I remarked.

"Yes, all is well, all is well," Father said.

We exited the pier and walked down a narrow cobblestone road, where we found one of the oldest citizens, Rebecca, walking her pet tortoise across the street. I believed she named him Phillip. Odd name for a tortoise. When Rebecca saw us, a smile spread across her wrinkled face.

"Oh, hello, Mayor, and welcome back, Captain. I'm so glad to see you safe and sound."

"Good afternoon, Rebecca." Father tipped his feathered top hat. "Mind if I pet Phillip?"

"Of course, Mayor, of course," Rebecca agreed and faced the tortoise. "Say 'hi' to the mayor, Philip."

Philip squawked in response.

Father hurried over to pat the tortoise's head. Philip nestled his head into Father's palm, who chuckled gleefully. "He's certainly delightful."

"Thank you, Mayor. Have a good day, and you too, Captain," Rebecca said, now facing me. "You should come over to my place sometime and have some of my home-made almond cookies. Phillip helps me bake them." She patted Phillip's head. "Isn't that right, Phillip?"

Phillip responded with another squawk.

"Uh, sure," I said, not knowing how else to respond.

"I look forward to it. Good day." Rebecca bowed and continued her exceptionally slow walk down the street.

"We should really get a tortoise," Father said.

"Go ahead, I'm barely home, anyway." I shrugged indifferently.

"Do you know what Caleb wants?" Father inquired. "He wants a whale. I told him that wouldn't be possible, but he keeps telling me he'll take good care of it and feed it every day and —"

"Can we please change the subject?" I asked.

We were now walking up a steep slope and passed by some small houses, on which the windowsill of each sat lit candles. A couple of their owners either swept the doorsteps or watered plants. They waved at us before resuming their tasks.

"Ah, right," Father agreed and then let out a small gasp. "Oh, how was battling that terrible Black Sting? None of you are hurt, right?"

"No, we're all good," I said. "But unfortunately, we weren't able to kill the Black Sting. It got away." I then muttered under my breath, "You told everyone that we killed it, didn't you?"

"No, I told them you were coming home, but I guess they'd assumed that you killed it. You are part of *The Raging Storm*, after all. But I'm also quite surprised ... I also assumed that you killed it." Father scratched under his chin and pursed his lips. "You've always completed the tasks successfully —"

"I know, and that's why we need to return to the sky as soon as possible," I exclaimed, raising my voice a little, but not too loud that it would catch anyone else's attention. "Right now, we're taking a break, but only for a while. We're going to finish the job and I can't have anyone know that we haven't killed that creature yet."

"Cor–"

"Cora!"

A flash of red flew into me, nearly throwing me off my feet. Caleb picked his head up and smiled up towards me.

"Welcome back!"

I reluctantly patted Caleb's head before lightly nudging him off me.

"Yes, I'm back."

"Did you get me a present?" Caleb asked, bouncing a little.

An orange scarf hung loosely over his shoulders and it bounced with him. His brown boots padded into the ground, creating a soft beat. Caleb's hair, his most distinctive feature, practically blazed like fire when the sun's light got lost in it.

I dug into my pocket and tossed Caleb a couple of coins that he caught. Caleb's mouth formed an 'o' and he whistled.

A delicate and talented hand had etched a detailed design of whales into the coins.

"Cool!" Caleb exclaimed. "Where did you get 'em?"

"They're from the Western Isles. We passed by them while heading back here. Buy anything you want with them," I told him.

"Awesome! Thank you!" Caleb exclaimed. "I dunno what to buy, so I'll keep them for good luck!"

"Sure, go ahead." I shrugged and my attention focused on the sky. I saw nothing, but my paranoia didn't cease.

3

– EAMON –

D IEDRICK DRAGGED ME INTO HIS HOME, where his twelve siblings were apparently waiting for us. When they saw me, they immediately tackled me to the ground. They laughed as they tried to hug me to death, and I couldn't help but smile, but I needed to breathe.

"Oh, Eamon!" Aunt Lulu's voice rung, but was drowned out by her children's squeals. "Kids, please get off your cousin."

"Yes, Mama!" The kids hopped off and gathered themselves at my aunt's side.

Aunt Lulu shook her head and sighed. "I am so sorry, Eamon."

"It's all right, Auntie," I said with a chuckle. "How are you doing?"

"Very well. Dinner should be ready soon. Mind helping me set up the table?"

"Sure." I nodded and followed Aunt Lulu into the kitchen.

The kitchen was so spacious that a tree had grown in its center where a marble island surrounded it. Fifteen stools stood at the island and all the children hopped over. I helped Aunt Lulu set down utensils and plates, and my cousins bounced on the stools, awaiting their food. They looked over at their mom with such enormous eyes that I was sure that they were going to pop out. Aunt Lulu didn't seem to mind as she hummed a little tune to herself with a smile lighting her face.

"Ah, Eamon, dear." Aunt Lulu turned to me. "Do you want to see if your parents would like to join us for dinner?"

"I did but, um ..." I paused and whispered in my aunt's ear, "they didn't want to deal with thirteen kids. They like it quiet."

"Oh," Aunt Lulu pouted. "But Aster, Amber, Odette, Georgy, Georgiana, Diedrick, Laurel, Zack, Phillipe, Penelope, Bastion, Basil, and Baster are well-behaved kids."

"Yes, they are, but there is a reason why I'm an only child," I said.

I was so sure we've had this conversation before. Aunt Lulu was always convincing my mom to get more kids, but, apparently, I was such a troublemaker when I was younger that my parents refused to go through the trauma again.

Aunt Lulu cupped a chin with her ring hand. "That is such a shame ... Anyway, how is the captain and the rest of your crew doing?"

"They're good, though, the captain is a bit stressed ..."

"I'm not surprised," Aunt Lulu said. "She has such a huge responsibility for her age. Do you ever get vacation days?"

"Yes, but they're short," I said.

"Well, when you do get a vacation again, I suggest going to Soarum Island. There's a great resort there where you're served passion fruit, pineapple and coconut smoothie, and it's the best drink — wait, it has alcohol in it. Well, I guess being part of such a famous crew will give you leeway." Aunt Lulu giggled.

"I don't think so."

"Oh, come now, you all are free to take down awful monsters, but you can't have alcohol? That's ridiculous."

"I'll be turning eighteen in two years. I can wait," I said with a shrug, but Aunt Lulu rolled her eyes and dropped the subject.

"I still think you all should have longer vacation days. It's not good for your health if you keep doing your job all the time."

"I've tried telling the captain that," I said, "but she won't want us to stop until the task is done."

"Well, you've all defeated the Black Sting, right? You all should be able to take a long break now."

"Yeah ..." I trailed and then turned to the oven where smoke spewed.

"Fire!" The triplets, Bastion, Basil, and Baster collectively flailed their arms up.

"Oh, no!" Aunt Lulu hurried to turn off the oven and brought the food out.

Fortunately, the food wasn't burnt that much, but my aunt still looked distraught. She loved cooking, and having any of her food burnt practically meant the end of the world for her. But even though the food was just a tad burnt, it still tasted good, and I thanked her for the meal.

In the middle of eating, Uncle Vinci arrived home from work and, just like his children, tackled me in a great bear hug. "What a surprise to see you, Eamon!" Uncle Vinci exclaimed as he smothered me in his bulky arms. "Welcome, welcome!"

"It's nice to see you too, Uncle," I coughed, struggling to breathe. I was sure my face was turning purple.

"Dear, Eamon is about to lose air," Aunt Lulu remarked, though she was clearly finding this amusing, considering the smile crossing her face.

Uncle Vinci gratefully released me, but slapped my back as he burst out a laugh. "So, Eamon, how has it been? Haven't seen you in quite a while."

"I'm well," I said and cleared my throat. I was sure Uncle broke something.

"Good, very good. Hey, do want us to call your parents and have them come over?"

Aunt Lulu groaned. "Selene and Glenn prefer to eat in silence, apparently."

"Really? I didn't know ..."

"I'm fairly sure my parents have said that," I piped in.

"They just don't understand how wondrous it is to have more than one child," Aunt Lulu said. "Anyway, my dear, you must eat before the food gets cold. And, Eamon, since your parents won't be joining us, would they like to take some food home?

"Yes, thank you." I smiled. I couldn't say no to my aunt. She gladly piled the food into a container and handed it to me.

"There you go. Oh! Do you want any cookies? I baked some yesterday and there's still a couple left."

Diedrick piped in, "I thought you said they were all gone!"

"The ones that are left have raisins in them," Aunt Lulu remarked, but whispered in my ear, "They don't, actually."

I smiled, even though Aunt Lulu baked and cooked a lot, she made sure that all her children don't get fat. She would go berserk if that ever happened, so she made them exercise by running from their house all the way to the lighthouse every morning. She convinced me to come along one time too, and, of course, it rained that day. It was fun, though. Diedrick was the fastest of his siblings and almost beat me. He wanted to be part of our crew when he grew up, and I wouldn't at all be surprised if he made it. It would be pretty cool if he joined us.

Aunt Lulu collected the cookies, tied them up in a bag with a bow, and handed them to me.

"There you go dear, tell your parents we said 'Hi'."

"I will, thank you."

4

– MARK –

M Y FAMILY WASN'T HOME. It would've been nice to see them after being gone for three weeks, but I suppose I'd see them later. Still, it would've at least been nice if they greeted me when we arrived back here.

I entered my house and glanced at the empty foyer before me. I never enjoyed walking into an empty house. It was so quiet and dark. Even when I switched on the lights, there was still an unwelcoming silence and made me slouch.

I wandered into the kitchen and switched on those lights as well. Checking to see if there were any snacks, I picked out a bag of chips and tossed a few in my mouth. The saltiness was a delight for my tongue, and, as I munched, I circled the kitchen and winded up the stairs that led to my bedroom.

Switching on that light, I found that my room had been cleaned up. The books in the bookshelves were all lined up in alphabetical order, the walls were repainted since the old paint had been chipping off (it was now a clearer blue), and my bed was made with brand new covers. I assumed Mom did this since she was passionate about cleaning. Though, there were some things that she wouldn't touch, like my lighthouse clock that sat next to my lamp. Mom had called it cheap and tacky looking, but she knew how much I liked it, so she never threw it away.

The clock was ceramic dyed in red and white paint. It produced a little ticking sound and, when the arms met the hour, the lantern flashed a light several times, depending what hour it was.

Out of boredom, I watched the seconds tick away while finishing up the chips. When I finished, I crumpled up the bag and tossed it away in the trash. I should probably cook myself something for dinner soon and drink something too. The saltiness of the snack burnt my tongue a little. It tasted good, though; couldn't deny that. Still, I really should cook something. Can't just be eating bags of chips all night.

Before I headed out, I tossed off my boots. I should've taken them off earlier, since pebbles somehow got stuck in them and had jabbed at my toes. How did they even get in there, anyway? I inspected the boots and noted the small holes punctured at their soles. They probably appeared during the Black Sting's attack. I shuddered by the memory. My life had practically flashed before my eyes when I toppled from the ship.

Thankfully, the captain saved me. I definitely owed her something, but I didn't know what. Perhaps I could give her a gift. Maybe a necklace? No, she didn't wear necklaces, or that much jewelry for the matter. I don't know; maybe I could ask Eamon what she'd like. He knew her better than everyone since he was the chief mate.

As my mind drifted to what gifts I could give the captain, I rummaged into my closet in search for boots. However, I couldn't find a pair suited for trips on *The Raging Storm*. The boots I needed had to be sturdy enough that they could withstand momentum during attacks and not tear easily. Well, I guess I needed to buy new ones.

•   •   •

The shoemaker's shop was right in the middle of town, next to the square. Sculptures of shoes stood around the bricked building, giving the place a fun and unique touch. Above the wooden doors a wooden sign said: Jim-Jim's Shoe Palace. It was a fairly small shop, so the irony in its name was amusing.

As I entered the store, a bell announced my presence. The owner of the shop, Jim-Jim, poked his head out from around one aisle. His bright and bushy greenish blue beard always made him distinguishable from the muted colored shoes lined up at every corner of the shop. He also wore a top hat that sported a different bow practically each day. Today, the bow had polka-dots on them.

"Ah, Mark! Welcome! What can I do for you this fine evening?" Jim-Jim asked in a deep, but friendly tone.

"Hi, Jim-Jim. I'm looking for new boots, similar to these ones." I brought out my old pair from my bag and showed him.

Jim-Jim studied them before snapping his fingers. "I got just the pair, come around back." Jim-Jim led me to a back aisle where a variety of boots were stacked. As he searched about, he told me, "It's great to have you all back. How did the fight go with that Black Sting fella? Bet it was tough, right? Hey, how's the captain? She didn't look too happy when you guys came back."

"She's tired; it's been a long trip," I only said. I didn't want to go further into the conversation, but Jim-Jim was eager to chat.

"Mmmm, don't blame her," Jim-Jim said, "I'd be pretty tired out too if I had a job like that. I wonder how you guys do it."

"A lot of training," I simply answered.

"I see, I see." Jim-Jim stroked his beard. "You know, you all should be proud for what you do for us. There should be a holiday dedicated to you guys or something."

"I don't think that would be necessary, but thank you."

"No, no, thank you — ah, here we are." Jim-Jim pulled out a pair of black boots with buckles strapped to them.

I tried them on and they fitted perfectly. "They're great, I'll buy them."

"Very good."

Jim-Jim took the boots to the register, and I paid for them. They were a tad expensive, but I needed them anyway.

I exited the shop and traversed along the cobblestone path, listening to the way my new boots hit against the stones and crunched upon fallen leaves. It was pleasant and made me relaxed. I couldn't be happier spending these next few days of leisure.

As I walked, I watched as couples took strolls nearby and children raced one another. The sun went down and hung just below some cream-colored clouds. Birds flew right over the white buildings, and dogs barked as they attempted to chase them. One neighbor ran to chase their dog down.

I moved to the square where our tallest clock tower stood at its very center. Made from tin and copper, its hands were made of bronze. The clock struck six as the biggest hand slide over to its smaller counterpart. Three small compartments on the clock's face opened and little figurines popped out holding bells in their hands. The figurines rung their bells six times before returning to their compartments.

I sat at the stone bench that circled the clock tower. Glancing up, I saw more birds flying overhead, but this time they carried rolls of paper in their beaks. They were delivering messages to and from the post office just around the corner. And above those birds the stars were peeking out. It made me think about all the undiscovered places we've yet to explore, and where we would go from there. Right now, I was contented to be where I was at the moment.

5

– CORDELIA –

I VORY LIGHT BLOSSOMED from the two-tiered chandelier. The remnants of the sun dripped through the tall windows and splashed into the foyer. Paintings of lighthouses and flowery fields decorated the walls and climbed up to the oval ceiling.

One of our servants greeted us at the double doors, bowing his head and announcing that dinner was going to be ready soon. Father and Caleb thanked the servant while I walked by and climbed up the stairs to my room. I stated that I was going to change and be back down shortly.

I switched on an oil lamp and the room was suffused in a faint caramel tint. The glow washed over the white paneled walls where several maps hung. A clock in the guise of a compass faced the four-poster bed. It ticked quietly in the room; a hypnotizing sound that could lull anyone to sleep. A wooden carving of a ship hovered from the sky painted ceiling. Tiny wires locked onto each corner of the ship, holding it perfectly still in the air.

I fell back on my bed, sighing at the familiar comfort. Sinking into the mattress, I stretched out my arms while my legs slouched over the bed. I lifted my head to the ship figurine before turning on my side. After kicking off my boots, I folded my knees over to my stomach. Despite that, my body was finding rest, but my mind wasn't. I was plagued with thoughts about the crowd earlier, and of the Black Sting.

We should've gone after that creature …

If I hear another person congratulating me, I'm going to explode, I bitterly thought, crushing the sheets with the impact of my hands.

Just calm down, calm down … we'll get it later.

Rolling to another side of the bed, I pressed my body further into it. I chewed on my lip and emitted a groan.

But what if we don't?

I rolled on my stomach, face-planting into the bed.

Shut. Up. We're going to kill that creature soon. Right now, relax. Just relax.

I rolled over one last time and was now on my back. My body spread out and my focus returned to the floating ship.

I'm trying to relax … but I can't when that creature is still out there.

I sat up on my bed and shut my eyes, massaging my temples.

"And I don't want to fail …"

"Cordelia?"

Father knocked on my door before his head peeked through the doorway.

"Your dinner is going to get cold. You should come down and eat."

"Fine," I said and rose to my feet. I went over to my dresser, plucked out my earrings and placed them in a small jewelry box.

"Is something the matter?" Father asked.

I slammed the jewelry box shut with a sharp snap. My father flinched at the sound, and his hand that locked onto the doorknob trembled. I released my hands from the box; they were trembling too, but I stepped back so I touched nothing else.

"I'm just a bit stressed, that's all," I said.

"It's about the Black Sting, isn't it?" Father guessed.

I nodded, facing away from my father, and turned my attention to one map on the wall.

Father walked over to me and placed a hand on my arm. He gently patted it and glanced up at me. He was tiny compared to me; I always stood tall and stiff, but right now my posture was almost breaking from how unsteady I stood, as if I was going to collapse. Father continued to pat and hold my arm as a means of support.

"Cordelia," Father's jovial tone descended to a softer tone, "you are a brilliant young lady, but sometimes a brilliant mind can be overwhelmed, and that's understandable. This job is not easy, you will always face obstacles, but sooner or later you will overcome them. Right now, I want you to settle down, come downstairs and eat dinner.

"We'll talk more about this after you've eaten. Or better yet, tomorrow when you're fully rested. Okay?" Father insisted, pulling up a tiny smile that was partially visible through his mustache. His gray eyes appeared to smile as well, and they gleamed by the oil lamp.

I inhaled through my nostrils and gave myself a moment. *Relax ...*

I exhaled, shutting my eyes and opening them to face my father. I gave him a small nod and headed out of the room.

"Fine ... we'll talk about it tomorrow."

"Good, excellent," Father said and followed me down the hall. "You're going to love tonight's dessert. It's your favorite: strawberry parfait! Now that should cheer you up!" Father patted his potbelly and released a short laugh.

We entered the dining hall, where Caleb bounced on his chair with a knife and fork in hand.

"Awesome! Cora finally came down, now we can eat!"

Caleb stabbed a large piece of ham with a knife and tossed it into his mouth, but he had trouble chewing it. His face contorted and his eyes twitched, struggling to tear the ham into smaller pieces and swallow.

"Caleb! Let me cut your food first!" Father cried, grabbing his head.

"Em ungy!" Caleb slurred, his face repeatedly puffing and deflating like a balloon. His eyes watered after nearly choking on a piece, but regained color as he continued his scuffle.

"Don't talk with your mouth full!" Father rushed to Caleb's side and grabbed his napkin. He held the napkin under Caleb's chin while also supporting his back. "Spit out the ham. Now."

"*Mmm, mmm!*" Caleb frantically shook his head, his cheeks puffed up once more.

"Caleb!"

"*Mmm–!* Ugh! Ah!" Caleb choked up again and eventually spat out the meat before he turned into a cherry. Caleb gasped for air and grabbed a glass of water. He slurped down the liquid before slumping over the table, spilling out incoherent words about his near demise.

"Don't ever do that again, Caleb. Please let me or a servant cut your food first," Father insisted, clutching his chest as if he was going to have a heart attack.

I rolled my eyes and sat at the farthest end of the table. I glanced down at my plate that contained ham, rice, and vegetables.

Can I return home once with none of this commotion starting? I asked myself. *Maybe I should've gone over to Eamon's ... wait, no, he's with his little cousins. No doubt they would act the same as Caleb.*

"Ah, Cora! Cora!"

"What?" I muttered, glaring over to my brother, who had apparently forgotten about his near-death experience.

"Tell us 'bout your fight with the Black Sting! Did anyone get hit with its tail and die?"

"Caleb —" I started, but Father held out a hand and patted Caleb's hand.

"Cordelia is not in the mood to talk about her travels right now," Father said.

"But I wanna know 'bout the tail!" Caleb cried with much enthusiasm.

I huffed. "If I tell you, will you be quiet afterwards?"

"Yup!"

"Well," I fiddled with my fork before aiming it upwards. The silver glistened vaguely from the chandelier hanging from the arched ceiling. "The very tip of the Black Sting's tail is the deadliest part of the body. If you've taken a direct hit from it, then the Black Sting's poison seeps into you and slowly causes your body to turn as dark as coal."

"And then you die?"

"Yes, but it's a slow and painful process ... Depending how strong someone is, it could take days or even weeks before the poison takes you over."

"Ooh, have you ever seen it happen?"

"No, but I heard about it," I said dryly. "What brought you to ask about the tail, of all things?"

"It's cool!"

"Humph, it wouldn't be cool if you were poisoned. Considering how small you are, you wouldn't survive longer than —"

"Ahem!" Father loudly cleared his throat. "Can we please not spoil our meal with such a gritty subject?" he pleaded, darting his eyes between Caleb and then I.

"He started it." I jabbed a thumb to my brother.

Caleb stuck out his tongue in response.

"I don't care who started it. Let's stop talking about it," Father remarked sternly.

"Whatever." I rolled my eyes and started cutting my ham.

I chewed slowly. Unlike Caleb, who acted like he was in a competition. He unceremoniously chomped into the meat while Father repetitively told him to slow down or else he'd choke again. I rubbed a temple and shut my eyes; Caleb's obnoxious chewing was driving in a headache.

"All done!" Caleb exclaimed, freely dropping his knife and fork onto his now empty plate.

"Be careful with the silverware, Caleb!" Father cried, grabbing the utensils to make sure there weren't any marks.

"Can we have dessert now, Dad?" Caleb asked with an innocent gaze. He clapped his hands and shuffled in his chair eagerly.

"After you promise me, you won't eat so sloppily again," Father instructed, waving a finger in the air.

"Pro~mise!" Caleb sung.

Lying little brat.

"Fine, fine ... but I really want you to eat slower. You don't want to hurt yourself," Father said.

"Yeah."

Caleb tilted his head to the side, glancing over Father's shoulder to see Chef Javas bringing out a trolley with tea and strawberry parfait. Caleb bounced off his chair — nearly knocking it over — and rushed to the trolley.

"Ah, Master Caleb." The chef halted the trolley in front of the excited boy. "Happy as always. Would you mind if I serve the first parfait to Mistress Cordelia? It is her favorite dessert after all, and I'm sure I —"

"Just give the first one to Caleb before he explodes," I snapped.

I directed the chef's attention toward Caleb, who wouldn't stop bouncing and panting like a dog. A thin trail of drool seeped through Caleb's widened mouth and his clasped hands shook. Chef Javas blinked, pursing his lips for consideration, but turned back to me.

"Are you sure, madam?"

"Do I have to repeat myself?" I threw a glare, and he shuddered.

"No, madam, I apologize."

Chef Javas quietly served our desserts before briskly heading back into the kitchen.

Father tapped his fingers onto the table while glancing over at me. "That was rude, Cordelia," he said.

I sipped my tea until there was nothing left. I set the cup down and picked up a small silver spoon.

"I simply told the chef to do a job — that was it."

"It wasn't necessary," Father stressed. "You can't act like you can say whatever you want and get away with it just because you're a captain. You're at home, not on your ship."

"I'm well aware of that, Father."

"Please be more mindful of what you say," Father insisted, trying his hardest not to raise his voice.

"Fine, whatever." I stabbed the spoon through the creamy substance of the dessert.

"I'm serious, Cordelia," Father stressed and turned to Caleb. "And you need to be respectful as well, Caleb. You have to be patient and courteous to others, all right?"

"Yeah!" Caleb exclaimed.

"Good, good, now that that's settled." Father picked up his spoon and dug out a giant strawberry. "Let's finish up our meal —"

"Yay —"

"— quietly," Father emphasized, briefly giving Caleb a side-eye.

"Ah ..." Caleb nodded, slowly comprehending, but I knew that Caleb had the attention span of a bird that flew into the same window too many times.

I rolled my eyes and finally got into my dessert. The vanilla cream cheese melted in my mouth, and the addition of fresh strawberries enhanced its sweetness.

Before I knew it, the silver glass that the dessert came in was empty. I placed the spoon down, wiped my mouth, and scooted back my chair.

"I'll be excusing myself now," I said before getting up and walking out of the dining hall.

•   •   •

Fireflies sprung out from their hiding places like tiny fireworks, bursting in flashes of gold and white. The tiny creatures glided under the canopy of stars, whizzing around the garden of tulips that blanketed the backyard.

I watched the fireflies from my balcony. They skipped along the tulips like little dancers performing for the moon that hung right above the lighthouse. The bright beam from the tall stone structure circled about, streaming light across the sky like a shooting star that never stopped soaring.

I wore a robe over my nightgown to shelter myself from the chilly night air. My hair lay draped over my shoulder and the chilly breeze gently played over it. I brushed a few strands back when they got into my face and placed a hand on the balcony's ledge. My fingers tapped a small beat into the marble, but paused when I heard the pitter-patter of small feet approach me from behind.

"Cora?"

Caleb stood at the doorway, carrying both a large stuffed whale and a picture book. His orange pajamas stood out against the shadowed doorway. His abundance of red hair consumed his head, proving that he had already rolled around in bed too many times.

"It's late, Caleb. Go back to bed," I told him.

"I can't sleep ... Can you read me and Blubby," Caleb limply waved the whale, "a bedtime story?"

I huffed and slapped a hand to my hip. "Fine, but just one story. What's it about?"

Caleb handed me the book.

I read the title, "'The Great Adventure of the Elphida'? What's that? A type of fish?"

I raised an eyebrow, now staring down at the cover. A group of little kids raced across a golden wheat field.

"No!" Caleb burst into a laugh, clutching his stomach. "It's an animal that grants wishes!"

He took back the book and opened it to the first page. It showed a peculiar-looking creature with antlers that lay partially hidden within a large, golden mane. White feathers covered the creature's ridged body, supported by eight long legs. Three glassy violet eyes stared back at me.

I frowned back at it. "It looks strange ..."

"It's really cool! It lives on an island far away where there are rivers of honey and the trees are blue and grow giant, juicy fruit that are this big!" Caleb stretched out his arms for emphasis.

I rolled my eyes. "That sounds ridiculous."

"But you travel to many, many different islands! And see many, many creatures! You must've seen something that's like this!" Caleb pointed out and handed back the book.

I flipped through the pages and shook my head while I grimaced.

"No. This is just a fairy tale to make kids like you feel happy and hope that they can get some dumb wishes. What would you even want, anyway?"

"More coins!" Caleb remarked while throwing Blubby in the air. He caught the stuffed whale and hugged it. "What would you wish for, Cora?"

"I don't have anything," I said.

"Oh, c'mon! You gotta have something!" Caleb insisted, bouncing on his feet. His orange slippers patted softly into the marble.

"Wishes are for kids, Caleb. I'm not a kid anymore."

Caleb pouted and mumbled into the stuffed animal. "That doesn't mean there's nothing you want. There has to be something."

I puffed out some air and crossed my arms, glancing ahead to see the fireflies still frolicking in the moonlight. The tiny specks of gold and white spiraled upward before gliding through the many tulips.

"Something I want ..."

I turned my attention to the town sleeping on the cliffs. The houses were bathed in the moon's blue and silver rays, and all the lights were out. Nothing had stirred, and everything was settled in a peaceful stillness. This silence pleased me, and I couldn't help but smile faintly. My back was turned on Caleb so he couldn't see my smile.

"I guess ..." I started, my voice lowering to a gentler tone as my focus stayed on the town. "I guess I'm afraid of failing, and I don't want that to happen."

"Why do you think you would fail?" Caleb asked, blinking curiously. "Aren't you one of the best captains?"

"I'd like to think so, but —"

"I think you're a great captain!" Caleb cheered. "You have nothing to worry 'bout. The island will always be safe as long as you're around, right? Right?"

"Yeah ..."

My attention stayed on the sleeping town. A light flickered on in one window. Its bright orange light stood out amongst the moon's rays. I watched that light for some time before turning back to Caleb.

"It's getting late, let's get to bed," I said.

"But what about the story?" Caleb whined.

"I'll read it to you tomorrow. Right now, I'm exhausted."

"Mmm," Caleb pouted, emitting a whiny sound. "Can I sleep in your bed then?

"No."

"Please? I haven't seen you in a while and I missed you," Caleb remarked pleadingly. "Sometimes I sleep in your bed when you're gone ..."

"You sleep in my bed?" I asked slowly, gritting my teeth, but my anger subsided when I saw the glum look in Caleb's eyes.

"Yeah ... I get lonely," Caleb mumbled. "Can I please sleep with you tonight? It'll be a big help. Just for tonight? Please?"

Caleb widened his eyes and puckered his lips together, attempting to look like a lost puppy needing a home. The little boy stood on his tippy toes, hugging his stuffed whale so hard that its beady eyes looked like they were going to pop out.

"Fine," I groaned, running a hand through my hair. "Just don't end up rolling on top of me."

"Yay! Thanks!" Caleb cheered, bouncing about.

"Yeah, yeah, c'mon," I said, and Caleb immediately bounded back inside.

I gave one last solemn glance to the town before heading back as well. The bright light from the window flickered off.

6

– CORDELIA –

M Y EYELIDS CRACKED OPEN, but I quickly closed them when the sun's light hit my face. I groaned into my pillow before finally giving in and pushing my upper body up. I wearily glanced around and saw Caleb practically hanging off the bed with his stomach sticking out. His arms stretched over the bed's edge while his legs lay mangled in the sheets. He slurred out gibberish in his sleep while drool leaked out of his mouth.

"How do you even get into that position?" I asked him.

I reached over to get him off the edge, but then the piercing sound of sirens screeched from outside.

Eeeeeeeeeeeeeeeee!

I instinctively flung myself out of bed and rushed to the window. For a split second, I'd forgotten how to breathe, as if something had grabbed my throat and squeezed it. A familiar black figure came whizzing frantically in the air and headed towards the island at an incredible speed, releasing dreadful, pained howls.

"It's the Black Sting!" someone outside yelled, calling over the sirens that woke the entire town.

Eeeeeeeeeeeeee!

"No ..." I whispered under my breath, slowly shaking my head.

Eeeeeeeeeeeeee!

"No ..." I took a step back while the sirens shrieked louder, followed by the screams of people.

Eeeeeeeeeeeeee!

"Everyone! Stay in your houses!" someone else cried.

Eeeeeeeeeeeeee!

"It's going to destroy the island!" another exclaimed.

Eeeeeeeeeeeeee!

"Where is Captain Cordelia? Didn't her crew kill the beast?" another person demanded

That person's words rang the loudest in my ears. Sweat broke out of my skin and my stomach churned. I yanked myself away from the window and darted to my closet.

"Cora ..." Caleb yawned, rubbing his eyes. "What's that sound? It's so noisy." Caleb yawned again, weakly pulling his body up before falling face first into the mattress.

"Whatever you do, stay in the room, Caleb," I ordered abruptly, reaching to the top of my closet and retrieving my crossbow.

"Why? What's going on?" Caleb asked, pulling himself up once more. He blinked drowsily at the crossbow and the many arrows that I had collected in my arms.

"I can't explain now. Just stay here," I ordered him once more.

Tossing the arrows in a quiver, I strapped it over my shoulder. I grabbed my boots and yanked them on, but I didn't have time to change out of my nightgown.

"What 'bout you?" Caleb tilted his head; his bangs flew over his eyes and he waved them away.

"What about me?" I asked.

"Will you be okay?"

My gaze fell, and I reached into my dresser to pull out a dagger. I strapped it into my left boot.

"Yeah, I'll be fine, don't worry," I said with a quick nod. I presented him with a small smile of assurance before disappearing out of the room.

Flocks of birds dashed away in fright, becoming nothing more than fleeting dark specks against the crimson dawn. The sun rose steadily, pouring out streams of red light that stained the hills and buildings. Light gray mist swept the island in gradual waves that covered the cobblestone streets. The mist rose, crawling upon cream walls now dyed with red.

The alarm continued to blare out as people ran and hurried back into their homes. They locked their doors and shut the blinds of their windows. Some people were too frightened to move. They stood frozen in the middle of the streets, staring up at the Black Sting with fallen jaws.

The creature loomed above them and blocked out the sun, mimicking an eclipse. The sky darkened for a moment, and the island seemed trapped inside a cavern. The Black Sting then broke away, releasing the rest of the sun's light, engulfing the island in a cascade of gold and red. The Black Sting's body swerved about, sweeping the town with its large, dark shadows. The creature rose back up and soared towards the highest peak of the island — the lighthouse.

As I dashed towards the lighthouse, a few of my crew followed close behind, including Eamon and Mark.

"Some of you take to the left. Everyone else follow me!" I exclaimed. We had to separate so we could corner the creature.

The Black Sting circled around the lighthouse before it swung its great tail and coiled around the narrow structure. As the Black Sting tried to tear the lighthouse from the ground, my crew and I hastily ascended the cliff, not once stopping as we climbed higher and higher to the top.

"Quickly!" I yelled, but realized that we weren't going to reach it in time.

Grunting, I climbed onto a large enough rock to get myself to an offensive stance. I loaded my crossbow, aimed it at the Black Sting, and, when I finally found a clear opening, I fired.

The arrow whizzed through the air, rising past the sun. The sun's light briefly brushed through the tip, painting the metal red. The arrow struck the Black Sting in the eye. The creature screeched. Blood squirted out of its eye and it released its hold of the lighthouse. Its body twisted and coiled, slashing its tail all over until it crashed into the fragile light room, knocking the lantern out of its enclosure. The lantern, with its flames still dancing, fell like a shooting star onto the town below.

Screams rose as the lantern crashed into two of the houses, immediately setting them ablaze. The fire quickly spread, blazing against the already burning sky. Smoke ascended and circled about the still and dark lighthouse.

Orange and red flames filled my vision. A mixture of screams and yells wailed in my head, but I could barely register them. I dropped from the rocks, rushing down to assist in the rescue, but halted when a quick flash of black blurred my vision for an instant, followed by a sharp slap and a sting that threw me back against the rocks.

"Captain!"

I nearly fell off the cliff, but grabbed hold of the ledge. I turned back and saw the Black Sting coming in for another attack, but an arrow pierced its head before it could continue. I looked to see where the attack came from and saw Eamon firing another arrow at the spastic creature. I pulled myself up on the ledge and winced at the pain on my shoulder. Backing up against a wall, I clutched my stinging shoulder. A burning pain rippled from my limb, as if thousands of needles prickled my skin at the same time. I shut my eyes as dizziness took hold and a headache started to form.

"Captain!"

Someone grabbed my burning arm, and I flinched away. I opened my eyes and saw Eamon in front of me.

"Eamon ... where's ...?" I stopped, glancing around but didn't spot the Black Sting, nor heard it anymore.

"It's gone, Captain ... we killed it."

"We — ugh —" I faltered; I freed my shoulder and glanced at the blood on my hand.

"C–Captain ..." Eamon studied the wound. "You ... you were hit ... the poison ..." A long cut slashed across my shoulder. The skin around the wound transitioned to a light gray color. Blood leaked out of the wound and looked darker than normal.

"N–no, I'm fine, it's nothing," I dismissed, hiding the wound with my hand.

"Captain, you need medical attention. Now." Eamon urged and lent his hand. "Let's get down where we're safer."

I nodded slowly. Dizziness still lingered in the back of my head, so I followed Eamon down at a slow pace. My head rocked from side to side as I tried to keep focus as we moved along, finally reentering the town. I raised my head and saw the fire still burning, eating away the houses while screams continued to disrupt the dawn. I could vaguely see burnt bodies being taken out of the buildings. Clutching my head, I dropped to my knees.

"Captain!"

Eamon helped me back up, and we continued our way through the town before we were stopped at the town square.

"Captain Cordelia!"

Several of the townspeople approached us, yelling out in unison.

"What happened?"

"We thought the Black Sting was dead!"

"The island could've been destroyed! We could've all been killed!"

"Five people have died from the fire and eight are injured!"

More and more townspeople surrounded us in a semi-circle. They kept shouting out questions, frustrations, and concerns. The pain beat into my head like a hammer.

"Please, everyone!" Eamon exclaimed, managing to yell over them. "Let us speak!"

I took a step forward and clutched my bleeding shoulder. The blood flowed down my skin like trails of ink. Some people noted my wound, but didn't say anything. Even so, most them were losing their patience, and their expressions turned bitter. For the first time, I felt vulnerable with all those eyes staring straight at me.

I gave myself a moment before speaking, breathing in before quietly saying,

"Our deepest apologies." My arm shook; now it felt like a knife had struck the skin and was slowly slicing into it. "We had fought the Black Sting beforehand, but we were unable to kill it because we were exhausted from the travel, so we came back here to take a break. But I knew it was a terrible idea. If we had killed it before, then ..."

My eyes trailed over to the destroyed houses. The flames were dying down as hoses of water sprinkled amongst them, but smoke continued to choke the blood red sky.

"We're truly sorry ..."

"Sorry is not going to bring back the dead!" one man yelled, his voice boomed across the cool morning air. "What kind of captain are you if you're not able to protect us?"

"Gideon!"

Father stepped through the crowd. He rushed over to Eamon and I before shooting Gideon a glare. He was a bulky man that dwarfed Father in size, but size was unimportant here.

"It's not Cordelia or anyone else's fault that they're dead," Father said. "Don't put the blame on my daughter. None of you should put the blame on her. Cordelia and her crew still saved us in the end, and, if it weren't for them, we would've lost much more."

A grunt crawled out of Gideon's throat. "If Cordelia wasn't your daughter, would you still protect her like this?"

"That's enough from you, Gideon," Father scolded. "I understand your frustration, and I can see that you aren't the only one, but please understand that Cordelia and her crew are only human and have done the best that they can to protect us."

"Father —"

"The Black Sting is dead because of them, be grateful for that at least."

Gideon emitted another grunt and rolled his eyes. Father caught the gesture of disdain, frowned deeply, but ignored it and continued, "Let us not allow this event to change anyone's minds about the crew of *The Raging Storm* — or any other crew for that matter. This isn't the only time that our island had been attacked, as you may recall from a few years back."

"And we hoped that would've been the last," Gideon muttered under his breath, but Father could hear him.

He opened his mouth, but I cut in. "Look. I'm sorry for what had happened here," I said, digging my nails into my shaky palms. "I truly, truly am. I can't do anything but continue to protect you all, and that's what I'll do. I'll make sure nothing like this ever happens again —"

"Cordelia —"

"What, Father?" I barked, then noticed Father slowly raising a finger and pointing at the wound on my shoulder.

"The wound ... your skin ... oh no ... oh no." Father's lips quivered, struggling to mouth the words. "Oh, no ... Cordelia ..."

I covered up the wound, but the black blood kept flowing out.

"We need to get help. There has to be a cure, right?" Eamon asked abruptly.

"The antidote is extremely rare," Father responded. "We don't have it here, but ..." he paused, twisting his lips and struggling once more to spill out the words. "I know someone who might ... but ..."

"But what?" I asked.

"His name is Theron, he's a doctor, the best that I've ever known. However, he and I have a bit of a troubled history and I worry that it might be dangerous if you seek his help. He might still have a grudge and transfer it to you."

"What happened between you two?"

"It's a long story, but I believe it would be better if you see one of the doctors here. They should probably —"

"If you say this Theron guy is the best option, then I should go see him instead, right?" I inquired.

"Well, yes, but I still believe it would be best to see one of the doctors," Father repeated, dismissing the idea altogether. "We should meet with one of them now, before it gets worse."

7

– CORDELIA –

I UNRAVELED MY SLEEVE, showing the doctor the wound. Dr. Jonah was one of the top doctors on the island. She was well in her forties, with red hair transitioning to light gray that she usually wore in a short ponytail. Her blue eyes studied the wound behind wired glasses. With gentle hands, she cleaned the cut while I stared at the many certificates and photos hanging against the white wall of the office. Many of the photos showed Dr. Jonah and her twin boys, smiling with ease at the camera, and presenting a warm ambiance to the room.

"How does the wound feel?" Dr. Jonah asked, taking my mind away from the photos that had comforted my mind.

"It stings," I said. "It first started on the shoulder and now my arm stings too."

"Hmm ..." Dr. Jonah observed my arm once more. The skin had also turned a bit gray in the area as well. "I'll see what I have."

Dr. Jonah finished cleaning the wound, wrapped a bandage around it, and walked to a cabinet in search for medicine.

"Do you know who this Theron guy is?" I asked curiously, rubbing the bandage.

"He was an old friend of your Father's." Dr. Jonah didn't hesitate to answer as she rummaged through one shelf and then another. "Extremely smart man — he could find the cure to pretty much anything. But he kept all the knowledge to himself. That didn't please your father, especially since they were friends. The mayor suspected that Theron was hiding something bigger from all the research he was doing, so the mayor had his house inspected and found he was performing illegal experiments —"

"What sorts of experiments?"

"He was testing on animals. Trying to get some sort of remedies from them, but that wasn't allowed. Us doctors only work on plants, and that's supposed to be it. Once he was discovered, he went to jail for a few years, and then moved away to another island. We haven't heard much from him. It's been twenty years now."

"Do you know where he is?"

"He lives on a small island south of here. Rumor has it that he's been doing intensive research on his medical studies."

"What about the animals?"

"There has been no word about that ... Whatever he does, it's none of our business now unless it affects us. But who knows, perhaps he learned his lesson. It has been decades."

"If so, I should see him in case nothing works out here."

"Let's not get too carried away. We have to have something here for you," Dr. Jonah said, briefly reading the labels on one bottle.

She muttered incoherent things to herself, frowning at her inability to find the right item. Dr. Jonah soon picked up something and returned to me.

"Drink this." Dr. Jonah handed out a bottle filled with purple liquid. "It will relieve you of pain for a while, but take small sips, you'll become drowsy if you drink too fast."

"All right." I took the bottle and drank cautiously, but cringed afterwards. "That was disgusting."

"You'll thank me in three minutes."

Dr. Jonah returned to the cabinet and continued her search. After a while, I felt like hope was dwindling, though I stayed quiet. I looked back at the photos to assure myself.

"How are your boys doing?" I asked.

"They're good. They've both built a toy boat for a contest at school and won second place. Austen was thrilled, but Adam ... not so much. He was grumpy that he didn't win, but once I made him his favorite meal for dinner, he cheered up."

"Sounds like Caleb," I said dryly.

"That reminds me — he's due for his flu shot soon."

"Do you have any lollipops that'll keep him from screaming?"

"Yes. You're also due for your shot soon too. Would you also like a lollipop?"

"I'm a bit old for those," I said, though I suppose I wouldn't mind if there was a strawberry flavor.

A while later, a knock sounded at the door, and Father and Caleb entered the small office. Once Caleb stepped through, he hurried over to me, clutching his stuffed whale in his arms.

"Are you gonna be okay, Cora?" he asked, his eyes brimming with tears.

"I will soon," I said, though I wasn't too sure myself about it.

"You should find the Elphida and wish to get better!" he proposed, jumping on his tippy toes.

"The Elphida?" Father questioned.

"Yeah!" Caleb piped up. "It grants any wish! It can help Cora get better."

"It's a fairytale, Caleb," I huffed. "I told you —"

"It's real!" Caleb exclaimed, tears shooting out of his eyes. "If you find it, it'll be able to help you!"

"Caleb, this isn't the time," Father said, resting a hand on Caleb's shoulder. "My apologies, Dr. Jonah. My son is just really upset right now."

"It's no problem, Mayor. I understand," Dr. Jonah said.

"What's the situation?" Father asked, his bloodshot eyes trailing over to me and then at the doctor.

"Well ..." Dr. Jonah started fixing her wired glasses. "I looked and I have nothing that'll get rid of the poison. I gave Cordelia something to get rid of the pain, but there's nothing else that I have on hand. You could take Cordelia to another doctor, but I doubt they have anything. Her best chance is to go to Theron."

Father pinched the bridge of his nose as he paced about the room. After a minute of consideration, he broke the hold of his nose, which left two small marks on the bridge.

"Fine ... I'll send Theron a message —"

"We don't have time to send a message — let's just go see him in person," I offered.

"Cordelia —"

I hopped off the chair, and my boots made a hard thump. "Father, just focus on getting the island back together while I deal with this. I'll find Theron myself and get the antidote from him. I want to get this done and over with as soon as possible. I don't care if Theron did some stupid experiments in the past that ticked you off. That was twenty years ago. I doubt he's still angry about what happened, and, even if he is, he needs to just get over it — and so do you."

I stormed out of the room and marched down the hall of the hospital. The morning light streamed through the paneled windows and lit up the white-washed walls. I continued walking until —

"Oh, Captain!"

Eamon came into view through a crowd of people. In his arms, he carried a bundle of white and pink carnations tied by a red ribbon. The petals fluttered about and the leaves swayed from side to side as he rushed over.

"Eamon, what are you —"

"Are you alright?" Eamon asked, his face flushed from running. He took a moment to catch his breath.

"Could be worse," I said simply. I eyed the flowers with mild surprise and became quiet, speechless.

Eamon cleared his throat, lending the flowers forward. "Oh, uh ... these are for you," Eamon mumbled. "I'm sorry if this is improper, but my mom grew these in her garden, she wanted me to give them to you." Eamon rubbed the back of his neck and his eyes dropped. The redness on his cheeks gradually grew.

I took the flowers as gratitude. "Thanks ..." I said, my voice drifting off and, holding the flowers in my arms, felt a sense of warmth surfacing. However, that soon disappeared when I shook my head in dismissal and chided him, "Listen, Eamon, right now I'm running out of time. We're going to get the medicine from Theron — he's my only chance for a cure."

The redness disappeared, and Eamon's eyes widened. "But, your father —"

"What he says doesn't matter," I said. "We're going to Theron. Now."

"Are you sure about this?" Eamon asked, apprehension evident in his voice.

"What other choice do I have?" I snapped, throwing my arms outward and causing the flowers to shudder. "If you know any other solutions, by all means, tell me. It's not like I'm currently dying from poison right now."

Eamon clamped his mouth shut and his shoulders slumped. After a moment, he huffed out a sigh and said, "I'm sorry, I'm just concerned for you and I want to make sure you're making the right decision."

I pinched down on my lower lip. I glanced at the flowers in my hands and my hold around them tightened.

"Let's get going, we don't have much time."

•   •   •

"Where does this guy live again?" Flint asked, unrolling a map and placing it upon my desk.

Five of my crew members — Flint, Eamon, Mark, Fable and Edna — who had come in case I needed backup, surrounded the desk, glancing at the map brightened by the stained-glass ceiling above us.

"He lives on Green Crescent Island, far south from here," I said, jabbing a finger at Domus first and trailing it downward until I spotted it.

The island was crescent-shaped and engulfed in forest. Written in delicate cursive above it read 'Green Crescent Island'." Much smaller in scale in relation to Domus, it was like comparing a grape to a watermelon.

"It's tiny," Edna commented.

"Yeah, I guess it's not very populated," I said. "I don't really think Theron cares about that though."

"I remember hearing a lot about him," Mark said. "I hope he's not experimenting on animals again. I own two pet shrimps and I can't imagine what kind of experiments he could do on them."

"Relax." I rolled my eyes. "We're only stopping by for an hour at the most. I don't think he'll give us a tour of his lab or something."

"Ah, right, sorry," Mark said, accompanied with an awkward laugh afterwards.

"How's the shoulder, Captain?" Fable asked, changing the subject. Her tone of voice was much sterner and clearer than Mark's.

"It's fine, just stings a bit." I dismissed the question and rolled up the map. "As I said before, we will not stay too long. Just get the medicine, give him whatever amount of money he wants, and leave. But keep your guard up in case something suspicious happens. If this doesn't work, we'll look somewhere else. Got it?"

"Yes, Captain," my crew members said, and they left my cabin, all except for Eamon.

He noticed that I had put the flowers he had given me in a vase. "They're nice decorations," I said bluntly. "Is there something you need to tell me? Or are you going to stand there gawking?"

"Uh, no, sorry, Captain," Eamon cleared his throat and backed to the door.

I held up a hand. "Wait," I said. "Could you do me a favor, actually?"

"Yes, Captain."

"Could you send a dove to scout Green Crescent? We need to make sure it's safe to set foot there first."

"Of course, Captain."

"Thank you, you're excused."

Eamon nodded and left my cabin.

I turned back to the flowers he had given me. They did make for some nice decoration and I couldn't help but smile.

•   •   •

Later we all gathered at the deck to have lunch. We packed little since we were in a hurry, but Mark had made us all tuna horseradish sandwiches. Honestly, I wasn't a big fan of them, but it was either that or cabbage soup. I was so tired of cabbage soup.

As we ate, Mark told us jokes to lift our moods, but I barely paid attention to them. I was too focused on my bandaged shoulder, but then I heard the flapping of wings and we all glanced to the sky. A dove carrying a flower swooped down to us before landing on the deck. The dove released the flower before it disappeared.

"A flower means that the island's safe, right?" Mark asked.

"Yes," I said. "A root says otherwise. Regardless, we should bring our weapons for precaution."

I picked up the flower and examined it: it was a white rose, which was rare here, at least in Domus. *I think I'll place it with the ones that Eamon had given me.* It was nice, I admitted to myself, and made me wonder what kind of place the island was if it had such a flower.

"What if there was an island that didn't grow flowers?" Mark suddenly asked. "What does a dove bring?"

"A leaf," Fable answered for him.

"What if an island doesn't have trees?"

"All islands have trees. Don't be silly." Fable rolled her eyes and got back to eating her sandwich.

"Right ..." Mark mumbled to himself and bit into his own sandwich. "So, yeah, how long should it take us to arrive at the island?"

"A couple more hours," Flint answered, glancing up at the clear sky. "Good thing there are no signs of a storm."

"Yeah," Mark agreed and took another bite from his sandwich. "Mmm, is everyone liking the sandwiches? Usually my mom makes them, but I wanted to make them for the first time."

"It's good, Mark," Eamon said.

"You did a good job," Edna agreed.

"Yeah," Fable nodded. "Though, I think some mayonnaise would make it better."

Flint raised an eyebrow. "Mayonnaise? No, that'll ruin it."

Edna shrugged. "I'd like to know how that'll taste."

"We have mayonnaise in the kitchen," Eamon said. "Should I get it?"

"No," Flint argued.

"Yes." Fable nodded.

"Sure," Edna agreed, "but I like the sandwich either way. You really did do a good job, Mark."

"Thank you." Mark timidly smiled. A soft blush rose in his cheeks and he awkwardly coughed, quickly turning away.

Everyone knew he had a small crush on Edna, since he was horrible at covering it up, but we didn't want to embarrass him about it.

Eamon disappeared to retrieve the mayonnaise; I had forgotten that we even had it in the fridge. I wasn't a fan, but Caleb was. He liked everything he got his sticky hands on. I wouldn't be surprised if he grew up fat.

Mark spoke up again, "What is mayonnaise exactly? Like what is it made of, I mean?"

"You really like asking random questions," Flint said.

"I want to lighten the mood," Mark insisted.

"It's not really helping," Fable said. "But if you must know: mayonnaise is made up of egg yolk, vinegar, and oil. Sometimes lemon juice is added to it."

"It does sound gross when you say that ..." Mark said.

Flint nodded. "That's because it is gross."

"I personally think it's the best thing to put in a sandwich," Fable said.

This whole talk about mayonnaise also made me not want to have any mayonnaise, but at least it was something to put our minds off things for a while. It had been strenuous, and I supposed a random conversation like this was ... nice. It's not a topic I would have had in mind to pull up, but it was better than anything else at the moment. Really, it was, and I was grateful I brought along some of my crew. I didn't want to admit it, but I don't think I would've handled going on this mission by myself. If I was alone and this mission turned out to be a failure, I ... no, I didn't want to think of it. I can't. I can't.

"Captain?"

Eamon was at my side with a hand on my shoulder. Everyone else had fallen into silence and were looking concerned.

"You're pale, do you need to lie down?" he asked.

"It's nothing, I'm fine," I said, nudging my shoulder away. I wasn't.

8

– CORDELIA –

A T MID-AFTERNOON, WE ARRIVED at Green Crescent Island. The island was nothing more than a vast forest; evergreen trees rose seventy feet in the air. It was hard to see what was behind their wide, brown trunks and the drooping branches that resembled spider legs. The sun sat on the treetops, forming ivory halos that blended into the green. Red-eyed crows sat on the branches, cawing at our incoming ship before taking flight.

There was another ship docked at the far end of the pier where we headed. That ship was a bit smaller than ours, with rows of green sails tied to its masts. Below the bow of the ship was a wooden carving of a vulture with hollow eyes. I glanced at the ship curiously with a small frown.

I don't recognize that ship ... Does Theron own it or is it someone else's?

When the ship came to the pier, Flint was the first to get off as he worked to steady the ship. He used a couple of long cords to hook the ship to the pier by locking them onto a long, metal bar. After the ship finally steadied, my crew and I stepped off the ship and stood upon the edge of a forest, gazing up at the tall, looming trees.

"It looks a bit ominous," Mark mumbled to himself.

"Let's get a move on," I ordered and led my crew into the forest.

We wandered for several minutes, and, as we moved further and further into the forest, the narrower the path got. It felt like the trees were closing in, nearly squeezing us. It was getting hard to navigate, as it was not just cramped, but also darker, as the sun's light could barely stream through the trees.

Eventually, the trees finally gave way to a great stone mansion that stood amid a clearing. Thorny vines wrapped themselves around the marble columns that supported the tall portico. Narrow, arched windows adorned every wall of the mansion. A glass dome wrought in iron dominated the roof.

"This should be the place," I said, walking up the stone steps of the portico.

"It's huge," Mark whistled.

I ignored his comment and brashly knocked on one of the double mahogany doors. Mark cringed at the loud sound while the rest of the crew remained still. Our swords were strapped to our belts, and we placed our hands on them as a precaution. After a moment, the door opened, and a short man with crinkly, pale skin and wearing black attire stared back at us questioningly.

"Yes?" the man asked, in a slow, raspy voice.

I took a step forward and said: "I am Captain Cordelia Thomasthan of *The Raging Storm*, and this is my crew. I must speak with Theron. It's urgent."

"Oh?" The man's eyes gradually widened at my name and his lips curved to an 'o'. "Is the Master in trouble?"

"No, but if I don't see him this instant, he just might be," I warned, seizing the hilt of my sword as a warning.

The man swallowed a huge gulp, and he shook. "Ah, yes, give me a second, please. I must inform the Master." His speech hurried just as quickly as the speed of the front door slamming shut.

"I think you could've been a bit calmer, Captain," Eamon commented.

"I want to hurry this up," I said, tapping my foot upon the porch and stared sternly at the closed doors. "I wasn't actually going to hurt him, you know. Enough people have gotten hurt today."

Eamon opened his mouth to say something, but then closed it. He glanced over to me and then his attention returned to the double doors. After a few minutes of impatient waiting, the door opened fully, and the man returned, but this time opening his hands.

"The Master will not see you unless you put away your weapons. I'll take them for you and put them in the storage. You'll get them back when you leave. The Master wouldn't feel comfortable if you carried them inside his home."

I narrowed my eyes, and a tinge of paranoia surfaced. My fingers twitched alongside the sword's hilt, which I swore felt colder than usual. After a moment of consideration, and not wanting to waste any more time, I reluctantly released my sword from its belt and prompted my crew to do the same.

"Here." I presented my sword to the man, and he gratefully took it, along with everyone else's.

"Thank you, the Master will be pleased." The man smiled and backed away for me and my crew to step inside.

We entered a spacious foyer lit by twin globe-shaped chandeliers that circled one another by wires attached between them. Heads of animals mounted on the green-paneled walls caused Mark to cringe and look away. But at every corner, unblinking, black eyes stared back at us.

A spiral staircase stood in the center of the foyer, flying past the second floor, and halted at the third. I gazed up at the staircase before the man beckoned us to move forward.

He led us into a long hallway lit by sconces upon the walls. We passed by many rooms before stopping at the very back where there stood another pair of double doors. The servant opened both doors, revealing an atrium.

Strands and strands of rose vines hung from the glass-domed ceiling and hovered over the bookshelves that surrounded the room. The crowns of trees swayed above the glass dome. The sun's light could just barely bleed through the branches and glass, giving the room a dusky shimmer.

The room was furnished with ornate furniture draped in fancy coverlets and tassels. An elderly man sat upon one couch, reading a book with an intrigued expression written on his aging face. Small, wired glasses sat on the brink of his crooked nose. The glasses flashed subtly in the sun's weak light, and, when the light dispersed, faint blue eyes were distinguishable behind the glass.

The servant cleared his throat. "Excuse me, Master Theron. Captain Cordelia Thomasthan and her crew are here."

Theron closed the book and settled it on the table in front of him. He spread his arms in a hospitable gesture.. "Captain Cordelia Thomasthan. What an honor for you to come into my home. Truly, it is an honor. I've heard so much about you and your crew. Please, have a seat." Theron gestured toward one of the many couches and chairs that surrounded the room.

"No thanks," I said. "What I'm here for is something that shouldn't take too long."

"Oh?" Theron raised a thin, gray eyebrow. "Well, that's unfortunate, I rarely get guests, and I hoped that we could have a long chat."

"I'm afraid that can't happen." I dismissed the invitation. "Maybe another time when I'm not in the middle of a problem."

"A problem?" Theron echoed. "What sort of problem?" He leaned forward, attentive.

"Long story short: my island has been attacked by —"

"Attacked you say?" Theron cut in, frowning, pulling himself back into the couch. He rubbed his chin. "That's strange, I thought Domus was one of the most protected islands in the entire sky. Isn't that why I was exiled? So that the island could stay protected?"

"Can we just cut to the chase?" I asked, gritting my teeth at the instant I was interrupted.

"Humph, impatient, aren't we?" Theron inquired. "And you just got here. Whatever it is, it must be urgent. But it shouldn't be so urgent that you can't just sit down and have some tea. Clyde?"

"Yes?" the servant asked. He still remained at the doorway and grew stiff at the mention of his name.

"Bring us all tea. Mint will suffice."

"Right away, sir," Clyde said and disappeared from the room.

"You all look exhausted," Theron noted with pursed lips. "Was it hard getting here?"

"No, it's just been a long day," I responded.

"I see ... well, do sit down. Please. It's not good to stand around when you look like you're all going to drop at any moment."

I frowned and glanced at my crew. They were clearly exhausted, judging from their bloodshot eyes; none of them had slept after the battle, nor could they shut their eyes much during the trip to Crescent Island, since they were concerned for my well-being. I exhaled sharply and prompted my crew to sit down. I sank into one cushion and pulled myself up before the cushions could squeeze me in more.

"Good, good, tea will be here shortly," Theron said with a curt nod.

"We're not staying long. We only need something from you," I stated.

"Oh?" Theron again raised his thin eyebrow. "I see. Is this in relation to what happened on your island?"

"Yes, we were attacked by the Black Sting."

"Oh, how terrible!" Theron exclaimed much too loudly. "Did anyone get hurt?"

"Yes ..." I answered. "Including me, I was struck by the tail."

Theron shook his head and clicked his tongue. "The great Captain Cordelia Thomasthan was struck by the tail of the Black Sting ... that is indeed terrible. I would have never imagined that could happen."

"Do you have a cure?" I asked in an almost demanding voice.

"Of course, I have the cure ... I'm not the greatest doctor in the world for nothing," Theron said. "But it does come with a price."

"I know it comes with a price; I wasn't expecting you to give it to me for free. What is it? Money?"

"Mmmm, perhaps ..." Theron trailed off while tilting his head from side to side.

He lifted himself from his seat and wandered about the room. In between two of the bookshelves stood a tall cabinet made from glass and cherry wood.

"I believe I already have enough money now. After your father exiled me, I made my business on this island. I continued with my research and my experimentations and earned a great deal of money off them."

Mark spoke up, "What kind of experiments? You don't ..." he hesitated at the next words. "You don't still test on animals, right?"

"Of course, how else would I carry on with my hard work? I have to find side effects in my remedies."

"That's not right!" Mark exclaimed, shooting up from his chair, his knuckles hitting against him.

"Mark, sit down," I ordered sharply.

Mark sucked in a breath of air and slumped back into the chair.

I yanked Mark's collar and whispered harshly in his ear, "This isn't the time right now."

"I see I struck a nerve, my apologies," Theron said. "Don't worry, I only test on rodents, nothing more. Now, where was that vial ..." He mumbled the rest to himself, fumbling through the glass shelves of vials and bottles.

Eamon spoke up, "You've been able to keep quiet for a while. I'm surprised no one has spotted this mansion and brought up any questions."

"I was already quite rich before my exile," Theron said. "Since this is my island, I simply expanded my wealth upon it. Besides, my affairs shouldn't be of any concern to you all."

"Does no one else live on the island? Besides you and your servant?" Fable asked.

"I have a couple more servants, though I would say they're more like bodyguards and associates on my projects, rather. One of them, Elliot, owns the ship at the pier. *The Green Vultures*, he calls it — bit of a boring name. *The Raging Storm* ... now that's a powerful name. Who named it?"

"Mayor Thomasthan did," Eamon answered.

"Oh, he did, didn't he?" Theron inquired, glancing over his shoulder once more, passing a look of curiosity. "How is he doing, by the way?"

"He's fine," I said shortly, not wanting to say anything else as my patience was wavering. "Do you have the medicine or not?"

"Patience, Captain," Theron said. "Didn't I say I have it?"

I slumped back on the chair, and I touched my shoulder, which had started stinging again. I softly inhaled and exhaled to keep myself calm, but it felt like a knife was cutting into my skin again.

"Ah, here we are." Theron picked out a vial and unscrewed the stopper. "Nectar squeezed from the rare cerasis flower. This remedy shares the same color as the fruits that grow on the golden willow tree. Do you know about this tree, Captain?"

"I've never heard of it," I said with a small frown, watching as Theron picked up a glass and poured the golden liquid into it.

"The golden willow is exceptionally rare. There's only one in existence, and it grows on an island, far, far away. This island is like no other. The rivers on the island are streams of honey. The trees are white and bear blue flowers, except for that one tree. And the landscape is covered in fields of grain that are said to feel exactly like bird feathers. The island is home to this rare creature called an Elphida."

My eyebrows rose, taken aback at the familiar word over which Caleb had been obsessing. *Now why would he ...?*

"Fairytales make it out that the Elphida grants wishes. That's absurd, of course, but it's much more interesting to hear about an animal than a plant, isn't it? Though the only thing that the willow helps with are its fruits, that are said to cure anything. The Elphida guards the tree, and the only way to get past it is if you have a strong desire —"

"Why are you telling us this?" I interrupted in a now vexed tone. My patience has now ended and my blood boiled like fire.

"Because that's what I want you to do. I'd like you to search for the Elphida, the rarest of all treasures, and then I'll give you your remedy."

The servant shyly entered the room with a cart filled with the tea. He picked up one of the fancy cups and handed it over to me. But, like lightning, I smacked the cup out of his hand and it crashed into the floor. I shot up from my chair and stomped my foot.

"Is this some kind of joke?" I snapped, my voice bouncing off the walls. "I'm not looking for some make-believe creature! Just give me the medicine and I'll pay you back whatever you want."

A crooked smiled crossed Theron's lips. "Ah, I knew you wouldn't like the proposal."

With a flick of his wrist, the medicine flowed out of the glass and stained the carpet. I paled, and I stumbled back into the chair while my crew emitted inaudible gasps.

"If you want to be saved, you will now have to find the Elphida and the tree it guards. It's the only way to save yourself."

"How do I know that you're not lying and you have another antidote in there?" I asked, masking dread as I gritted my teeth.

"I don't."

Theron snapped his fingers and the doors behind us burst open. The crew rose, but halted when a group of ten men, all wearing masks that concealed their faces, held up daggers toward our general direction. Dressed in all black from head to toe, they looked like shadows as they all stood behind us.

Their masks bore the shape of a vulture's head — perfectly round, with a stark black beak pointed downward like the heads of a harpoon. Their eyes were barely visible, ranging from stark gray to bright green. One of the men with blue eyes lifted his knife to my neck. The cold metal touched the side of my throat and I remained motionless, glaring at Theron, who rose from the couch and walked over to me.

"What do you want?" I demanded, flinching when the knife pressed into my skin. At the corner of my eye, I caught Eamon about to rise, but was shoved back down by his captor.

"I've been looking for the Elphida for so many years, and now I finally found the chance to get to it. You. *The Raging Storm* can track down anything, so I'm sure you can track down the Elphida. It'll be beneficial for the both of us," Theron remarked with a low chuckle.

"The Elphida doesn't exist," I spat. "I had enough of your nonsense. You're crazy."

"Crazy, eh?" Theron fiddled with the word, a smile widening upon his lips and revealing a dull golden tooth. It looked like an old coin was caught in between his decaying teeth. I grimaced at the smirk and turned away, but Theron forced me to look at him by grabbing my chin and straining it forward.

"You can say whatever you wish, but that won't stop me from getting what I want." He roughly pulled away and came back to the center of the room.

"If you don't cooperate with me, I may have to take matters into my own hands." He raised a hand. Golden rings covered in rubies donned each digit. Upon the sun's dim light, the rubies glistened like tiny sparks of fire. "With the simple snap of my fingers, all of your heads will end up rolling off your shoulders. But I'm sure you don't want that to happen, and I don't want the carpet to get any messier. So, let's make a deal, shall we? No harm will be done."

I ground my teeth until my jaw ached to the point that it felt numb. My shoulders tensed up and my eyes darted to each individual crew member. I could see in their eyes that they were scared, but could muster strength to keep themselves composed and quiet.

Eamon gave me a small nod and a subtle smile for reassurance, though I could see cold sweat traveling from his brow. I slowly inhaled and my shoulders dropped before exhaling.

"Fine," I said. "We'll do what you want. Though I don't know what good I will be, considering how much time I have left."

"Humph," Theron chuckled. "Knowing you, I'm sure you will be able to help me find the island before your time is up. You are an excellent traveler, after all; a little poison shouldn't be a bother. I heard that if you're strong enough, you'll be able to stay alive for about a week. Aren't you strong, Captain?"

"Of course," I exclaimed, baffled by the question.

"Then there's nothing to worry about," Theron said. "You're a renowned captain, the youngest to rule her own ship, so of course you're strong. But I'd like to test your strength. Prove to me that you are strong, that you still hold the strength to find the Elphida and your life will be spared. Now," Theron returned to his chair and folded his hands, "let's make our deal. You find the Elphida for me, and you get the fruit that grows from the golden willow. That's a fair exchange."

Eamon spoke up, "Why exactly do you want to find this creature?"

"Who wouldn't want to find it?" Theron inquired. "The Elphida is a rare creature — the true wonder and mystery of the sky. Yes, it is indeed believed to be a myth, but that's because the idea of it is too alien for most people to comprehend. Captain, as someone who has traveled throughout the entire sky, and would have encountered so many wonders, I am shocked that you don't believe in the Elphida. Now, that would be troublesome for you to hold this claim since finding it will help you. Elliot." Theron gestured to the young man with the knife at my throat.

"Yes, sir?" Elliot asked. His voice was soft, a different sort of tone that I wouldn't have imagined behind the gritty vulture mask.

"Prepare your ship. We'll be setting off soon."

"Yes, sir," Elliot repeated and then departed.

Theron continued, "In the meantime, let's have some lunch. I'm sure you all haven't eaten yet and you should save your strength. It'll be quite the journey and it'll be a shame if any of you lose energy. Clyde." Theron now turned to the servant.

"Yes, Master?"

"Tell the chef to prepare lunch. It'll be a grand feast. After all, Cordelia and her crew are honorable guests and we want them to feel welcome. It's a celebration."

"Right away, Master," Clyde said and disappeared from the atrium.

"Now," Theron returned his focus to us, "it'll be a while until lunch. Why don't I give you a tour of the house?"

"First, you need to release the rest of us," I said. "I don't think my crew members are comfortable with knives aimed at their necks."

"Ah, certainly." Theron nodded to his bodyguards, and they gave the crew their space. Tension reduced just slightly in the room, but my crew kept their guards up and remained still.

"You're honored guests, after all. I don't mean any harm," Theron said.

I narrowed my eyes. "How ironic of you to say that. Just a minute ago you threatened to kill us."

"I merely wanted to grab your attention," Theron insisted. "After all, you wouldn't believe me if I didn't take any action. It was a persuasion, nothing more."

"I think you could've thought of a better approach." I hissed.

"Mmm, perhaps," Theron considered, shrugging his shoulders. "But what fun would it be if I didn't send your blood flowing? I'm sure your hearts were beating so fast once my bodyguards stormed into the room. I could see the alertness in your eyes. It was amusing." He chuckled and leaned back in his chair. "Messing with the crew of *The Raging Storm*. When will I ever get another opportunity to joke with the most renowned crew in the sky?"

"You're pretty sick if you thought that was amusing," I spat.

"I enjoy dark humor every once in a while," Theron responded. "But in all honesty, I wouldn't hurt any of you. Why should I poison those who are already poisoned? You all are still recovering from what happened on your island — hurt, troubled, confused — must've never felt these feelings before, considering how brave and successful you all are.

"As I look at you all now, tired from all the fighting and concerned about your well beings — especially you, Captain — I see that I should give you all a break, and you should all take my word for it. I'm the host, and the job of the host is to treat you all with respect. So," Theron got up from his seat once more, "allow me to give you a tour of the house. It's the least I can do before lunch," he offered with a smile.

I wasn't completely convinced by the man's words, and I was sure my crew weren't either. But having no other choice in this matter, and not wanting to risk the lives of my crew, I huffed and reluctantly agreed, "All right, we'll follow your lead."

Eamon passed a worried glance to me and turned back to Theron, who smiled and clapped his hands together.

"Very good, come along now." Theron moved past the crew and exited through the doors, but not before gesturing them to follow him.

We all got up uneasily while all of his bodyguards stared at us like the vultures they were. Then they nudged us out of the room and the doors were shut behind us. We followed Theron into another hall and he began talking about some of the animals mounted on the walls.

While he talked, I gently nudged Eamon to grab his attention and, silently and swiftly, communicated with him through sign language.

'I don't trust this man, no matter what he says. When we get the chance, we'll find our swords and get out of here,' I signaled, occasionally looking over to Theron to make sure that he wasn't looking, but his back remained turned on us the entire time. Fortunately, the Vultures weren't around either.

Eamon signaled back: *'Let's not make any rash decisions, Captain. Let's do what he says. I'm not sure if we'll be able to get our swords easily. He has his bodyguards and they could be spying on us right now. All we can do is be cautious.'*

A low sound of retort escaped from my throat, but Theron didn't hear it since he was talking:

"— and over here is one of my studies," Theron commented, looking ahead at a particular locked door. "I conduct some of my research in there, while I perform my experiments in the lab below." He tapped his foot upon the carpet. "We won't go down there — it's rather messy and I don't want to feel embarrassed. If I knew you all would be coming sooner, I would've had the servants clean it."

"That's all right," I said, pretending to be engrossed in the conversation. We returned to the foyer and I ensured that the Vultures weren't spying on us as Eamon had speculated. My focus then went to the stairs. "What's at the top?"

"My bedroom, of course, a library, and another study. I like to work in different places of the house. It is just me here, and the servants, but I own most of the rooms and I like to occupy most of them for my work. It can get boring working in one room all the time."

"So that's all you do? Work?" Edna asked.

"Usually, but I have a garden in the back that I enjoy tending to every once in a while. And my books in the library and atrium that I read at my leisure," Theron responded. "Before you all came here, I was reading *Wreath of Violet Roses* — it's a marvelous piece of work. This is my fourth time reading it. Have any of you read it?"

The crew grew quiet, all knowing that this was a silly question coming out of a man who had threatened to kill us. The crew only shook their heads in response.

"Oh, that's a shame." Theron presented a gloomy look. "It's a beautifully tragic story about the last man and woman in the sky, I won't give away the ending, but it'll leave you breathless. I'm sure your library back at home has it. It's a bestseller."

"I've heard of it, but I'm not interested," I said dryly. "I'm not much in favor of tragedies either."

"Hmm," Theron mused. "Well, if you change your mind ..." He shrugged and moved on.

Leading my crew around the house for a while, he pointed out more of the mounted animals and other decors, such as statuettes sitting on stools and decorative plates. The walls, primarily painted in green, gave the mansion an elegant, but dark look.

Mirrored candle sconces lit up the long halls, and small glass-ball chandeliers filled a majority of the rooms with ivory light. I kept glancing about to see where our swords could be hidden, but had no luck. I couldn't wander off, nor have any of my crew members do it. Like Eamon said: it would be too risky.

"— and over here is the billiard room," Theron continued, opening a door and revealing a dimly lit room where light cascaded onto a pool table made from mahogany. At the end of the room stood a bar with shelves filled with glasses and bottles in different shapes and colors. Theron walked over to the bar and picked up a cigar case sitting on the counter. He lit a cigar with a match, propped it in between his lips, and inhaled before exhaling a small trail of smoke. He offered the case to the crew.

"Would any of you like a smoke?" he inquired, but then chuckled. "Or will you smack the case out of my hands? You really startled my servant when you knocked the cup from him. He nearly jumped out of his skin."

"None of us smoke," I declined, ignoring his last statement.

"Ah, right, you all are still young for a cigar, my apologies." Theron nodded and closed the case. "I don't think your father would be pleased if he found out I gave you a cigar, anyway."

"He's not pleased with me coming here either," I noted.

"Oh? Is he still mad about what happened so many years ago?" Theron asked with a curious glint in his gray eye. It shone like an old, glass marble.

"Father was completely against the idea of me coming here for help, so yes."

"Oh, Theodore ... Theodore, Theodore, Theodore ..." Theron placed the cigar back into his mouth. He breathed in shortly before letting loose another trail of smoke that trailed upward towards the glass chandelier. "I wish we could've settled this like old friends ... It's been twenty years, hasn't it? Mmm, I still remember that day, when I was thrown in jail, locked up with the thieves and murderers as if I had done a crime as treacherous as theirs ..." Theron walked about the room, passed the landscape paintings, the pool table, the dart board, and the fireplace before finally sitting down at an armchair and continuing:

"I was renowned ... respected ... praised ... Why should a great doctor like me be taken to jail and then banished from his home? Humph, pathetic," he muttered, flicking the cigar now perched between his middle and index finger. He sat there for some time, thinking, twisting his lips, and scrunching his eyebrows together.

The atmosphere in the room grew thicker than the smoke drifting about. My crew and I watched him warily, exchanging glances before turning back to the man who finally sighed and shook his head.

"Ah, never mind ... that was a long time ago. I have my own place. I continue my work. I make money. Why should I still be bothered?" He shrugged his shoulders and perched the cigar back to his lips.

"You shouldn't, and neither should my father," I said.

"Indeed ... we shouldn't allow this strife to extend any longer," Theron said, lifting himself off the chair. "It's getting rather stuffy in here; let's go outside. This should be our final stop before lunch."

He led us out into a small courtyard behind the atrium. The glass dome could be seen looming overhead along with the trees that surrounded the mansion. Cypress trees lined the stone walls. A fountain made from black marble stood in its center. Surrounding the fountain, a field of red and white roses sprung up to catch the ivory droplets of the sun's light that bled through the treetops. The trees enclosed the mansion under a giant canopy of curved, green branches that swayed with the wind, causing leaves to tumble and twigs to shudder.

Theron perched himself on a stone bench and took in a breath of the fresh, cool air. The only sound in the garden was the fountain in which the statue of a woman poured out water.

"Ah, this is much better ... you could just sit here for hours ..." he mumbled primarily to himself, and closed his eyes. "Just listening to the water flowing as if it was a little waterfall ... smelling the rich scent of the roses ... I planted them all myself. Beautiful flowers they are; they stand out against this gloomy forest. Oh, and then there are the birds. Every day they sing. Singing songs to one another. Happy songs. Sad songs. It keeps me at ease. Takes my troubles away for a while. Ah ..." He opened his eyes and released a short chuckle.

"Why am I telling you this? You probably don't want to hear an old man ramble on about his garden; it's boring. But you must admit, it's beautiful here. Like a little utopia. If I didn't have my garden ... if I didn't have my books ... if I had nothing except for my interminable work, I would go mad."

Theron fell quiet, and I glanced about the garden. The red and white roses danced quietly in the breeze and birds chirped nearby, singing a cheerful song that indeed brightened the dark forest. A blue bird sprung up from a branch, its bright feathers a stark contrast to the glum backdrop of the trees. It swiftly flapped its little wings, chirping a quick song as it glided about. It swept upward to another branch, joining another blue bird that sat upon a nest. The birds chirped together a little tune and their song echoed amongst the tall trees.

Utopia was a strange word to define this lonely place ...

I turned my attention to my crew, who stood by quietly. They had nothing to say, and I felt there was nothing to speak of either. We just stood there and listened to the birds singing songs — sweet little tunes that rung a pleasant melody. The water continued to flow into the pool, and, if the woman's statue could speak, she would be humming along to the bird's tune. Just humming along while endlessly draining out the vase.

Gradually, the tranquility of the calm atmosphere swept over to my crew and eased some of our tension, but it was just for a fleeting moment as Theron finally spoke up,

"Let's go to the dining room, shall we?"

•   •   •

Candle-lit sconces and a blazing fireplace lit up the oval-shaped dining hall. Landscape paintings hung on the green paneled walls, showcasing gloomy images of mountains and valleys. The gray head of an elk, mounted above the fireplace, stared back at everyone seated at the long, golden-clothed table with wide, glass eyes. A vase filled with red and white roses stood on the black marble mantle, giving off a sweet, rich scent that glided about the dimly-lit room.

Servants brought out golden plates filled with food and settled them in front of my crew and Theron. Then they brought out extra plates when Elliot and his group appeared and sat down as well.

This time, Elliot and the others weren't wearing their masks, but they stayed in their flowing, black cloaks. All ten Vultures appeared to be around our ages. Elliot, being the leader, looked no more than seventeen, with sleek black hair and blue eyes that looked like they could pierce through anything. To my disgust, Elliot sat down next to me, but Eamon sat on my opposite side. Eamon gave Elliot a quick side-eye stare, but let it go and turned to Theron, who sat at the very end of the table. Theron clinked his glass with a golden fork to grab everyone's attention.

"I would like to make a toast," Theron said, "to the brave crew of *The Raging Storm*. The Vultures and I shall help you on this journey to save your beloved captain, and, in exchange, they will find the great Elphida. May the journey be victorious!"

Theron raised his glass, followed by everyone else.

"Oh," Theron continued, gesturing to his Vultures seated around the table. "Allow me to properly introduce you to Elliot and his crew of *The Green Vultures*. They're very faithful companions to me. I sell them medicine and they bring me back priceless possessions for my home."

"I've never heard of *The Green Vultures*," I commented.

"That's because we're from Avem," Elliot responded. "It's a small island far east from here — it's quite easy to miss, just like this island." He took a sip of wine to clear his throat and continued. "We're also unlike you, *The Raging Storm* ... While you go protecting your homeland and other islands, we have more personal objectives. We take things that could be valuable to us, and to Theron, while he gives us what we need."

"So, you're thieves, then," I argued.

"Thieves is a bit of a harsh word," Elliot said with a frown. "I would say ... collectors."

"Humph," I said and picked up my glass, peering down at the wine. "What sort of things do you collect then?"

Elliot leaned back in his chair and said, "All sorts of items — you saw them when you were touring around the house: mirrors, paintings, candles, statuettes ... Theron has a rather classy taste."

"Thank you, Elliot," Theron said. "My dear Vultures have been helpful. They also serve as my bodyguards in case some sort of dilemma arises ... and I pay them all fairly for their contribution. We help one another in need, and now they and you, *The Raging Storm*, will set off on your most important mission yet." He smiled to everyone and turned to Eamon. "You're the one who asked about why I wanted to find the Elphida, correct? Eamon, was it? The Chief Mate of *The Raging Storm*."

"Yes, that's right," Eamon said.

"Your name suits your position," Theron noted. "It means 'guardian' ... I assume, as chief mate, your job is to guard your captain with your life, correct?"

"Yes," Eamon repeated without hesitation.

"Well," Theron folded his handed on the table and smirked, "bearing in mind your captain's condition, you will have to put your skills into good use, or else you'll fail your duty."

Before Eamon could speak, I cut in, raising my voice. "I don't think Eamon needs to be reminded of his position, and I don't need to be told that I need protection. Eamon may be my chief mate, but I can take care of myself."

"Really?" Theron inquired. "You can take care of yourself? Mmm, seeing that you're poisoned, and your life is slowly being taken away by the minute, saving yourself on your own accord may be difficult."

I grimaced and my fingers impulsively curled around a golden knife. Theron caught the subtle act, and he shook his head.

"Ah, ah, ah, don't be careless, Captain," Theron warned. "Don't forget that you're sitting next to my Vultures."

Elliot gave me a crooked smile. Reluctantly, I released my grip on the knife and fell back on my chair. I cringed when a pain shot through my shoulder, but I chose to ignore it as I kept myself composed.

"Very good, Captain," Theron praised mockingly. "Remember, following my lead will save your life. So, I advise you to choose your words and actions wisely. Now, let's continue eating, shall we? We don't want the food to get cold."

"... Fine," I could only say. There were so many threats I wanted to spit at Theron's face. If I had the chance, if I wasn't sitting next to Elliot or any of the other Vultures, I would have this man at my mercy and force him to get me another cure because I was damn sure that he was hiding another one. Instead of giving it to me, Theron was forcing my crew to take on this ridiculous wild goose chase.

After a few minutes of eating in order not to appear suspicious, I said, "I need to go to the washroom. Where is it?"

"It's outside the door to your left," Theron responded.

"I'll be right back," I said and walked out of the room.

I headed to the washroom and shut the door. I glanced at myself in the mirror: exhaustion and irritation were evident all over my pale face. I stood there silently for quite some time, contemplating my situation.

How are we going to get out of this place? I tried to think of some strategies, but my thoughts were cut short when a knock sounded at the door and Elliot's voice followed.

"Captain?" Elliot asked.

"What?"

"Just checking to see that you're in there."

"You seriously thought that I wouldn't be?" I asked.

"It was an assumption. My boss wouldn't want guests to be wandering off."

"Well, 'guests' don't want their host to be breathing down their necks all the time. Ever heard of privacy?"

"Of course, but you've been in there for a while."

"Why should it matter how long I've been in here? I think you should mind your own business."

"I'd advise returning to the dining hall soon, Theron isn't a patient man, and he would like all of us to finish so we can leave."

I rolled my eyes. "Oh, *he* isn't the patient one?"

"I'll give you five minutes," Elliot informed me before walking off.

I turned back to the mirror. My shoulder started hurting once more, like a knife repeatedly scraping the muscle. I curled my hand around the shoulder and mumbled out a small sound of distress. I shut my eyes, trying not to linger on the pain. My hand wrapped itself into a fist and raised upward with a sudden impulse to strike at the mirror. However, I managed to restrain myself and backed off until I hit the wall behind me. I slid to the floor and stared up blankly at the ceiling, unable to do anything. I was held within the talons of the Vultures.

9

– CORDELIA –

F LINT UNROLLED A MAP and placed it over a desk. The map was so large that it covered the entire desk and some of it dropped off over the edge. My crew and the Vultures surrounded the table, looking upon the map that showed all the islands within an oval. A majority of the islands were named, while others were not, and the latter ones were either on the uppermost of the circle or the southernmost.

"So ... where is this island? What's it called?" Flint asked. He eyed Elliot, who had poured himself a glass of wine.

"It's called Aer, but it's nowhere on the map," Elliot answered and took a sip of his drink.

"So how do we know it really exists?" Flint asked.

"Oh, let's not start this again," Elliot said, rolling his eyes. "The island exists; it's hidden, that's all. It's said that the island is seen like a shard of gold floating in the sky since its grass is golden instead of green, and has rivers of honey instead of water. The golden willow is believed to be in the center of the island. And of course, there's the Elphida that lives there. It'll be your job to get it for us."

"I believe we're already aware of that," I said. "Where do we find the island?"

"We have to follow the constellation Ave," Elliot said. "If we keep going north, we'll find the constellation, eventually. The constellation is that of a bird, and the island will show up as the bird's eye."

"Great, so we have a lead," Flint said.

"Yes," Elliot nodded. "Now, we should get moving so that we don't waste any more of the captain's precious time." Elliot gave me a sly look before he started for the door. "Now, where are my crew members sleeping?"

"We have a couple of extra cabins in the back, but some of you may have to share," I answered, and then bitterly asked, "Is there really a reason why you all have to come with us? You have your ship, don't you?"

"It'll be easier if we all came together instead of us going on our respectful ships. Besides, you could try to run away."

"So, you're pretty much holding us hostage on our own ship," I said.

"You think too harshly, Captain," Elliot said with a false hint of hurt in his voice. "We're working together for our own benefits, so don't believe that we'll turn on you."

"Then could we have our swords back?" I inquired. "It would appear suspicious if you kept them from us."

"Of course." Elliot nodded with a smile curved on his lips.

I grimaced at his smug look and stomped over to him until we were inches apart. "I have some ground rules for you. Since you're now on my ship, you have to follow my orders. I'll do what you want, but you also have to do what I want. Got it?"

"Of course, Captain," Elliot remarked. "It is your ship after all, but you certainly can't order us to walk off the plank."

"No, but If you treat me with respect, I'll treat you the same. Just so we're on equal terms with each other," I explained.

"Whatever you say, Captain." Elliot emphasized my title, keeping the smirk that I yearned to smack off his face, but managed to restrain myself and turned away. "Where's Theron?"

"He's collecting a few more items from his home. He'll be here shortly and we'll be off," Elliot informed.

"Alright." I focused my attention toward one of the windows. My shoulder started to ache again, so I wrapped a hand around the wound and rubbed it.

"Do you need any medical attention?" Elliot offered.

I glared at him. "No. If you'll excuse me."

I exited the cabin and returned to my bedchamber. Dr. Jonah had given me medicine to relieve the pain, so I took a couple of pills and sat down at my bed.

A knock sounded at my door.

"Who is it?" I asked groggily. If it was Elliot, I swore —

"It's only me, Captain," Eamon's voice came through and he opened the door. He held my sword in his hands.

"Theron just arrived with our swords," he said.

"Have they been tampered with?" I asked, raising an eyebrow.

"On the contrary," Eamon said and handed me the sword, "they've been polished and look brand-new."

"What?" I inspected the blade: its silver shone brighter than before, and all the scratches that proved of its long usage were gone.

"I suppose they want to polish our shoes next?" I scoffed.

"They want us to trust them."

"Rather hard to do that when we're being held captive here," I argued.

"Captain, I agree that we're in a tight spot," Eamon said, "but we don't exactly have any other choice. Let's follow the Vultures' lead and sooner or later it'll be over."

"Yeah–ah." Pain shot through my shoulder and I groaned as I clasped it again.

"Captain?"

Eamon came to my side, but I raised a hand.

"I'm fine, it just stings a little."

I was lying. It felt as if fire scorched through the skin and my shoulder burned through the bandage. The pain was getting worse.

"Did Dr. Jonah give you any medicine?" Eamon asked.

"Yes, I took it," I said.

"I see ... Well, please rest easy, Captain." Eamon bowed his head before leaving the cabin.

10

– EAMON –

I SHUT THE CAPTAIN'S DOOR and proceeded down the steps to the deck. I tightened the bonds that connected my sword to my hip and observed the Vultures unloading their equipment. Elliot was shouting some orders that I chose not to pay attention to, but, when he noticed me, he strolled over with a hand on his hip and another over the hilt of his blade.

I straightened my back and offered a smile. "It was kind for your crew to polish our swords."

"Of course, we went off on quite the bad start, I thought it would've been appropriate if we showed hospitality. After all, we'll be on this trip for some time. We don't want to raise tension."

"That's thoughtful of you —"

"Though, I'm curious to know how well your blade is. Care to spar?"

I raised an eyebrow and noted Elliot's sword: a vulture's head was sculpted at the hilt. A pair of black stones were its eyes, and its beak was of pure gold.

"That's fine craftsmanship," I commented. "Would be a shame if I damaged it. Are you sure you want to spar?"

"I would gladly take on the captain's chief mate, no matter what," Elliot remarked with a smirk and unsheathed his sword. The blade was so clear it could've been mistaken for glass.

"Very well."

I unsheathed my own sword and pulled myself into a fighting stance. Elliot lurched forward, but I blocked his attack. Our swords emitted a metallic sound when they clashed. Elliot jumped back to prepare another attack. I dodged this time and aimed to knock him off balance. Elliot pivoted away, his feet tapping with diligence. But that diligence disappeared when he struck his sword forward. My sword clashed with his once more. We clashed and clashed again until Elliot struck his sword in a way that I could only dodge. I leaned my head back and the sword flew just inches from my face.

I caught a glimpse of my reflection within the blade, and I was met with the vulture's stone eyes. The eyes stared down at me, shinning dimly against the sun's light. I struck my hilt upward, striking the vulture, shattering one of the stones. The impact forced the sword out of Elliot's hand and it clattered to the ground.

Before I could snatch the sword from Elliot, a shimmer of gold flashed before me, and I instinctively shielded myself from the blow. I nearly tripped from the surprise attack, but, when I regained composure, I saw that Theron had blocked me with a dagger crafted from gold.

"You fight well," Theron said and tucked the dagger back to his belt.

"I didn't realize that you had a hand in combat," I said.

"I know some simple moves, that's all," Theron said and turned to Elliot who retrieved his sword. "Any damage?"

Elliot raised the hilt where the vulture's eye had been smashed. "It appears I need to see a blacksmith. I suppose I shouldn't have offered a sparring, but I hadn't faced a worthy opponent in a while. Thank you."

"It's my pleasure." I wasn't sure if that compliment was sarcasm or not, but I decided not to dwell on it.

"Where is the captain?" Theron asked.

"She's resting," I answered. "It wouldn't be wise to see her now. If there's anything to discuss, I'm here on her behalf."

"Ah, you really are quite loyal," Theron noted. "Well, it's good that the captain is resting; it's been a hectic time for her. So, should we set sail?"

"Yes, I'll inform Flint that we're ready," I said and headed to the upper deck.

Flint was there, leaning at the helm, checking his compass. He snapped it shut when he saw me.

"Are we ready?" Flint asked.

"Yes," I answered.

"All right."

He huffed and his shoulders dropped. Flint stole a glance to the lower deck, and I followed his gaze. A couple of the Vultures, including Elliot, had gathered themselves and were talking in a circle.

"I can't believe we got ourselves wrapped up in this," Flint muttered under his breath.

"I know," I said, "We can only hope that everything goes accordingly."

"Yeah, yeah."

Flint moved to the side and released the ropes that bound our ship to the pier. Then he released the sails and returned to the helm. From there, he steered the ship away from the island, and allowed the wind to move it forward.

I stood by as I watched Flint at the helm, and he picked up his compass to check on it. "North, right?" he asked

"Yes."

"Gotcha." Flint then dug into his breast pocket, plucked out a toothpick and placed it in between his lips. He did this to calm his nerves. I could even spot a bead of sweat at his temple.

"Do you have anything in mind to help our situation?" I asked.

"Mmm," Flint pondered as he chewed on the toothpick. He eyed the Vultures down below again and his chewing halted. "I told you that my dad was once a sailor, right?"

"I believe so."

"Years ago, a group of thieves took my dad and his crew hostage — kind of like our situation here. But unlike these guys, the thieves were really dumb. My dad served them tons and tons of alcohol until they were so drunk that they could barely move. The crew tied all the thieves up and took them to the nearest jail. The thieves were wanted criminals, so my dad and his crew were paid handsomely."

"Interesting story."

"Yeah, too bad we don't have any alcohol to give these guys."

"Elliot did bring some with him," I said. "But it won't be enough to get them all drunk. There's about eleven of them."

"Mmmm." Flint resumed chewing on his toothpick. "I suppose all we can do is hope this plan works, and it doesn't kill us."

"Yeah."

"So, I saw you sparring with ... uh, what was his name again? Emmet?"

"Elliot."

"Right. Too bad Theron had to cut it short. I would've liked to see you take down that guy."

I chuckled. "Maybe if we have another spar."

"Mmm, y'know, I don't believe we ever sparred."

"Really?" I raised an eyebrow, taken aback.

"I believe so," Flint said. "I mean, I'm not that great of a fighter, but we should spar sometime. Maybe after all this is over."

"I look forward to it," I agreed.

Flint accidentally broke the toothpick from the constant chewing and searched for another one. As he did so, he said, "So anything we can do for the captain in the time being?"

"No, she's resting now, so we have to leave her be."

"Mmm." Flint stuck another toothpick in his mouth and chewed it. His head rocked from side to side, and he plucked out the toothpick to say, "Y'know, we should cook her favorite meal for dinner. That should cheer her up. What was it again? Potato and leek stew?"

"Potato and rice," I corrected.

"Yeah, we should make her — wait," Flint paused, "we don't have the ingredients, do we?"

"The Vultures brought in several bags; I'm sure some of them contain food. If not, we'd have to make a stop to gather ingredients, but we don't have time for that."

"Mmmm," Flint hummed once more. "Whether or not we do have the right ingredients, we should still cook a nice meal for her."

"Yes," I agreed, and then my attention shifted to the Vultures below.

They had separated and Theron now hung by a mast, reading a book. His casual posture showed that he was comfortable, as if this was his own ship. He had this smile on his face. It was hard to describe, but I knew that if the captain was around to see it, and to see how comfortable he was, she would be furious.

Then there was Elliot, who sat polishing his sword. He had a sour look on his face, obviously disgruntled that I ruined his hilt. I couldn't help but smile, but it dropped when we made eye contact. It lasted only a moment before he returned to his business. I knew I should return to mine, too.

•   •   •

It turned out that the Vultures did indeed bring food, but the only ingredient missing was onion. The captain never cared much for onion anyway.

As I cooked the meal over a stove, Mark entered the kitchen. He carried himself with slouched shoulders, but his head perked up when he sniffed the stew.

"That smells great!" Mark commented. He slid to my side and glanced at the boiling pot. "Is that potato?"

"Yeah, the Vultures were generous enough to give us some of their food," I said. "Though I can't say how much more generous they can be. How are you holding up, by the way? With all of this?"

"As well as can be."

I nodded and added a dash of salt and garlic into the pot before stirring. The Vultures had been onboard for a few hours now and, so far, they haven't done anything suspicious. I even taste-tested each ingredient to ensure that nothing tasted funny.

"What about you? How are you holding up?" Mark asked.

"All right ..." I said. "Theron and his crew haven't done anything, but I'm still keeping my guard up. This whole plan ... them being onboard our ship ... finding this unknown island ... I'm not wholly in favor of it, but if this'll eventually save the captain, I'm willing to go with it. This might not be the best plan, but ..."

"It's what we got, yeah ..." Mark agreed, biting his lip and falling quiet.

Usually, Mark was very talkative whenever we interacted, but this time he was as tense as everyone else. Uncertain of what was to come, and I hoped to assure him, but didn't know how. I wanted to see more good in the Vultures, but I was sure they were plotting something cruel against us, and we all must stay on our guards to be sure they didn't do anything rash.

"I think I'll be sleeping with one eye open tonight, just to be safe." Mark released a nervous chuckle.

"I might do the same," I said, and we both shared a short laugh.

"Do you need help with the soup?" Mark asked.

"I'm almost done ... Why don't you make a salad? The soup's for everyone, but I don't think that would be enough."

"Sure, what kind of salad?"

"Mmm," I glanced at the other ingredients we had. "How about tomato and mozzarella?"

"Sounds good." Mark gathered a couple tomatoes, washed them, and cut them into thin slices.

While he did so, I asked him, "Your uncle's a blacksmith, correct?"

"Yes, why do you ask?"

"Do you know anything about golden blades? Theron wields one and I don't think I've seen them before."

"Yeah, golden blades are a rarity, as it's also a soft metal, so it doesn't make for a very strong blade on its own unless it's blended with something sturdier. Plus, gold's too valuable to be wasted on fighting, so maybe Theron has one to show off his wealth."

"That's possible," I said. "He did say he only knows a few basic moves, but I don't want to find out if he's bluffing."

"Yeah," Mark agreed. He then fell silent as he finished up chopping the tomato, and then moved to cutting the cheese.

The soup was ready now, so I gathered a bunch of bowls to serve it.

"Do you think ..." Mark began, "since we don't have much time ... we should visit Angela? Hasn't she been working on a boat that's much faster than this? We could use it."

"That's not a bad idea," I considered. "But I fear we might be wasting our time if it turns out the boat isn't ready."

"The crew could split," Mark suggested. "The captain should stay here in case the plan doesn't work. But if it does, we'll go back to pick her up."

"I'm sure some of the Vultures would want to come along too," I said. "They might think that some of us are running away, and it's best to tell them what we're doing so we don't face anymore problems with them."

"Yeah." Mark nodded, though there was reluctance in his voice.

"We'll talk some more tomorrow," I said, and poured soup into one bowl. "Would you mind telling everyone that food's ready? I'll take this to the captain."

•　　　•　　　•

I knocked on the captain's door, but there wasn't an answer. *Was she still sleeping?* I knocked again, but still no answer. Waiting a few moments, I glanced about to see everyone gathering around the deck for dinner. Flint handed out bowls and plates, while Mark handed out the huge pot of stew in case anyone wanted seconds. He then returned to the kitchen to grab the bowl of salad he'd made.

As everyone chatted about in the distance, I turned back to the captain's door, where I pressed an ear to it and was met with silence. I waited a few moments longer, hoping that the captain would answer. But the longer I waited, a weight pressed further and further into my chest as a sudden fear arose.

It was against code, but I entered the cabin without the captain's permission. My worriedness had gotten the best of me, but I needed to know if she was all right.

As I stepped into her dark office, I moved past the mess that was her desk and entered her bedchamber. There, the captain lay sleeping beneath a heavy blanket. Blue moonlight touched upon her bandaged shoulder and, for a second, I swore I saw a splotch of blood leaking through. But my subconscious was simply messing with me.

As the captain was deep in sleep, I didn't bother waking her. She needed her rest, after all. Though, it was a shame that she couldn't try out the stew at least. That would've put her in a better mood — or at least I would hope so.

Not wanting to stay for too long, I departed the cabin and returned to the kitchen. I placed the bowl in the fridge to save for later; I couldn't let it go to waste. I really did want to know what the captain thought of it, but more importantly, I wanted her to eat as soon as she woke up.

11

– CORDELIA –

A BLOOD RED SUN BURNT THE SKY and cries echoed around me. I stood on a crumbling plain surrounded by shadowed figures burning amongst flames that grew and grew until the sky was consumed by smoke. Everything burned and the shadowed figures couldn't stop screaming. Arms shot out of their burning bodies and fingers struck at my direction as they shrieked:

"You did this!"

"This is your fault!"

"We're dead because of you!"

"How could you!"

"You were supposed to protect us!"

The cries blared into my head, and I shut my eyes. I dropped to my knees. This was a dream. Only a terrible dream. But why wasn't I waking up? Wake up! Wake up! But when I opened my eyes, there stood a shadowy figure with eyes *glowing a deep, deep red. It pointed a shaky finger at me and a gaping red hole of what should be the mouth widened.*

"You did this."

"No. No. No." I shut my eyes once more. "Go away. Go away."

"You did this!"

"Stop!"

I opened my eyes, and I gasped. Before me, the shadow figure had disappeared and was replaced with Caleb. He looked smaller than he usually was as his back was hunched and his pajamas hung loose on him. Caleb's hair was in disarray and his eyes were swollen and red from the tears he was shedding. His cheeks were almost as bright as his hair and his body shook as if it was freezing, but it was hot, so hot that sweat had broken out and my hair stuck to my skin. Caleb had his arms wrapped around his small body, staring at me with those wide eyes of his, but they were filled with so much anguish. I've never seen him this upset before.

"Cora ... Cora ..." Caleb hiccupped, rubbing his eyes. "Why did you ... why did you put us all in danger? Don't you care about us, Cora? Don't you care?"

"Of course, I do, Caleb," I said. I took a few steps forward. But each step I made, Caleb drew further and further away from me.

"Then ... then ..." Caleb hiccupped some more, his words choked up in his throat. His body shook still, and he struggled to speak. Finally, he burst out words that caused my heart to stop:

"Then why are we dead? Why are we dead, Cora? I thought you were going to protect us!" Caleb screamed and cried and he dropped to the floor where he thrashed his arms and legs.

"Caleb!" I ran to him, and still he was too far away for me to reach.

"You lied!" he wailed. "You lied! You lied! You lied! YOU LIED!" Caleb screamed to the top of his lungs. He screamed so loud that I swore my eardrums were going to burst. I wanted to scream too, but I couldn't. All I wanted to do was get to him. But when I finally managed to grab his arm, his body melted

before my eyes and became nothing more than a puddle. I looked at my hand, which once held Caleb's arm, and it started to shake. The cold was getting to me now.

I dropped to my knees and watched as the melted form of my brother leaked across the plain and fell off the edge. I looked up at the blood red sun that was nearly extinguished by smoke. The silhouette of the Black Sting flew through the smoke and its cry echoed throughout the area.

Suddenly, the fire had gone out, the shadow forms vanished, and the smoke evaporated. All that was left was that sun glaring down at me, but it didn't give off much light. It was like an eye, just staring while darkness filled everything else around it and me. The plane had disappeared, and I found myself floating in the dark, staring up at that blasted sun while the cries of the Black Sting echoed before me. But what sent me shaking were the screams of the townsfolk shrieking in my head.

Then, the sun exploded. It didn't make a noise, but balls of fire shot out everywhere, lighting the sky with blinding flashes. I caught the sight of stars trying to bring light, but to no avail. Darkness returned to coat the area while the fire flew like shooting stars. The screams had ended all together, and there was silence as I watched the fire and the remnants of the sun fly towards me. Red and white and yellow and orange blended together, and I watched as it drew closer and closer before it became the silhouette of the Black Sting. The creature released a scream so terrible that my heart dropped and I couldn't help but scream as well. I screamed as I was embraced by the fire.

•   •   •

I woke with a choked gasp, staring into the darkness of my room. Panting, I rested a hand on my chest and waited for myself to calm before getting out of bed. Rising, I grabbed a robe and walked outside. I needed a breather, and so it felt comforting when the chilly air of night brushed by my face.

My bare feet tapped gently across the deck. The only other sound was the wind that whistled a quiet lullaby, attempting to lull me back to sleep, but I couldn't do so right now. I was wide awake and still overwhelmed by the nightmare. A sickening feeling resonated within me because I knew that it wouldn't be the last one.

I huddled the robe close to my body and leaned against one of the masts. Staring up, I thought about climbing it and getting a better view of the sky, but then I realized how ridiculous that would be, especially if anyone saw me do. I chuckled to myself.

A pathetic one at that. I really needed to get back to sleep, didn't I?

No, I knew that the nightmare would come back ... It was so damn clear.

I took in a breath and sucked in more of the cool air. The air refreshed me somewhat, but the sting in my shoulder remained constant. A constant burn. I pressed my hand into it and rubbed some circles, considering taking some more medicine. But before I retracted myself from the mast, I heard the soft taps of slippers hitting the floorboard.

Edna approached with a cup of tea in her hands. I got a whiff of chamomile and I almost yearned to get myself a cup too, but I remained at the mast.

"Evening, Captain. Couldn't sleep either?" Edna asked.

"Not really," I simply said.

"Mmmm."

Edna took a sip of her tea, albeit loud as she drank it. She even slurped it, which I found annoying.

When she finished, Edna traced a finger around the cup's rim. "I heard that drinking tea when you're outside can help you sleep."

"Is that so?" I inquired.

"Yes, would you like me to make you some?"

"Please," I said, and then added, "make it mint by the way."

"Of course, Captain." Edna gave me a quick bow before she skipped below deck.

I sighed with gratitude as silence returned. Not that I didn't like company; I just found it better being by myself. Closing my eyes, I focused on nothing in particular in my moments of solitude. But it wasn't long until Edna returned with the tea.

"Here you are, Captain," she said as she handed me the cup.

"Thanks," I said and gulped down the warm substance. It soothed my dry throat, and it brought me to smile a bit.

"Did you add sugar to it?" I asked.

"Yes," Edna said, but then gasped, "Wait, is that bad?"

"No, it's good with sugar."

"Good, good." Edna chuckled with some nervousness lurking in her voice.

She and Mark were fairly similar in terms of shyness.

Perhaps they should get together … but that's none of my business.

"Where did you hear about drinking tea outside?" I asked out of curiosity.

"Oh, I overheard a conversation in the city square not too long ago, forgot who exactly said it, but I thought it sounded reasonable."

"I see …" I trailed off.

Even if it was true or not, drowsiness did return as my eyes started to droop, but another question crossed my mind. It was something I didn't necessarily want to ask, but it came out. "What do you think … everyone back home thinks of us now?"

Edna went quiet for a moment, but she said, "I'm sure there are no hard feelings. After all, it was mainly Gideon who was angry. Everyone else was confused or worried. They know how difficult this is for us, so I'm sure they understand."

"Yeah …"

"And when we come back home, I'm sure they'll be happy to see us. In the end, we're all like one huge family," Edna added.

"What about Gideon? I'm sure he won't welcome us warmly ... Same with others no doubt."

Edna pinched her bottom lip. "Well, we can't make everyone happy ... but it's only a few. It's not like everyone's against us. Like your father said: we're only human."

"Right ..."

I gulped down more tea, but did so quickly. I nearly choked from it, but managed to keep it down and sighed.

"Thanks again for the tea."

"No problem, Captain." Edna smiled, and she skipped back a few steps. "I think I'm going back to bed. Good night."

"'night," I said, and Edna bounded back beneath the deck.

I was left alone again, back in my own space as I drank my tea in peace. I attempted to push back the negative thoughts that threatened to intervene, but I couldn't help but worry what everyone else at home was thinking. It couldn't just be Gideon who was angry; there had to be others. This was a mistake too big to be ignored, and I still blamed myself for it. I really did, and the guilt was only going to intensify — just like the nightmares.

Just like the nightmares.

I swallowed a mouthful of the cold air and closed my eyes. I needed to push these thoughts out of my mind. Taking more sips of the tea, I hoped that the warmth would push away the coldness that shrouded me. It didn't help much. All I could think of were the flames. The screams. The cries. Caleb. I never cared much for the brat's thoughts of me, but I wondered now.

12

– CALEB –

I PRESSED MY FACE TO THE WINDOW as I watched a shooting star fall from the sky. It was so cool.

"Caleb, what are you doing up?"

I turned to see Dad, who had crossed his arms and gave me a sad look. I didn't like to see him sad.

"I couldn't sleep," I said, but pointed to the window. "But look, look! There are shooting stars in the sky!"

"You should really go to bed," Dad said, and he yawned.

He yawned funny. He sounded like a whale when he yawned. I've always wanted to see a whale. I wondered if Cora could ever take me to see one.

I sniffed and my eyes started to water.

"Oh, Caleb, why are you crying?" Dad asked and came over to me.

"I miss Cora," I said and sniffed some more. I wiped off some boogers with my sleeve.

"I miss her too," Dad said. "But she will be back, don't worry."

"When will she be back?"

"I can't say," Dad said. He sniffed as well, but he didn't cry.

I don't recall ever seeing Dad cry. I imagined his big mustache would get all wet.

"Dad?"

"Yes?"

"Have you ever cried?"

Dad looked at me funny. "What brought this up?"

"You sniffed like you were gonna, but I never seen you get really, really sad. Have you ever cried, Dad?"

"Yes, Caleb," Dad said. "Everyone cries, but that's okay. Crying shows that you care about your sister."

"But I've never seen you cry."

"If I don't cry, it doesn't mean that I don't care," Dad said. "When I'm sad and don't cry, my heart is crying."

"Your heart cries?" I asked, tilting my head. "How can it cry?"

"If you're really upset, it cries. Right now, my heart's crying because I'm worried about your sister. But even though my heart's upset, my mind tells me that she'll be alright and come back safe and sound."

"So, does the mind cry?" I asked and rubbed my messy sleeve on my shirt.

Dad noticed, frowned, but didn't say anything about that.

"It's ... different," Dad said. "You see, the mind is what helps you to think and imagine things. What were you thinking when you watched that shooting star?"

"Mmm." I turned back to the window and saw another shooting star passing by. "I was wondering 'bout how Cora was doing and if I could help her. Could I fly on my own boat and see her, Dad?"

"That would be difficult," Dad said. "But maybe someday you will be the captain of your own ship and have a boat. Would you like that?"

"Yes!" I said, jumping up and down, but then I stopped and frowned. "But what can I do to help Cora?"

"You can write her a letter."

"A letter?"

"Yes," Dad nodded, "I'll help you with it tomorrow. Now, I believe you should get back to sleep."

"Mmkay," I said, though I wanted to stay up to watch the stars some more.

I crawled onto my bed and Dad put the blankets over me.

"Goodnight." Dad kissed my forehead, but I wiped the slobber off.

"Night, night!" I said out loud and Dad smiled.

I liked it when he smiled. His cheeks grew as if balloons were stuffed in his mouth and his mustache curved like it could smile too.

Dad walked over to the door, but I sat up on the bed.

"Dad?"

"Yes, Caleb?"

"How do you help a crying heart?" I asked. "You can't hug a heart or tell it to get better like you can with a person."

Dad paused and looked at me for a bit before he answered. "That's true, you can't hug a heart or tell it to get better, but what you can do is allow your heart to get better by doing things that won't upset you more. For me, I like to eat ice cream to cheer myself and my heart."

"Oh," I said and patted my heart. "My heart's crying too, can I have ice cream too?"

Dad laughed. "Very funny, Caleb, but you really need to sleep."

"But I don't wanna sleep with a crying heart," I sniffed and puckered my lips. "My heart won't be happy."

"And your stomach and head might ache afterwards."

"No!" I exclaimed and hoped off the bed. "Every part of my body loves ice cream! If ice cream makes your heart stop crying, it'll stop mine. Please? Only a couple of bites and then I'll go to sleep." I clapped my hands together and jumped up and down. "Please, please, please!"

Dad sighed. "Fine, fine, but only a couple of scoops and it's back to bed."

I gasped excitedly, and I jumped up and down again. I ran up to hug Dad, but I was so small I could only hug his legs.

"Oh, thank you, I love you so, so much!"

Dad patted my head. "I love you too."

"My heart loves you too, it's gonna be so happy!"

Dad smiled, his cheeks puffed up like balloons again. "Mine as well. Now come along before I change my mind."

"What?" I covered my mouth in fright. "You wouldn't do that! No way!"

Dad chuckled and shook his head. "I'm kidding, I'm kidding."

I chuckled as well. Dad was so silly, I wished Cora was as funny as him. He makes so many funny jokes. I think Cora only made one joke as far as I know but she was always frowning so much, or maybe ...

"Dad?" I asked. "Do you think Cora's heart cries too?"

"Yes," Dad said, his voice became sad again. "Like I said, everyone cries, whether it's in the inside or out."

"What does Cora do for her heart?"

"Well, being around family helps," Dad said. "It might seem that she doesn't like to be here, but deep down she cares about us and our home more than anything else."

"Ooh," I said. "I hope Cora can come back soon so she and her heart can feel better!"

"I'm sure she will."

13

– MAYOR THOMASTHAN –

I COULDN'T BLAME CALEB FOR STAYING UP LATE. I haven't been sleeping well either. After I finally managed to get Caleb into bed, I went for a walk. I wouldn't be long; just a walk around the neighborhood would suffice. I needed to clear my head.

I put on my coat, wrapped a scarf around my neck, and checked to make sure that the house was securely locked before venturing off. Leaving Caleb with the servants for only a few minutes wouldn't hurt. Everyone was asleep anyway.

Traversing the cobblestone streets, only flickers of candlelight from the windowsills gave life to the houses. I appeared to be the only one awake. That was fine. I preferred the quiet, especially on nights like these where all the stars were out, and the moon shined so brightly that it made the town glow a bluish-silver color. Wind chimes from some of the houses rung from the chilly breeze. They cast a sweet melody when they all played together. It made me think that I should get a wind chime for the house too. It's a delightful sound, and this was a delightful night to feel right at peace.

I wandered to a field and spotted a patch of caeli flowers growing. The dark blue flowers were one of Marisa's favorites. *Oh, Marisa.* I decided I'd visit her. Collecting some flowers in my arms, I carried them to the cemetery that was up ahead on a hill. Just like the town, the cemetery was quiet, but there were no wind chimes to lull the inhabitants in their eternal slumber. However, the moon's light on the headstones made the stone glow almost like diamonds. It was a wondrous sight. But the most wondrous was Marisa's grave that sat just below a willow tree.

A marble vase formed her headstone with an intricate design of her profile carved into it. Cordelia and Marisa looked almost identical, save for their eyes. Cordelia's were gray, while Marisa's was the loveliest blue I've ever seen. When I looked up at the night sky, I saw her eyes.

"Marisa, dear," I said, as I placed the flowers in the vase, "I brought you your favorite flowers, I hope you like them." I smiled and made sure the flowers were arranged well. "I was going to visit next weekend on our anniversary, but I decided to see you sooner. I hope you're doing well over there." I paused as if waiting for an answer. The only thing I received in return was the cold wind blowing and nearly knocking over my hat.

"Our little girl is out there again," I said. "Well, she's not little anymore, but she's still our child. She's strong though, very strong, but I still worry for her. She was struck by the Black Sting and she's off finding a cure. There's a part of me that fears she won't make it, and it makes me feel so scared. Oh, Marisa, if you could hear me, please watch over her. Make sure she's safe. Please."

This time I really wished I could get an answer — something to acknowledge that my beloved was truly listening and would take care of our child. Our little girl. I'd lost Marisa three years ago; I couldn't bear losing Cordelia. Caleb barely remembered his mother, and now there was a chance that, when he gets older, he might barely remember Cordelia if she's gone too. I couldn't bear thinking of it. My heart was hurting thinking of it. I remembered Caleb wondering if hearts could cry, and, as a matter of fact, they could. My heart was crying right now, and it felt so painful.

"Mayor?"

I looked over my shoulder to see Rebecca approaching. Her shoulders were wrapped in a shawl and she carried a boutique of flowers.

"It's a pleasure to see you this evening," she stated in her sweet little tone of voice. "I see you're visiting Marisa this evening." She plucked a couple of flowers from the bouquet and held them forward. "May I?"

"Please."

Rebecca placed the flowers into the vase and she kneeled down beside me. "I pray that she's resting easy and watching down on us. Such a wonderful woman she was."

"Yes." I nodded and glanced at the flowers she held. "Who are you visiting tonight?"

"My husband. You remember Henry, don't you?"

"Of course," I said. "He was one of the funniest men I've known."

Rebecca chuckled lightly. "Yes, yes, he was." Her chuckle faded to a solemn sigh. "It's a shame that Gideon doesn't share any of his good traits, I'm sorry for what he said to Cordelia that day. I should've put him in his place, but I was just so shocked by what had happened."

"All is forgiven," I said. Although I was still a touch vexed by Gideon's words, I didn't want to upset Rebecca more than she already was. Instead, I patted her hand in reassurance. "What is Gideon up too now, if you mind me asking?"

"Oh, he's out there again," Rebecca huffed. "Didn't bother telling me where he went but ... I'm not surprised anymore."

"I'm sorry to hear," I said.

Rebecca remained quiet for a few moments before getting to her feet. "I should go visit Henry now. Have a good night, Mayor."

"You too."

14

– CORDELIA –

M Y SHOULDER DIDN'T HURT AS MUCH as it did the previous night, but its coloring had changed to a darker tone of gray. I covered it up with my red overcoat and, when I had finished changing, I marched out to see the early morning sun bathing ivory light onto the deck.

"Good morning, Captain."

Theron carried himself as if he owned the ship — smugly and with pride. He was dressed in his own overcoat, but this one was forest green with gold buttons trailing down the opening. He smiled towards me and I frowned in return.

"Did you sleep well?" he asked.

"None of your crew members snuck into my cabin to slit my throat, so I suppose I slept well," I said dryly.

Theron sighed. "You're so harsh. Why, I'm not complaining about your own crew doing the same."

"That's because they don't threaten other people's lives," I hissed. "Now, if you'll excuse me, I'm going to get breakfast."

"I've already made breakfast, actually." Theron gestured a hand to the east end of the deck. Some of our crew members were seated in a circle, eating eggs and sausages from plates. Eamon was even in that circle, chewing quietly while Mark was telling a joke. No one laughed, but I noticed a smile tugging at Eamon's mouth.

"Why don't we join them?" Theron suggested, and he ambled over to join the circle.

He grabbed a plate from Flint, who was serving everyone, and he took a seat next to Elliot. I sat down as well, since I didn't feel like arguing, plus my stomach was begging for food. I helped myself with some eggs and roasted potatoes and sat down next to Eamon.

"How are you feeling today, Captain?" Eamon asked.

"All right," I mumbled and bit into a potato. It was smothered in butter and rosemary. It tasted surprisingly good.

"How is the food?" Theron asked. "I don't normally cook, but I wanted to show my hospitality to you all."

"It's delicious," Edna said, and the rest of my crew nodded in agreement.

I couldn't help but agree too, but it was best to continue eating in silence.

"It is thoughtful," Eamon said. He chewed and swallowed his food before saying, "We have a proposal for you."

"Oh?" Theron raised an eyebrow.

I also glanced at Eamon with curiosity.

"We were thinking that, since we don't have much time and our ship is too slow, some of us could go to Helium and visit Angela, who we know is crafting a boat that can take speeds of one hundred miles per hour. If the boat is ready, we'll take it and go on our way."

"That is a clever idea," Theron said, rubbing his chin. "What do you think, Captain?"

"It is good," I agreed. "When did you come up with this, Eamon?"

"Mark came up with it, actually." Eamon gestured to Mark, who sheepishly nodded. "We were talking last night, and he suggested it. This is the first time we're bringing this up to everyone."

"I appreciate that," I said. "I like the proposal ... You suggest that we should split up? How should we do that? This time I'd like to hear from Mark."

"Oh, well," Mark faltered when all eyes were on him, "I was thinking that I should be one of the crewmembers that goes to the island while you, the captain, stays here and continue on just in case the plan doesn't work."

"I'm sure we have enough time for all of us to drop by," Theron pipcd in. "Angela is an old friend of mine and I would be happy to see her as well, I'm sure we could make some arrangements to get the boat faster."

"I suppose ..." I said with some uncertainty.

"We'll simply be missing a few hours. It'll be no problem if we lose those hours," Theron continued. "Helium is on our way, isn't it?"

"Yes," Elliot answered.

"But if something happens —" Eamon started.

"Relax, everything will be fine," Theron assured. "You want a faster boat, don't you?"

"Yes, but —"

"Then let's go. It shouldn't be a long visit. If we don't get the boat, it's no problem. We'll simply be losing a couple of hours, that's all."

"You're not the one who's losing time," I argued.

"Your ship is quite slow," Theron remarked as he glanced briefly to the sails. "Would be a shame if you miss the opportunity to find a faster route and ended up being stuck here."

I gritted my teeth, and it took me a moment before I could compose myself. "All right," I agreed. "We'll go to Helium."

"Good, good." Theron said and bit off a piece of sausage.

He indulged himself more in the food. But I've lost my appetite altogether. I wasn't keen about this idea, but ... if we were to get a faster boat from Angela, we would be able to reach the island much faster. However, if that boat wasn't ready, we'll only be wasting more time. I placed a hand over my shoulder. Pressure weighed on it as if something tried to push it down. It was hard to ignore it.

I got up and excused myself to my cabin, telling everyone that I wanted to be left alone. There was no way I could tolerate anyone at the moment. All I wanted was peace and quiet.

As I sat at my desk, I stared up at the stained-glass ceiling that hovered above me. The sunlight started to dim as clouds blocked them. Gritting my teeth, I hoped that a storm wouldn't show up; I couldn't deal with anymore problems. I had enough on my hands and I just wanted to shut my eyes for a while.

However, I couldn't enjoy myself long as the skitter-scatter of a familiar little rodent disturbed my solace. As I shot up from my chair, Amabel scurried from her hiding spot in a corner and dashed across my cabin. In seconds, I caught the annoying ferret by the scruff of her neck and lifted her in the air.

"You really do like to pinch my nerves, don't you?" I inquired through gritted teeth.

Amabel yipped in response, and I glared at her in return. She tilted her head and blinked her beady eyes. But that didn't do anything to lighten my mood. Amabel might just be a little bit cute, but that was it, and I didn't want to deal with her right now.

Before I could call for Eamon to get her, there came a knock at the door.

"Who is it?"

"It's Mark, Captain."

I huffed. "Is this important?"

"Not really, but I wanted to give you your food — you didn't finish it, and you know what they say: breakfast is the most important meal of the day." Mark chuckled at the end, but I frowned in return.

"I've lost my appetite," I bluntly said and cracked the door open. I shoved Amabel through the opening. "Give the rest of the food to Amabel."

"I don't think she can eat that stuff," Mark stammered.

"Just keep her out of my sight." I handed Amabel to Mark and, before he said anything, I closed the door.

Groaning, I returned to my desk and ran my hands through my hair. I shut my eyes once more, massaging a temple with two fingers. All I wanted was peace and quiet as I ignored the burning pain on my shoulder.

15

– MARK –

A MABEL MEWED IN MY ARMS, as if she knew that the captain wasn't fond of her. I patted Amabel's head to cheer her up, but the ferret kept mewing and dug her face into my jacket. *I should probably hand her back to Eamon*, I thought.

I soon returned to the others and, once Amabel saw her master, she jumped out of my arms and wrapped herself around Eamon's shoulders.

"Amabel was in the captain's cabin again," I told him.

"I figured," Eamon said. "I'll try not to let her wander in there again."

"That's a lovely ferret," Theron said, leaning forward. "She's yours, Eamon?"

"Yes." Eamon nodded. "Her name's Amabel."

"Where did you find her, might I ask?"

"My parents gave her to me as a gift," Eamon answered. "I'm not sure exactly where she came from."

"Ah." Theron nodded. "Can I see her?"

A spark of reluctance flashed in Eamon's eyes. Not wanting to initiate any trouble, though, Eamon handed Amabel to Theron.

At first, Amabel shook, but once Theron scratched her behind her ear, she nuzzled her head against his palm.

"You found her favorite scratching spot," Eamon commented.

"Yes," Theron said. "I've actually used to own a couple ferrets when I was a really young lad. They were both twins, and I named them Boo and Foo. Yes, yes, those were silly names. Again, I was really young." Theron then scratched under Amabel's chin and said, "Those two lived a long life, but ... when they died, I couldn't part with them. So, I had them stuffed."

I gulped heavily while Eamon appeared eager to snatch Amabel back, but he said, "That's one way to remember them by."

"Indeed, the bond between human and pet is powerful," Theron stated. "They lived for twenty-two years, in case you were curious. Actually, the mayor and I had been friends for those many years too. Or perhaps it was twenty-three? Hmmm."

"That is a long friendship," I commented.

Theron only nodded and handed Amabel back to Eamon. He appeared lost in thought now, and I considered walking away before he noticed.

"Anyhow," Theron cleared his throat, "we should move on to a lighter topic. I dislike it so when our conversations turn solemn. Anything you all have in mind?"

We all exchanged brief glances until Elliot said, "Why don't we play a little game? That should brighten the mood."

"A wonderful idea," Theron praised. "What game do you have in mind?"

Elliot dug into his pocket and brought out a wooden dice. "How 'bout some 'Even and Odds'? Rules are simple: you roll an odd number, you do a dare; you roll an even, you tell a truth. I'll go first."

Elliot rolled the dice across the deck and got a four. "Someone ask me anything and I'll tell them the truth."

There was a short pause until Eamon asked, "How did you and Theron meet?"

"Good question," Elliot said. "It was a few years ago ... My crew and I were selling a chest at a market, and Theron witnessed the bid and asked us where we had found such a find."

"Where did you?" Eamon asked.

"Starna. Forgot the exact location, but someone else found the chest first and took whatever was inside. Unfortunately for them, the chest was also quite valuable as it was made of a rare material." Elliot paused to pick up the dice. "Anyhow, Theron wanted to hire us to find precious items for him, and in exchange he'd give us a greater sum of money as well as supplies for our ship. We obliged, of course, and the rest is history."

"You agreed to help him immediately?" Eamon asked.

"Why, yes," Elliot said. "My crew and I knew of Theron before our initial meeting and were fascinated of his story. We wanted to be part of it." Elliot then tossed the dice to Eamon. "Why don't you go next?"

Eamon eyed Elliot for a split second, making me wonder what he could be thinking before rolling the dice. Eamon landed an eight.

"Truth, again," Elliot stated, "Interesting how we both got it."

"What do you want to ask me?" Eamon asked.

Elliot rubbed his chin while contemplating. After a few moments, he asked, "Do you have any feelings for the captain? You two seem to be awfully close."

A hint of red tinted Eamon's cheeks, but he said stoically, "She's my captain and friend, and I care for her as such and not in the way that you think. That's all."

"So why do you look flustered?" Elliot asked.

"You're asking a silly question."

"I'm simply asking the truth."

"And you just got it," Eamon remarked with restrained annoyance. He tossed the dice to me. "Your turn, Mark."

Even though I didn't really want to play, a chilly breeze from Elliot's direction compelled me to roll.

I landed a one. Odd.

"Okay, what should I do?" I asked.

"Hmmm," Elliot thought, and he glanced to a mast. "Why don't you climb that mast over there?"

"Uh, sure," I said and headed over to it.

I've never climbed a mast before, but I supposed I could try it out. I jumped and clung to the mast before advancing upward, but the mast felt so slippery that I didn't make it too far. I ended up losing my grip and landed hard on my butt. I heard Elliot laughing behind me, and now *I* felt flustered. I got up again to do it once more, but I only ended up on my butt again.

When I attempted it a third time, I heard Fable yelling out, "All right, I think he has done enough!"

I sighed and returned to sit with the others. I turned to Fable, whom I swore was about to explode into a rant, but she simply shot daggers at Elliot. Elliot just smirked.

"Thank you for the show," he said. "Now, who else wants to play?"

Fable crossed her arms. "I believe we've had enough. We should be preparing for Helium, anyway."

"That is correct," Theron said. "Maybe next time, then."

If there was to be a next time, I hope I wasn't dared to climb the mast again. My butt was going to ache for a while.

16

– CORDELIA –

H ELIUM WAS ONLY TWO HOURS from where we were. Like
our island, it had a lighthouse sitting on its tallest peak
and a village built into the cliffs. Angela lived at the far end
of the island, inside one of the few manors. She was one of
the wealthiest inhabitants since she made a living building
boats. Angela had even designed *The Raging Storm*; it's one
of her proudest achievements. Some of her older models
were stationed at the pier right next to her home.

Unlike the inhospitable invite back at Theron's home,
we were welcomed warmly by a servant who led us into a
cozily-lit sitting room. Paper lanterns hung down from the
barrel ceiling, and the room was furnished with furniture
that we practically sunk into because of how soft they were.
A bright pink carpet dressed the floor; our feet sinking into
it as well. A sickly sweet smell glided about the room. I
wasn't sure where it came from — or wanted to know, since
it was such an odd smell.

After a few moments of waiting, Angela ambled in with a cane and cigarette in hand. I couldn't recall a time where I didn't see her holding a cigarette. A small, elderly woman, she wore glasses that were much too big for her piggy-shaped nose. She fixed her glasses before she sunk into a winged chair adjacent to the fireplace.

"It's been sometime since I've seen you all — especially you, Theron; I thought you were still rotting in jail," Angela said in a hoarse voice. She passed him an odd look before snorting out her nose.

Theron released a hearty laugh, slapping his stomach. "No, no, I got out years ago."

"I see. Well, I hope you don't do anything else dangerous again," Angela said. "Believe me, jail can be quite troublesome."

Mark's jaw slacked open, staring in awe. "You've gone to jail, Ms. Angela?"

"Yes." Angela replied. "They were the best and worst years of my life." She appeared lost in thought for a second and then continued, "Ah, that's a tale that would take hours to explain. So, let's cut to the chase: what are you here for?"

I leaned forward with hands crossed on my lap. "We're in a hurry and need a fast boat. Do you have one available?" I asked with urgency and determination in my voice.

Angela placed the cigarette between her heavily painted lips and inhaled deeply. Then, she exhaled a stream of smoke that spiraled towards the ceiling. She maintained direct eye contact with me, and seemed to be enjoying my impatience as a smile crawled on her wrinkled face.

"Ah, yes," she finally said. "I have a few that have been ready for quite some time. But, of course, they come with a price."

"Of course —"

"It's been a long time since I've seen any of you, so the price will be big," Angela remarked, raising a crinkly finger. "Let's see, let's see."

Angela stood from her chair and paced the room. She traced her hand upon bookshelves and tacky knickknacks, and then stopped briefly at a mirror to fix up her hair. She picked out a bird's feather that somehow got stuck between the strands, and tossed it away. Satisfied with herself, Angela puckered her lips at her reflection, and then moved onto another part of the room.

She appeared to be surveying every corner as she mumbled gibberish. Angela tilted her head from side to side. Her gibberish rolled to a little hoarse whistle thanks to her croaky throat. The sound pierced my ears and Mark cringed. Theron sat by without a care in the world with that ugly smile on his face. I had to wonder if he was deaf.

After several drawn-out minutes, Angela stood before a strange-looking plant. She picked up the plant with both hands and lifted it in the air with one hand while she carried the cane in the other one. In the center of the plant's purple and yellow leaves, sat a newly bloomed orange lily.

"This is the 'Deadly Beauty'. It's poisonous if you consume it, but grind it up, it makes the perfect skincare product. I need about ... oh, five more of them. I would gather them myself, but the cave that they live in is now crawling with termites that like to peel the skin off your fingers, and I don't need anything else damaging my skin."

My crew and I exchanged weary looks, and I cleared my throat to grab Angela's attention. "Excuse me, Angela, but we're on a tight schedule ... We would gladly pay you in exchange for the boat —"

"Please," Angela cut me off, throwing back her head in exasperation, "I have so much money that I've considered being buried with it all when I die. I don't need money."

I huffed and pulled myself from the chair. "I'm sorry, Angela, but we must depart. If you'll excuse us."

Angela frowned and stomped her foot. If the floor wasn't made of carpet, I was sure she would've broken through the floorboard. "You've come to my house after a year to demand a faster boat, only to turn it down just because you're in a hurry? Unbelievable! I thought better of *The Raging Storm*, but it appears I've been mistaken."

"Angela, please," Theron began as he stood as well. We are indeed in a hurry. We're searching for Aer in order to cure the captain of the Black Sting poison."

"The Black Sting?" Angela's eyes widened, and she slowly sunk back in her chair, the cigarette nearly falling out of her trembling mouth. "What exactly happened?"

"We were attacked," I said, shifting my eyes to the floor. "The Black Sting's tail struck my shoulder, but it was killed right afterwards. However, because of my carelessness, there had been casualties."

I closed my eyes and immediately the image of fire burning flashed through my mind and my stomach churned. A hand touched my shoulder. Eamon was at my side, providing me a small smile, offering me comfort.

"I'm sorry to hear that," Angela said with a sunken face. I don't recall ever seeing her so distraught before. She crushed the cigarette into a tray and ambled to me. Taking my hand in hers, she gave them a squeeze. "Please, allow me to give you the boats for free. Allow me a couple of hours to make preparations."

I stared at her down-turned eyes wordlessly as I considered her offer. Again, she looked and acted so different; it came out of nowhere. She had known me for a long time, after all; I was almost like her granddaughter. A small smile rose, but it fell just as quickly as the stinging returned to prick my skin. I flinched and absentmindedly forced my hand out of hers.

"No, wait," I said, taking a sharp breath. "It's not fair for you to give us the boats freely ... We'll get the plants for you first. It's the least we can do for you. Besides, getting those plants shouldn't take long, right?"

"Oh." Angela blinked several times and pressed a hand to her chest. "Thank you, dear, but are you sure?"

"Yes," I stated with confidence, though flinched again as the pain intensified. I soothed my wound with a careful hand and faced the others. I'd almost forgotten that Angela and I weren't the only ones in the room.

Eamon and Theron each passed me a different look: Eamon's was that of concern; while pride sat etched in Theron's eyes, and a ghost of a smile crossed his lips. Eamon turned away, but Theron kept his eyes on me. It was hard to ignore that face. It was hard to ignore that ugly gold tooth that also poked out. But it was his eyes that I loathed the most.

They always held amusement — a sort of amusement that was cruel and unwarranted — and he would keep maintaining that look for as long as he possibly could. That look had been burned into my mind for quite some time now, and, the longer he stared at me the more disgusted I felt.

I forced myself to turn back to Angela, who had returned to her seat. She brought out a new cigarette and leaned back into her chair, staring at us all with intent.

"All right, well, retrieving the plants isn't that hard," Angela remarked as she lit the cigarette. "They live in a cave next to Lakit Lake. Go over the twin hills east from the town, and the lake is below the slope. Should take you at least fifteen ... maybe twenty minutes to walk there. After which, you get to the cave, that's where you need to look out for those termites; they are nasty little buggers. Fortunately, they're the only things you have to worry about."

"The only things?" I repeated.

"Must I have to repeat myself?" Angela frowned, plucking the cigarette out of her mouth. "Yes, that's all you have to worry about. Now, return here by sundown. I'm going to make some roasted vegetables and potatoes, which I grew all by myself. thank you very much."

Theron rubbed his hands together. "That sounds delicious."

"Yeah, yeah, get going now." Angela prompted us with the wave of her hand.

I nodded and said, "Thank you, Angela."

17

– EAMON –

T HE CAPTAIN WANTED ONLY ME to come along with her. Mark and the others stayed behind with the Vultures at Angela's. I wasn't keen on the idea of the captain doing the task though; she didn't look too well. However, I figured it was best to not say anything and finish the job as quickly as possible.

The late afternoon sun sat on top of the twin hills, causing the lake to turn to melted gold. The captain and I rounded the lake to reach the cave to find it surrounded by shrubbery. Leaves brushed our faces and branches scratched our skin. The darkness of the cave slowly engulfed our vision until we drew out flashlights that extinguished the darkness.

The cave was narrow, so we had to crawl our way through the passageway. The skitter-scatter of bugs whispered in our ears, and I watched to ensure that none were crawling on me — especially the termites.

We wandered for some time in silence, but the quiet bothered me. Something else was irking the captain, but I believed it best to discuss it later.

"Ugh!"

"Captain?"

The captain flung a spider off her finger and shook her hand. "It's only a spider."

"You didn't have to come here if you didn't want to," I said. "Angela offered to give the boats for free —"

"Yes, I know."

"Then why —" The captain turned around and shot me a glare. She barely ever did that to me and an uneasiness swept over me.

The captain didn't say anything and returned to crawling. After wandering for some time, we came across a fork in the path. Angela didn't provide us directions on which path to take, so we randomly chose left and went on our way. The ceiling heightened, allowing us to walk, but the walls still made the path narrow. We squeezed ourselves through the tunnels, and, whenever my hand brushed the walls, I felt something moist or sticky. It also smelled, as if some animal had died and was rotting away. I pinched my nose in hopes to block the smell, but it didn't do much good.

My hand brushed the wall again, but something felt loose. I pressed my hand on a stone and stumbled forward. Before I could emit a sound, I fell through and tumbled down a long slope. I rolled about until landing on my back. I must've fallen about twenty feet into a hidden cavity.

"Eamon!" I looked up to see the captain's flashlight almost blinding me. "Are you all right?"

"Yeah, I'm fine!" I called back and brushed dust off my pants. "I'll find another way back. Don't worry about —"

Before I finished my sentence, the captain slid down the slope and approached me. "Do you think I would leave my chief mate behind?"

"No, but —"

"Let's keep moving," the captain said.

We trotted forward, but before we got far, we came across a dead end.

"Damn it," the captain muttered, and she unsheathed her sword. "If you can't find a path, make your own, I suppose."

The captain slashed her sword at the rocks, breaking them apart effortlessly. However, before she could go any further, she cringed and dropped her sword.

"Ugh!" The captain clutched her shoulder and fell to her knees.

"Captain!" I exclaimed.

I approached her, but she raised a hand.

"It's nothing," she stressed and picked up her sword.

"Captain, you shouldn't strain yourself," I said. "Here, I brought this." I dug into my jacket and brought out a wrap and ointment.

"Take off your jacket please, Captain."

"I'm fine, Eamon."

I huffed. "Captain, please do this. It'll only take a second."

"Fine." The captain shook off her jacket and pulled down her sleeve to reveal her bandaged shoulder.

I unwrapped the old bandage and couldn't help but stare at the wound. It had grown to a long gray streak across her darkening skin.

"This might sting a bit," I warned, squeezing ointment onto my hand.

The captain released a dry chuckle. "I'm starting to get used to stings by now."

I didn't respond and rubbed the ointment gently over the wound. The captain flinched, but stayed calm.

"This should numb the pain for a while." I said, wiping off the ointment from my hands, and began wrapping the new bandage around her shoulder.

"Thanks." I heard her say.

"Hmmm?" I pretended not to hear.

"I said thanks," the captain raised her voice. She faced away from me.

"You're welcome."

The captain finally faced me, her mouth working on saying something, but it took a moment before she said, "Listen Eamon, I'm sorry that I've been quiet and deciding quickly on this plan even though I put it down but ... I can't shake away what happened back at home. The last thing I did was fail my own people, and I want to do whatever I can to help. If I were to ... you know ... not make it ... I don't want to be a failure."

"Captain," I finished wrapping the bandage and had her face me. For the first time, she looked genuinely hurt, "You are one of the strongest people I know and you shouldn't allow yourself to fall victim to the Black Sting's poison. You are not a failure; you've accomplished so much over the years and I've been by your side the whole way through. What happened at the island was not your fault; you had no control over the incident. Even though you're strong, you're only human and you can only do so much. But what you have done is great, and you will do more great things once we find the cure."

"Yeah ..." the captain said.

She shut her eyes momentarily and meant to place her hand on her shoulder, but accidentally placed it over mine. She opened her eyes and our gaze met once more.

"I'm sorry."

I was about to pull away, but the captain had laced her fingers around mine. I froze at the instant.

"No, you're right," she muttered under her breath. "I just ... the fire ... the screams ... They can't get out of my head. Because of this injury, I'm constantly reminded of it. I'm ... I'm practically desperate to make things right again."

"And you will," I assured. "First you need to get cured and we'll deal with everything else. We can't change what happened, but all we can do now is to keep going and stay strong. You are strong, Captain, and no one wants to see you doubt yourself."

"You're right," the captain said. "Thank you, Eamon."

"You're welcome, Captain."

Her soft smile slipped to a frown, and removed her hand from mine. "Now, if you ever tell a soul about this conversation, I might have to demote you."

I chuckled. "Don't worry, I won't tell anyone."

Her smile returned, and the captain slipped the jacket back on. "All right, let's break through this wall."

The captain picked up her sword and hacked into the wall several more times before it crumbled, revealing, not the darkness as we would've thought, but a peculiar ivory light in the distance.

We walked towards it and came across a large chamber with an underground lake. Thousands upon thousands of fireflies lit the entire chamber, presenting the lake a golden shimmer — a pool of honey. The fireflies surrounded the lake in wide circles, and their circles looped every so often. High above them on the curved ceiling hung large quartz sticking out — like dozens of chandeliers. The fireflies' yellow lights upon the silvery surfaces of the quartz gave off a rainbow glow.

The captain and I wandered towards the lake, utterly speechless at the sight before us. My jaw nearly fell, but I kept a professional composure as I soon spotted the Deadly Beauties on the other side of the lake.

"There!" I announced, gesturing forward.

But before moving on, the captain just stood there, staring up at the ceiling and all the fireflies drifting about. Her gray eyes shone and her mouth fell slightly. I've never seen her in such awe before. I felt somewhat hesitant to draw her back to reality, I, too, wanted to stay here and watch the view before me.

It appeared that time stopped for us and we were free to stand here and watch the fireflies glide by. I was reminded of the tranquility back in Theron's garden ... but instead of the birds chirping to provide songs to ease our troubled thoughts, here was a calm that was pleasant enough to let it all in and forget everything for one simple moment.

A moment of peace was what I wanted right now. Merely a moment. In that moment, thoughts of the future came to me. Thoughts of sailing that didn't involve protecting the skies. Thoughts of sailing, of simply traveling around. To explore new islands. To meet new, friendly people. To relax and enjoy life without the worry of losing it. That was all. That was all.

We stood there in that perfect silence for perhaps a few minutes too long, and for a second, I almost forgot why we were down here. Then my eyes wandered to the captain's shoulder, and a coldness struck through me as if I too had been hit by the Black Sting. The captain's troubles replayed in my head, but I wanted to put those thoughts aside ... She wasn't going to die. She was going to be cured. She was going to.

The tranquility of the moment disappeared, and I hurried to gather the plants in my arms. I returned to the captain's side and acknowledged her with a smile.

"We should leave now."

The captain nodded, but, as we were about to depart the chamber, we heard a rumbling noise and the ground shook. A shriek ripped through the air and, all at once, the fireflies fled away, leaving us in the darkness.

We switched on our flashlights and searched around for the noise. For a moment, we couldn't find anything except for the silence. Then we heard stone crumbling, followed by another loud shriek. The next thing we knew, we stared into the yellow eyes of a gigantic rat.

"Angela didn't tell us there were rats here — never mind a giant one!" I exclaimed.

"Hopefully there's only one of these damned things," the captain cursed and unsheathed her sword.

"Yeah," I agreed and unsheathed my own blade.

The rat shrieked and scurried right at us. Its glowing eyes never blinked as it raced over. It opened its mouth, revealing rows and rows of teeth smothered in saliva that leaked out of its hungry mouth. The captain and I dodged its attack, and it nearly slammed into the wall. The rat released another shriek. This time, it jumped in the air, throwing out its claws, prepared to strike us. As if we read each other's thoughts, the captain and I jumped up and deflected the claws with our swords. The rat's claws were so strong that our swords didn't even leave an impression. Nonetheless, we pushed the rat away and got ourselves back into position as we stood right at the edge of the lake.

Several fireflies returned and shined their ivory lights on the rat's horrid face. The glow of its eyes overwhelmed that of the fireflies. Saliva continued to drip from its mouth. The rat released another shriek, this time using its bony tail as a whip that slashed across the air, ripping off the wings of some of the fireflies. The tail swerved towards us, but the captain and I simultaneously slashed our swords forward and cut through the tail. The rat shrieked so loudly that it felt like our eardrums were going to pop. As we tried to recover from the noise, the rat crashed into me and pushed me into the water.

"Eamon!" I heard the captain yell, but her voice became muffled as water rushed into my ears.

I accidentally released my flashlight, which became a falling speck of light as it drifted to the bottom. Clutching tightly to my sword, I swam my way back to the surface and reached out for some ledge, but it was so dark only the tiny lights of the fireflies and the ghostly eyes of the rat served me as a guide.

I watched the captain fight off the rat within the quick flashes of lights that came by. Her labored breathing echoed and her legs staggered, but there was something in her that kept on fighting.

I found a ledge and lifted myself up. The captain struck the rat to the ground and, even though it was barely conscious, she stabbed the rat's head repeatedly. Blood sprayed her face, but she didn't seem to care. The captain kept hacking until I grabbed her arm.

"Captain!" I exclaimed and pulled her back. "It's dead, you can stop."

The captain huffed and wiped blood from her face. "I imagined that rat as Theron, not much of a difference in appearance." She stabbed the rat's eye and smirked in satisfaction.

"Let's get going, Captain," I suggested, "before it turns out that there's an army of these guys."

"Yeah, I had enough of this place." The captain wiped blood off her sword with a cloth and tossed it behind her. "I would like to have a little talk with Angela. She must've mistaken this cave for one that had finger eating termites instead of a giant rat. Not like I wanted to encounter termites, but I *definitely* didn't want to encounter a giant rat."

"There still might be termites here and we hadn't come across them. It's also likely that Angela didn't know about the rat."

"True," the captain muttered. "Still would like a talk with her though."

I took off my jacket and tried to shake the water out. My body shivered from the cold, but I tried to ignore it.

"Here." The captain took off her own jacket and tossed it to me.

"Captain?" I blinked several times, confused as I stared at her jacket in my hands.

"Just put it on, I can't be having my chief mate catching a cold," the captain said, but faced away from me.

I felt a blush crawl along my cheeks as I stared at the jacket before slipping it on. "Thank you, Captain."

"Again, if anyone asks, I might demote you," the captain said. "Once we get back to Angela's, get yourself cleaned up."

I smiled. "You're very generous."

"Again, don't mention it to anyone," the captain warned and started to walk ahead of me.

"All right, all right."

18

– MARK –

WHILE WE WAITED for the captain and Eamon to return, I engaged myself with some reading in one of the guest rooms that Angela provided us. There was a knock at the door and I turned to see Elliot at the doorway.

"Mark, was it?" He leaned himself against the doorway, acting like he owned the room.

"Yeah," I answered. "What is it?"

"My crew and I are going to the marketplace, and you and your crew should come with us. It's rather boring here, don't you think?"

"I'm fine, actually," I said, opening my book again. I wasn't keen on the idea on going out with the Vultures, but Elliot frowned and shot daggers at me.

"C'mon now, you're testing my patience."

"What will we even be doing there?" I asked.

"Shopping, what else?" Elliot looked at me like I was stupid. I gave him a frown as well.

I shut the book and got to my feet. "All right, fine. I'll go." He was just going to bother me.

"Good, come along."

Elliot led me out of the room, down the stairs, and outside where everyone else was. Edna, Fable, and Flint didn't look any better than I, but we might as well go along with the Vultures if we wanted to stay out of trouble. Elliot smiled a cocky smile at us with crossed arms and his head held high.

Theron walked out with his hands proudly on his hips and he breathed in the air. "Ah, a pleasant day to go to the market. Are you all ready?" he asked as if we were children.

My comrades and I chose not to say anything while Elliot kept up that cocky smile of his.

"Yes," he said. "Hopefully I can find a new hilt for my sword."

I remembered Eamon's and Elliot's spar together. Seeing Eamon in action was always inspiring. No wonder he was second in command of the ship. I wondered how he and the captain were doing in the cave. I was sure they were fine.

•   •   •

The market was filled with people crowded around vendors. Laughing children ran about. It was if a small festival was going on. Lights were strung up above our heads, and flags were toyed with by the wind. Someone was even selling cotton candy, and I couldn't help but indulge myself in the sugary treat. It tasted so good, especially when it melted right on my tongue.

"Tastes good?"

"Yeah —" I paused to see that it was Theron.

He gave me a crooked smile, showing off that ugly golden tooth.

"Great, I'm getting one as well. I don't think I have much time left, so might as well keep fattening this belly up." Theron laughed while patting his potbelly. He soon received his cotton candy and took a big bite out of it.

"Mmm, it is good." Theron sighed much too loudly. "Reminds me of childhood, I used to eat so much candy that my stomach hurt tons afterwards. I was sick for almost two weeks. My parents weren't pleased by that."

"Ah ..." I could only say. I really wasn't interested, but I was worried that my head would roll off my shoulders if I said the wrong thing or tried to leave.

"Here, let me show you something."

Theron led me to one of the little shops where they were selling figurines of a girl with stained glass wings. The wings were all sorts of colors: blues, oranges, yellows, greens. The figurines were crafted beautifully; the dress the girl wore spun around her body as if she was ready to jump up and fly away.

Theron picked up one of the figures and lifted it up for the sun to give it a golden shimmer. "Have you ever heard the tale about the Winged Girl?"

"I don't believe so ..." I said, tilting my head.

"Once upon a time there lived a little girl who dreamt to fly. She plucked out the feathers of all the birds she could find. Blue, green, yellow, orange and red were her wings, and she tied them all on her back. Her parents told her not to do this, for they worried she would fall, but she didn't listen to them. Instead, the girl closed her eyes and jumped off a cliff. When she opened her eyes, she was in the air.

"Her makeshift wings worked, and she flew across the land, becoming a symbol of good fortune as she reached her dream. It's said that if you had one of these figurines, you will have good fortune too. Perhaps your captain would want one. But that's just a suggestion." Theron shrugged and walked off without another word.

I stared down at the figurines and pursed my lips. Whether or not the figurines did give good luck, they were beautiful, and it did look like something the captain might like. After some consideration, I decided to buy two: one for the captain, and one for myself. In the end, it might've been a dumb decision, but I might as well use my money on something here besides cotton candy.

I stared at the figurines. Their stained-glass wings were so beautiful against the afternoon's light, I actually felt some warmth blossoming in my chest as I stared, wondering if good fortune could truly come from these wondrous looking pieces of art.

"Hey, what did you get?"

Edna peeked over my shoulder to check out the figurines. A pair of new bracelets with interesting flower designs encircled her wrists.

"Oh, I got these glass figurines of the girl who dreamt of flying. I got one for the captain and myself."

"Ah, I've heard of that tale," Edna said.

"You have?"

"Yeah, in the end the girl falls to her death."

I blinked several times. "Excuse me?"

"Well, that's one of the interpretations, but yeah, it's pretty gruesome," Edna said. "But it's just a story, it's not real."

"Yeah, but ..." I trailed, turning back to the figurines. "Isn't she still a symbol of good luck?"

"Good and bad luck, but people would say only good fortune so they can sell more," Edna said. "But who knows, perhaps luck will come to the captain's way. She does need it."

"She does," I agreed and then cleared my throat. "Um, so, I noticed you got new bracelets."

"Yes!" she excitedly raised her wrist up, revealing the bracelets that jingled melodically together. "They may be cheap, but they look stylish."

"They are nice," I commented. I didn't know much about jewelry, so I decided not to comment more. I simply offered a smile as we walked through the market.

We met up with Flint and Fable. The two were observing giant crabs crawling about inside cages.

"I used to own a crab," Flint commented. "It grew three times larger than these because I kept feeding it too much.

We had to get rid of him since I was such a bad pet owner." He chuckled to himself, but Fable wasn't laughing.

"I used to own a turtle. I think they're better to take care of since they do nothing all day." Fable shrugged.

"Eh, turtles can't back-flip."

Fable blinked several times at Flint. "Are you saying your crab learnt how to back flip?"

"Yes," Flint said without hesitation. "He also learned how to use a knife. Stabbed me on the finger. Here's the scar." Flint showed Fable a small scar on his digit.

"Uh ..." I stared also in disbelief. "Please don't tell me your crab did anything else with a knife."

"Nah, I was his only victim." Flint waved a hand. "I don't know how he ever learnt to use a knife, and I don't think I want to know." Flint shuddered, but I couldn't help but chuckle quietly. It was a funny image: a crab wielding a knife.

"Anyway," Flint said, changing the subject, "how do you think the captain and Eamon are doing?"

"Knowing them, they'll be fine," Edna said.

"Yeah," Fable agreed, "we shouldn't worry about them. Though, I do worry about the Vultures breathing down our necks. I swear, they're going to tackle us down out of nowhere."

"All we can do is act natural for now," Flint said. "Luckily, we're in a public place, so the Vultures can't ambush here or anything, but it's still good to keep our guards up."

"Right," I agreed and looked over my shoulder.

A couple of Vultures lurked amidst the crowd. It didn't look like they were listening in on our conversation, but they were certainly around no matter where we were.

I spotted Elliot nearby checking out some weaponry. He spotted me looking at him, but all he did was smile. All I could do was pull up a fake one. I turned my back to him, but, after a moment, footsteps approached us from behind.

"Have you all gotten anything interesting from the market so far?" Elliot asked.

Edna showed off her bracelets. "Just these."

"A whistle," Flint answered. "You?"

"I'm waiting for the blacksmith to fix my sword. Your second in commander is quite the fighter."

"He is," I answered.

Elliot smirked. "I wouldn't mind fighting him again. But, if he does wreck up my sword again, I won't be too happy."

Flint chimed in. "Perhaps you shouldn't duel with him again,"

"Hmmm," Elliot considered and shrugged. "We'll see."

He turned on his heel and returned to the blacksmith's. His presence alone unnerved me. I swore that Elliot was a ticking bomb ready to go off, but neither I nor my comrades wanted to think of it as we returned to explore the market. While we wandered, I held to the bag that contained the glass figurines and quietly prayed to myself that we'll be given good fortune for the rest of this journey.

19

– CORDELIA –

A S WE HEADED BACK TO ANGELA'S, I thought back to what Eamon had said to me in the cave. How I was strong and not a failure to anyone ... but I couldn't be certain that it would chase away my fears. I could still hear the screams, after all, and I dreaded another night of sleep, aware that the terrors would no doubt return.

Regardless, I walked with a confident stride to keep up with appearances as we passed through town. This town was much smaller than the one in Domus. The buildings were a similar cream-colored tone. Windmills overlooked the hills. One of the main differences was the vibrant and decorative tapestries that connected one end of a building to another.

The tapestries blocked out the sun's light, providing a dusky glow as we walked underneath them. Some tapestries had abstract patterns on them, while others had animals such as whales and snakes.

"Look at this one, Captain." Eamon pointed to one tapestry that had a ferret playing in a field of flowers. "This looks exactly like Amabel."

I frowned in return. "Speaking of your pet, you need to keep her out of my cabin."

Eamon's excitement vanished from his face. "Sorry, Captain."

Huffing, I glanced at the tapestry. The ferret did indeed resembled Amabel, but then again, all ferrets looked alike. I admit that the tapestry looked nice: the red fur of the ferret stood out against the softer tones of the flowers, and the blue sky in the background. A golden sun even peeked over the ferret's head like a little hat.

"Captain, look at this one."

Eamon had skipped over to the next tapestry and I went over to see. He raised a finger at a group of constellations in a massive circle. All the stars that made up the constellations were silver gems stitched into the blue fabric, and, in the center of it all, was a cluster of gold and green gems which I assumed represented the islands. I had to admit that it was mesmerizing, and I was somewhat curious who made it, but we needed to get back to Angela's.

As we went further into town, we found ourselves at a festival. Children bounced about with cotton candy. Musicians played instruments that drowned out the crowds' chattering. Almost everyone in town seemed to be here, celebrating with either laughter in their voices or food in their mouths.

Our clothes were wet and dirty from that rat fight, but no one paid any mind to us as they went about their merriment, although I was sure our grimy smell would've brought up some curious gazes. Regardless, the less attention, the better —

"Oh, Captain!"

Mark came running up to us with a bunch of bags swaying in his arms. He nearly tripped as he ran, and, once he approached, his nose scrunched up at the smell. But Mark being Mark, he didn't comment on that, instead a smile of relief curled his mouth.

"I'm glad you two are all right," Mark said. "Well, I knew you two would be all right, but it's still good to see you two in one piece, y'know."

"Thanks, Mark," Eamon said and glanced at the bags. "What did you get?"

"Oh, just little souvenirs from the vendors. There are a ton of cool things here," Mark answered as he rummaged through the bags. "I bought you this, Captain." He pulled out a glass figurine of the winged girl.

It was said that having one of the figurines brought good luck, though I didn't believe much in lucky charms. Still, it was thoughtful for Mark to get one for me, and I brought up a small smile.

"You didn't have to, Mark." I said as I received the gift.

Mark scratched the back of his head. "Well, I thought you would need it. And I got something for you too, Eamon."

"Oh?" Eamon stared with a curious look.

"Yup." Mark dug into another bag and pulled out a crossword puzzle. "I thought you might like this."

"Thanks."

Mark handed Eamon the puzzle and his attention went to the plants in my arms. "Was it hard getting the plants?"

"We had to fight a giant rat, actually," Eamon said.

Mark's eyes widened in shock. "A giant rat?"

"Yeah," I huffed. "Pretty damn sure Angela told us that we only had to worry about termites, but we never saw any of those pests."

"Huh," Mark said. "Maybe Angela didn't know that there were giant rats."

"That's what I assume," Eamon noted.

"Whatever, we got the plants, and that's all that matters," I said and started forward. "Let's head back to Angela's. Are the rest of the crew here?"

"Yes, and the Vultures," Mark said.

"Of course, they are," I muttered through gritted teeth. "Did they do anything suspicious?"

"No." Mark shook his head. "Actually, it was their idea that we come here ... They thought that we could use a break."

"I see ... So, they've done nothing."

"Yes, Captain."

I frowned, I was grateful that those rats didn't do anything while we were gone, but I kept my guard up. Glancing about the area in search of them, I couldn't spot them through the crowds of people. Keeping myself guarded, I carried on with Eamon and Mark close behind.

I surveyed the place until I spotted Elliot at one of the vendors. We locked eye contact for a moment before he headed right over. Instinctively, my hand wrapped around my sword's handle and Elliot broke into a chuckle.

"Captain, it wouldn't be wise to fight in public. You of all people should know that," Elliot noted with a smug expression.

"I am aware," I hissed and released my sword.

"Besides, you must be exhausted," Elliot added. "You just came back from your little adventure, after all. Why don't you enjoy yourself and buy something at the market? I saw some nice necklaces you might like."

"I don't wear necklaces," I spat and kept on walking. "I think it's time we get back to Angela's anyway."

"Theron's right," Elliot scoffed. "You truly are no fun." I ignored the comment and marched forward without halting.

20

– EAMON –

CLOUDS DARKENED THE SKY and obscured the sun. A storm was coming, but we've returned to Angela's right before it started to downpour. Rain beat against the windows while we ate dinner in the dining room, but Angela's strange tales lightened the dreary evening.

"And so, with a toothpick, a rod, and an eggshell, I escaped through that godforsaken place. But, due to my recklessness, I lost two of my toes," Angela stated.

"Oh." We all stared at Angela with surprise, and she looked at us like we were crazy.

"Don't believe me? Look." Angela raised her foot, slipped off a slipper, and revealed that her big toe and her middle toe were missing.

"How did that happen?" Mark asked.

The captain cleared her throat. "I'd rather us not hear it while we're still eating dinner."

Theron frowned. "Where is your fun, Captain?"

"I suppose it disappeared long ago," she answered bluntly with a shrug.

"Hmm, well," Theron turned back to Angela, "when the time is right, I'd be very interested in hearing more of the story."

"Thank you," Angela said, and then she turned to the window. Rain hammered at the window and thunder crackled in the distance. Angela shook her head. "It doesn't appear the storm will stop soon. Why don't you all stay the night? It's not safe to leave in this weather."

Theron nodded. "That's reasonable. The storm would only slow us down." He had cleared his plate and settled his knife and fork down. "Well, I'm ready for dessert. What do you have, Angela?"

"Raspberry pudding. I'll get it right now," Angela said and disappeared from the dining room.

Theron inhaled and sat back on the chair. "It's a good idea that we stopped here, would've been ashamed if we got caught in the storm."

"I suppose," the captain said.

She looked out the window and I could see it in her eyes that she was conflicted. However, she knew it would've been reckless to take the ship and leave. She inhaled and quietly finished her meal, the clinking of her utensils cutting and scrapping through the plate was drowned out by the rain that continued to beat on the windows.

"Well," Theron clapped his hands, bringing our attentions, "this stormy weather is the perfect setting for a story."

"What kind of story?" Flint asked curiously.

"I'm glad you asked," Theron said, showing us that golden tooth. "You know the forest that surrounds my house ... Well, sometimes at nighttime, I could hear strange noises from outside. It doesn't sound like it's from an animal, or even human, but regardless, I went out one night in search of the noise. The only thing I had was a lantern as I wandered through the forest. The trees surrounded me like tall, looming shadows with branches acting as if they could snatch me at any moment. Fortunately, I kept my guard up and so I continued my way, desperate to know what in all the islands that noise was."

"What did it sound like?" Mark asked.

"Ah, the sound …" Theron paused for a moment too long.

While we waited, we exchanged looks and listened to the constant beats of the rain.

"The sound," Theron repeated. "It's the sound you hear when an animal is wounded, but it was graver, like whatever it was, it was struggling, as if forgetting how to breathe and could only cry out with a sound that would make the toughest person's blood run cold, and my blood froze up. It was such a ghastly sound, but I needed to know where it came from, so I continued onward with just my lantern guiding my way.

"I was searching for several hours, and saw nothing but the wide eyes of owls and the curious looks of other critters that lived in the forest. There was nothing there but the animals and the trees that still loomed over me. Just when the sun was rising, I decided to turn back due to being so exhausted, but that sound … it still haunts me to this very day. I couldn't sleep at all the next night.

"I've had nightmares and woke gasping for breath, as if I was the owner of that sound and I had been attacked. Perhaps the sound and the nightmares are telling me something, or perhaps I just need to get my mind cleared. When I have these episodes, I go to my garden to meditate. I believe meditating is the best medicine for the mind, Captain." Theron turned to the captain who was too busy eating. "I'm sure you've been quite stressed lately … What do you do to keep yourself relaxed?"

The captain paused for a moment until she gulped down the final piece of chicken from her plate and placed her utensils down.

"Tea helps," the captain answered bluntly.

"Ah, a wonderful choice," Theron said with a bit too much enthusiasm. "Yes, I especially love drinking tea when I'm reading. Keeps my head cleared and focused. But I highly recommend mediating. It does wonders for stress."

"I know, I've done it before," the captain said dryly.

Theron chuckled. "It appears that it doesn't help you."

The captain closed her hand into a fist, but then she let it go. She inhaled softly, but, before she said anything, Angela came back with the pudding.

"Here we go." Angela set the plate right in the center of the table. "Help yourselves 'cause I'm not gonna do it for you."

"Thank you so much, Angela," Theron said. "It looks delicious."

"All of my food is delicious," Angela proclaimed and sat back down.

"Yes, yes, of course." Theron nodded and got himself a bowl of the pudding.

The other Vultures grabbed some pudding, but it seemed like our group had the same thought: we weren't in the mood for dessert, especially the captain. She sat there stern and still, glaring at the pudding while, in actuality, she wanted to glare at Theron and throw a punch at him. She was tired of all this, and so were we.

●　　　●　　　●

The rain pounded the windows, and I watched as the droplets slid down the glass. It was hard to see anything beyond the rain, and fortunately we weren't outside in that storm. I hoped the storm would settle by the morning, but right now there was nothing we could do.

I focused back on the letter I occupied myself with. I had written to my parents; I wanted to keep them updated on our travels. They didn't worry as much as the mayor did for the captain, but still it was nice to let them know how everything was coming along. Of course, I left out the part where we were stuck with the Vultures. I had to twist things around, so I said we had a misstep and needed to find the cure somewhere else.

Knock. Knock.

I stopped writing and turned to the door of the guest room. "Come in."

Elliot stepped in with a wooden box in his hands. He wore a strange expression that insisted he was up to something. Elliot closed the door behind him.

"I didn't catch you at a bad time, did I?"

"Not at all. What is it?" I asked.

"At the market earlier, I came across this vendor selling a gameboard that I hadn't seen since I was little. Have you ever heard of 'Glyphs'?"

"I haven't," I admitted.

"May I show you how to play? It's simple."

"Alright."

I placed the letter away and made room for the box that Elliot placed on the table. Elliot opened the box and inside it lay a wooden board with a double spiral carved into it. Strange glyphs were carved amongst the wood: some were painted black, while the rest were painted red. Elliot picked out four chips from the box and placed them on each corner of the board. Two of the chips were painted black, while the others were red.

"The objective of the game is to get to the end of the spiral," Elliot said. "By doing that, you must use both of your chips and land on only fifteen of the sixty-five glyphs here on the board." Elliot pointed to one of the glyphs with a squiggly design and dots surrounding it. "You can jump over a glyph only five times and go to any direction: diagonal, horizontal, even backwards. Our chips aren't supposed to cross paths with each other, so if I land on a glyph next to you, I take you out."

"All right ..." I said as I tried to figure this out. "Do I move my chips only fifteen times each?"

"Yes, but you only move a chip to one or two glyphs once per turn."

"I see, I think I understand now," I said.

"Let's get started then." Elliot smiled. "You can start first."

I nodded and moved my first chip to a glyph that resembled an anchor. "Is there a meaning for the glyphs?"

"I'm not entirely sure," Elliot answered as he moved his own chip. The glyph he moved it to resemble two tree branches twisted together. "It might simply be for decoration."

"I see …" I paused to see where I could move my chip again, but decided to move my second chip.

"Though I did hear that the glyphs could be a code for something, perhaps a trick to win the game."

Elliot moved his first piece again, but he didn't touch his second.

"That would be interesting," I mused and moved my second piece again.

"Mmmm."

Elliot nodded and stared down at his chip for a moment, then to my own. Finally, Elliot moved his chip over one glyph.

"Where did you say you found this game again?" I asked.

"At a vendor in the market," Elliot said. "The man who sold me this was selling a bunch of items from other islands. Ever heard of the Isle of Vena out in the west?"

"Yes, I have," I said as I moved my glyph. "One of its towns mysteriously burnt to the ground."

"Indeed, the vendor told me he was from there. He was able to escape the fire with his most valuable possession: a wind chime that he had hanging over his stand."

Elliot moved his chip once more.

"Do you think he knows what could've caused the fire?"

"No idea." Elliot shook his head. "Everything was right and peaceful until it all went up in flames in the blink of an eye."

"I see …"

"It's interesting though," Elliot added, "That an entire town could be destroyed all of a sudden. It leaves you wondering what could've caused it. If it was accidental or intentional."

"Mmm."

I finally moved my piece after some thought.

"Was the man trying to sell his wind chime too if he had it at the stand?"

"No, it was just a way to tell customers his story. Perhaps he's trying to find answers to what happened to his home."

"Ah."

I watched as Elliot skipped a glyph and placed his chip down. I realized he was heading towards my direction. I moved my chip two pieces away. A small smile tugged on Elliot's lips.

"What do you think could've caused the fire?" Elliot asked.

He moved two spaces over and hadn't even moved his second chip yet.

"Hmmm," I thought as I wondered what my next step could be. "Perhaps it was some sort of creature?"

Elliot chuckled. "I can't recall any creature that breathes or uses fire."

"Neither can I," I admitted. "But not everything in the sky has been discovered yet, so who knows."

"Right." Elliot nodded. "That's a frightening thought, a fire-breathing creature ... it's scarier than, say, the Black Sting. What happened to it again?"

"I killed it."

"How?"

"I shot an arrow through its head."

I moved my chip again.

"Fascinating." Elliot's smile grew. "How would you kill a fire-breathing creature?"

I clicked my tongue as I focused on my chips and then Elliot's. "I'll avoid going near it, so I might use my crossbow."

"Ah, do you prefer using long-ranged weapons?"

"I think I'm better with a sword."

"It's the same for me: I prefer swords too," Elliot said as he moved his chip closer to mine. He still hadn't moved his second chip. "You gain this sense of satisfaction when you feel the blade sinking into something ... or someone. I'm sure you've killed loads of creatures, but have you ever killed a person?"

I glanced up at Elliot and peered straight into his eyes. He had this ... look on his face I couldn't really describe. His face was absorbed in orange candlelight, as if wearing a burning mask. A faint smile sat etched on his lips, and his chin rose while he leaned himself forward. Then there were his eyes. A sick, twisted kind of curiosity lay wrapped up in those dark blue hues that nearly appeared black by the candlelight. It made my stomach churn just by looking at them.

"No," I answered bluntly.

"Ah." Elliot nodded and fell back into his chair. "That reminds me, we should spar again, I got a new hilt."

"We should," I agreed, and my shoulders dropped after I realized that they had tensed up.

I moved my chips two spaces that time.

"Tomorrow, perhaps?" Elliot suggested.

"That might work."

"Good."

Elliot moved his chip towards me again. He had also taken two spaces and still hadn't moved his second chip. But I found it best not to question it.

"I won't go as easy on you as I did before, so you best be ready."

"I'll be sure of it."

I moved my chip again and realized that I reached the center of the spiral.

"Congratulations, you beat me," Elliot praised, though there was a hint of disappointment in his voice. However, he held out his hand for me to shake.

I avoided eye contact as I took his hand and he shook it. He tightened his grip, and I smiled to hide my discomfort.

"We should do this again," I suggested, and immediately pulled my hand away once Elliot finally let go. My hand hurt from how strongly he had held it.

"Yes, I agree." Elliot collected the board and chips and placed them in the box. "The captain should play too. I'm sure she'll enjoy it."

"I think so too."

I got up as well and pushed in my chair. Elliot didn't push in his as he got up.

"Well then," Elliot held up his head and cradled the box in his arms. "Have a good night."

"You too."

Elliot passed me another of his smug smiles and left the room, leaving me with just the candlelight and my unfinished letter.

I finished up the letter, placed it in my coat jacket, and got ready for bed. Though before I went to sleep, I made sure that my door was locked.

21

– CORDELIA –

I WOKE UP IN A COLD SWEAT and stared straight into the darkness of the room. It was the middle of the night and aside from the recurring nightmares, the pounding rain that sounded like drums kept me restless. I slipped out of bed and stumbled into the bathroom. I splashed cold water on my face and studied the weary gray eyes that stared back at me. If my reflection could talk, it would wonder why I was up. But the nightmares would just come back to me. I kept seeing flames. I kept hearing screams. If I was the only one around, I would scream too. I wanted to scream so much right now.

I rubbed my shoulder. The grayness had now spread to my chest and crawled up my neck. It was if a shadow was preparing to choke me. A tightness wrapped itself around my chest, as if some heavy weight refused to let go. I feared that breathing was going to be a problem. Damn, how much time did I have left?

I splashed more water on my face. That was when my breathing fell short. I inhaled and exhaled slowly while I stared at myself in the mirror. Closing my eyes, I tried to clear my head. For just a moment I needed to clear my head. Just. A. Moment.

I wanted to scream.

No, I needed to calm down, just calm down.

Inhale ... I told myself as I breathed.

Exhale ...

Inhale ...

Exhale ...

I did this a couple more times before meeting my reflection again.

She stared back at me, giving me a cross look that said 'go back to bed now'. I complied and started to turn back to my room. But, before making it there, I spotted a light at the bottom of the stairs.

Curious, I wandered down and entered the parlor where I found Angela in a nightgown, smoking a cigarette by a fire. Angela inhaled sharply before puffing out a stream of smoke that drifted upwards before disappearing.

"Having trouble sleeping?" Angela asked.

"Ang–"

"Sit down." Angela cut me off and gestured to the chair across from her.

I sat down and noted the knitted cats sitting on the mantelpiece.

"Do you smoke?" Angela asked, waving about a box of cigars.

"No."

"That's too bad, this is some good stuff." Angela chuckled and placed away the box. "So ... what's the deal with you and Theron? Surprise you're with that son of a pig."

"It's a long story."

"I'm here until my sleep medicine kicks in and knocks me out." Angela blew out another puff of smoke and stole a glance at the clock behind her. "And that's in ... twenty-two minutes, I believe. Take your time with the story."

I sighed and decided to talk about everything that had happened up till now. Meanwhile, Angela continued to smoke and nodded her head as she listened attentively. Finally, she jabbed the cigarette onto the cigarette tray and smothered it.

"If I were you, I would get as far away from Theron as possible," Angela remarked in a harsh tone.

"I know, but I can't risk the lives of my crew if we escape," I said.

"Being involved with him is more dangerous." Angela pointed out and leaned forward. She checked first to make sure no one was listening and said, "Listen, first thing in the morning, you and your crew are taking the Arise Boat and getting out of here."

"I appreciate your concern, Angela, but this is risky. If we go, the Vultures will track us down and surely kill us."

"So, you'd rather stay as their prisoner?"

"No, but I don't want us to deal with any more problems."

Angela sighed and leaned back into the wing chair. "If I was you, I would take the risk and go. Did they mention what they'll do to you after you encounter the Elphida and get the fruit?"

"No, they didn't."

"Now that, that is a warning sign," Angela said, wiggling a finger. She adjusted herself in her seat, and placed a hand over her chest. "Captain, allow me to help you escape."

My mouth fell slightly at that proclamation. "If you get involved, you might be killed."

"Are you implying that I'm weak?" Angela raised an eyebrow. "Dear, a group of men invaded my home not too long ago, and I was able to defend myself just fine."

"How?"

Angela smirked. "I have traps hidden everywhere in my home in case someone dared try to steal from me. As one of the richest inventors here, I do have to be cautious, don't I?" Angela winked. "But I believe this time we need to be subtler. Come with me, dear."

Angela got up from the chair and led me into a storage room with strange bottles filled with liquids and powders. It reminded me of the bottles back at Theron's and I became wary.

"You make potions?"

"It's a hobby," Angela bluntly said, and I decided not to delve further into it. "Let's see ..." Angela mumbled to herself as she picked out several bottles before she found the right one. "Here we go." She plucked out the cork and gave me a peek inside.

"Uh, is that cinnamon?"

"Yes and no," Angela said. "This is a special sleeping powder designed to look and taste exactly like cinnamon. Got it from an old friend of mine. If anyone swallows this, they'll fall asleep within a minute. I was thinking that tomorrow during breakfast, I'll sprinkle the cinnamon on muffins and give them to the Vultures, and once they're all asleep, you all can escape."

"How long does the spell last?" I asked.

"A couple of hours, that gives you plenty of time to leave."

"What about you?"

Angela scoffed. "Are you still concerned about my well-being? Please, darling, I'll be fine," Angela remarked as she patted her chest with confidence. "Now, first thing tomorrow you're going to tell your crew the plan and we'll take it from there."

"Alright, thank you, Angela."

"You're welcome." Angela smiled. "Now, get back to bed. It's going to be a long day for you tomorrow."

"Yeah ..." I nodded and left Angela to her business. But before heading up the stairs, I got myself a glass of water. I carried the glass to my room, but was stopped by a shadowy figure at the corner of the hall. The figure stepped into the moonlight, revealing it to be Theron in tacky nightwear. That ugly golden tooth of his shone in the light as a smile spread on that punchable face.

"Can't sleep either?" Theron asked.

"I only needed some water," I bluntly stated, avoiding eye contact as I walked past him. My nerves tangled up inside me while I did so, but fortunately I remained calm.

"I have trouble sleeping too," Theron said. Before I could interrupt him, he continued: "Not sure if it's just my age or if I'm simply sleeping wrong, but I always need to walk around. Do you think Angela would mind if I walk in her garden? Thankfully, the rain had finally stopped."

"I don't know, go ask her yourself." I shrugged and took another step forward, but Theron stopped me once again.

"Might I ask you something, Captain?"

"What?"

"What do you think happens afterwards?"

"What do you mean?"

"Surely you must've thought about it considering your life's on the line. Death. I've always had a strange fascination with it. I was always keen to talk to someone who's life was at its brink."

"That's sick," I spat.

"It's curiosity."

"I'm heading to bed." I took yet another step forward, but the rat couldn't keep his mouth shut.

"I've dreamt of death once," Theron said. "I was lying in my own bed, and instead of looking up at the ceiling above me, I saw the embodiment of all my worries, all my pain, all my mistakes through life, staring down at me and a voice telling me, 'It's all over now.' I couldn't have been happier, and so I welcomed death like a friend, because all of those troubles that have weighted on my shoulders for so, so long, were going to disappear forever. I would be free. I wouldn't feel pain anymore. I would finally be happy. However, I woke up afterwards, and I'd never felt so much disappointment. I wanted to know if death truly was a gateway to true happiness, but of course, I wouldn't know until I have taken that final breath."

"Well, I wouldn't know," I muttered. "In truth, I'm not planning to know, because I am not dying anytime soon."

"Of course, Captain," Theron said. "I am sure that you will be successful." He smirked at me.

Damn I hated that smirk so much. I opened my mouth to say something, I wanted to yell something, but I chose not to. There was no point. I needed to sleep and not have his words consume my thoughts. My thoughts were my own, and he didn't have the right to get in my head. And so, I walked away.

"Have a good night, Captain," I heard him say before I shut the door.

●　　　●　　　●

"Cora, where's Mama?"

A knot tangled up inside me when I observed the confusion and sadness in Caleb's eyes. He was only three at the time. When exactly was it the right time to tell a kid about death? He sat there quietly in his chair; he had finished up lunch and was nibbling on the edge of his sippy cup. His big eyes blinked, and he tilted his head. Caleb's mass of red hair fell over his face, but he didn't brush any of them off.

We buried Mom that morning, Father didn't want Caleb to go to the funeral. He believed it would've been too upsetting for him. But all Caleb was, was confused. He kept looking at the empty chair where Mom used to sit, as if waiting for her to come right over, give him a kiss on the forehead before sitting down. It wasn't the case anymore.

"She's somewhere else," I simply answered.

"Somewhere ... else?"

"Yes."

"Where?"

I paused, damn I wished Father was here to help me out, but he was taking a walk to clear his head. I should've gone with him, but, either I or him would have to tell him, eventually.

"I can't exactly say," I started, fiddling with my words before saying, "but it's ... a nice place."

"Ooh," Caleb drawled out. "When is she coming back?"

The knot inside me tightened, and I inhaled a bit too sharply. I cleared my throat and tried to avoid looking at Caleb's confused expression, but it was hard.

"She can't." My voice nearly cracked at the end, and I cleared my throat once more. "It's ... difficult."

"Can we see her?"

I paused but eventually shook my head. "No, at least not now."

"When can we see her?"

"Later," I said. "If it makes you feel better, she's ... happy where she is, so you don't have to worry."

"Oh ..." Caleb trailed and then he smiled. "If she's happy, then that makes me happy."

I could only just nod to that and continued to eat.

•   •   •

I woke up in a cold sweat again. It was nearly morning now, and I didn't know whether to go back to sleep or not. There was that heavy weight again on my chest and all I could do was inhale and exhale. Just breathing calmly wasn't going to take this pain away. It wasn't.

I sat up and stared out the window. The sky was still dark, but I spied hints of reds and oranges in the horizon. I decided to get back to sleep, but it was too difficult. So, I just lay there, staring at the window and trying to ignore that dreadful feeling in my chest.

22

– THERON –

T HE RAIN HAD FINALLY STOPPED, and I couldn't be happier. I had asked Angela if I could take a walk outside, and she prompted me out without question. I was simply delighted. Stepping outside into the garden, I took in a good whiff of the air and sighed.

"Ah, this is nice," I said to myself.

I strolled through the garden with the moon being my guide, and I studied the plants growing around me. There was a variety, but the ones that struck me were the yellow roses budding near a pond. I couldn't help but pluck one out of the bush and observe it closely. Under the moonlight, the petals shined like gold. Rain drops dripped off them. I sniffed them and smiled. They smelled wonderful — like fresh honey mixed in with rain.

I continued my stroll down the garden, the moon still being my guide. It shone blue and silver light onto the plants. The lights from the house were also a comfort. The night was peaceful. Fireflies were out flying about, and there was silence. Complete silence. I was at ease and I could breathe easily. I sat down at a bench and allowed the silence to keep me company. This all made me want to return to my home; that was where I was really at peace. This was nice, too. Yes, this was really nice. I could stay here all night, but since it was a bit chilly out, I couldn't stay too long.

What a shame, though, that nothing could last forever. What a shame that time could pass in the blink of an eye. If I had one power — just one — it would be to stop time for as long as I could so I could appreciate moments like this. Yes, that would be a good wish. It would be a good wish indeed. Ah, I would love to be back home now. I missed the birds chirping, and the soothing sounds of the fountain. Even though I appreciated the silence here, the sounds in my garden are more satisfying. Either way, I was at peace. Yes, that was right. I could close my eyes here and not worry about anything. Nothing at all.

Ah, it really was nice here. If only I had my book with me so I could read. I supposed I could go back upstairs to grab it, but it would be a hassle to get it. Ah, well, relaxing here was good enough.

I opened my eyes and faced the moon. It shone down like a giant eye that watched over everything. A giant silver orb with a light that would never go out. Oh, how intriguing would it be to reach the moon and see what it had to offer? That would be impossible though, but then again, there were many wondrous and strange things here in this world, so perhaps reaching the moon wasn't so far-fetched. I wondered what could be up there.

Yes, I thought that was a valid question. What did it had to offer? Perhaps, after this fun little adventure, I'd embark on another adventure to the moon. We hadn't ever seen what was there. Perhaps treasure? Perhaps creatures never seen before? Who knew but the moon itself?

My thoughts on the matter ceased when clouds moved in to cover the moon. I feared that another storm was brewing, so I went back inside. What a shame; I was so comfortable. Time really did fly quickly. If only I had that power …

When I went back into the house and climbed the stairs to my room, it was even more quiet. No one seemed to be up, but that wasn't a surprise. It was late. I lost track of time, of how long I was sitting on that bench. It was more than several minutes, but less than an hour. Either way, it was nice, but nice things must end, eventually.

23

– CORDELIA –

WHEN MORNING ARRIVED, I went to each of my crew and told them the plan. They were all in on it, though Eamon did appear hesitant. Honestly, I was also hesitant, but what else could we do? We needed to get away from them.

When we entered the dining hall, the Vultures and Theron were already seated. We just needed to wait for Angela.

"How did you all sleep last night?" Theron asked.

"All right," I answered dryly once I sat down.

"Oh, Captain," Theron pointed a finger to my direction, "your neck is becoming gray."

"I'm aware," I said, facing away.

Eamon and the rest of my crew gave me concerned looks, but I had told them beforehand that the medicine's been helping. However, the stinging kept coming back and was now creeping to my chest and throat. I had to take in quick breaths and drink a lot to keep myself calm, but more importantly, I had to keep my head cleared. I had to, and I needed this plan to work. It had to work. I needed something to work for me for a change.

Angela walked in with a tray filled with food. In the center was a plate filled with muffins coated with cinnamon. She set all the food on the table and the plate of muffins directly for all of us to see. The muffins looked so good that my mouth started to water, but I warned my crew that we could only pretend to eat them and spit them out when no one was looking. So, we all carefully picked out a muffin and settled them on our plates. Theron and the Vultures did the same as well as they carried food onto their plates.

"Everything looks delicious," Theron praised as he clapped his hands together.

"Thank you," Angela said. "Please try the muffins, they're a special recipe I've made myself and I want to know what you all think."

"Mmm, don't mind if we do," Theron remarked and picked up one of the muffins. He twisted the muffin around while he examined it. "It looks quite delightful, and it smells good too. What kind of muffin is it?"

"It's banana and cinnamon." Angela answered.

"Mmmm, I love bananas," Theron said. "I once grew a banana tree actually, but the bananas were all blue for some reason."

Elliot chuckled shortly. "They tasted like pears."

"They did, didn't they?" Theron agreed. "I don't know what had happened, perhaps there was something in the soil."

"Perhaps." Elliot nodded.

"Well, I assure you that these muffins don't taste like pears," Angela said.

"Oh, we're sure," Theron said. "The muffins don't look blue either. Wouldn't that be something? Blue muffins."

"Yes, it would be something," Angela agreed.

"Blueberry muffins come to mind," Elliot said, "but those muffins aren't entirely blue."

"No, they aren't."

By Angela's tone of voice, she was growing patient and so was I. I had started to tap my fingers beneath the table as I watched the Vultures with great exasperation. Theron continued to ramble on and on about that dumb banana tree of his to what seemed like several minutes until finally, he took a bite.

Theron's eyes widened with awe. "Wonderful, Angela. Truly, you are a genius."

"Oh, stop." Angela cupped a hand over her cheek, feigning embarrassment.

The other Vultures took bites of the muffins and we pretended to eat them, but covered our mouths with napkins as we silently spat out the pieces. The muffin really tasted wonderful on my tongue, and it was almost aggravating that I couldn't swallow it. Then I heard a soft gasp and turned to Mark's direction. His eyes widened and covered his mouth. He had swallowed a piece.

Damn it.

"Are you all right?" Theron asked.

"Ah, yes," Mark coughed awkwardly, "the food went down the wrong tube." He drummed his chest and shifted his eyes to different directions.

"Why don't you have some water?" Angela suggested, gesturing her head to her left where the kitchen was.

"I don't — uh, right," Mark nodded and disappeared to the other room. However, it wasn't long until there was a small thump.

"What was that?" Theron asked.

"Oh, he must've dropped something," Angela excused, waving her hand.

"Shouldn't we help him?" Theron asked.

"He'll be fine," I said dismissively. "He's always clumsy."

"Ah."

Theron nodded and continued to eat his food. But it didn't take long for a yawn to linger from his mouth. The other

Vultures started to yawn as well. A small smile crossed my lips as I watched the Vultures' heads lull from side to side before they collectively fell lopsided. I released a breath that I held on for far too long and savored in that moment of relief, but it wasn't the time to celebrate. We needed to go now.

"Eamon and I will go on the Arise Boat and head for Aer," I said. "The rest of you go back on *The Raging Storm* and follow us. Send a letter to Domus and inform the rest of our crew what's happening and meet us in Aer. There's no doubt that the Vultures will come after us, so we need more help."

"Are there any fast enough boats they can take?" Edna asked.

"There are," Flint said, "but you do bring up a point: What if the crew doesn't make it and we're outmatched?"

I sighed. They did make a point. "Then we better hurry before that happens. We need to write a letter now then."

Angela stood from the chair. "Leave that to me."

"Thank you," I said and turn back to my crew. "Now, I doubt that the Vultures will go after you, but just in case, stay low in the sky so you're not spotted easily. If you are spotted, you know how to take care of them." I presented them a smile of confidence.

I trusted that my crew could take care of themselves, although there was a lingering feeling in me that feared for the worst. All I could do was assure them and hope for the best.

•   •   •

We settled Mark inside his cabin then returned to the deck where Angela had given us extra food and supplies. Hopefully she didn't pack any sleeping powder with it all.

"Now you all be careful," Angela said, patting my arm. "I'll keep the Vultures at bay as long as I can."

"Thank you, Angela."

I felt terrible putting Angela in danger. She was the wisest person I knew, and it was best for me to not convince her to come with us. Angela looked at me with a smile that was rare for her. She usually grimaced or gave me a snarky grin, but this smile was genuine. However, what surprised me more was her embrace. Her hug reminded me of my father's, considering how short they were. I hugged her back, and she told me that she'll send a letter to let me know that everything was fine. After that, I said my goodbyes to the rest of my crew, and Eamon and I went onto the Arise Boat.

The boat was small. It looked like it could only carry ten people. Eamon approached the helm while I sat at one of the many benches that filled the boat. I opened a bag, got out an apple, and tossed it to Eamon. He caught it.

"So, we head north, correct?" he asked.

"That's the plan," I said. "North until we find that golden island. With this boat we should be able to get there within two days, instead of four or however long it would've been before."

"Right."

Eamon unwrapped the sail, which sprung out and waved rapidly from the morning wind. He then unhooked the boat from the pier. It suddenly dropped through the sky. But, after a moment, its bird-like wings were released. They stretched out, cutting through the air as they ripped the wind current. The wings beat like those of a hummingbird before rising and soaring towards the north.

I watched as Helium and my ship became nothing more but specks in the distance. Soon clouds covered them up, and we faced the spacious sky all around us.

We soared across the clouds and swept by islands where their lighthouses flashed in our directions. We slowed when it was getting dark; it wasn't wise to fly at such a high speed in the darkness, we might accidently fly into something. So, Eamon lowered the sail, and the wings flapped gently, keeping the boat afloat.

•   •   •

Stars swept the night in a great sea of silver that stretched around us. No clouds were in sight, only the stars as they attempted to extinguish the black-drop of the sky. I gazed up at the stars above and spotted a shooting star soaring overhead. Eamon sat down next to me, but I barely noticed him until he spoke.

"How are you feeling?" he said.

"Alright …" I answered. Although my shoulder was hurting slightly, there wasn't much pressure on my chest. I had just taken some medicine, and was feeling drowsy. An odd sound echoed in the distance. It sounded like a deep, deep humming — something that was both melancholic but beautiful.

A pod of whales, both big and small, soared all around us, cutting out the lights of the stars as their shadows loomed over our boat. They continued to sing. Eamon and I felt the weight of their song as they carried it across the starry night. We both watched in silence, staring up and around and then to each other.

"Caleb would love this," I found myself saying. "Whales are his favorite animals, and he always wanted to see one up close."

"Perhaps you should bring him on one of our adventures sometime," Eamon suggested.

"Eh." I shrugged. "Maybe when he's older, I don't trust him to ride on my ship yet."

Eamon smiled. "I'm sure he'll be thrilled nonetheless."

I rolled my eyes. "Can we drop this?"

Eamon chuckled

What was so funny? I frowned and pulled out a blanket from one of our bags. It was getting cold, so I wrapped the blanket around my shoulders. The whales continued to sing their song as they flew amongst the stars.

"I've never seen so many whales in my life, either," Eamon said. "They barely show themselves in front of people. It's a shame that they're endangered."

"Yeah, I've heard," I said. "It's unfortunate ... I have to admit, they are beautiful creatures. Caleb would be devastated if they all disappeared before he could see them."

"Mmmm." Eamon nodded. He also got out a blanket and wrapped it around his shoulders. "How about this: after all this is over, we take Caleb on our ship to see the whales?"

"It is hard to find them, you know ... This was all sheer luck."

"Yeah, but there's no harm in trying. It's for your brother." Eamon tried to reason with me.

I sighed and said, "Fine," so he could get off my back on it.

"Great." Eamon smiled.

I had to admit, he always had a nice smile that jus drew me in. I don't know how to describe it, but whenever he smiled, I felt a warmth in my chest that blossomed and made me feel like I could float. And, underneath this bright sky, his eyes sparkled like the surrounding stars.

The whales had disappeared now. It was quiet. Just the two of us here on this boat. There was nothing but the stars to accompany us as we floated in the sky on our own personal cloud. It was peaceful, but drowsiness started to take its hold on me. I didn't want to go to sleep. Not yet.

"Eamon ..."

"Yes, Captain?"

"I ... uh ..." I paused, not so sure what I was going to say. I then shook my head and pulled back. "It's nothing, never mind."

"What is it?"

"It's nothing. We need to sleep, anyway." I turned away, but Eamon took my arm. But his hold was gentle.

"You can tell me anything, Captain."

I sighed and turned back to him. Eamon's eyes were filled with concern, as if I was hurting again. I wasn't, now that the pain had numbed thanks to the medicine. I was only sleepy, but ... something in me didn't want to sleep and I didn't know why.

"I just want to say ..." I paused again and swallowed some air. "I'm glad you're here ... with me."

"Thank you, Captain." Eamon smiled again, but then it transitioned to a frown. "Why are you acting nervous all of a sudden, though?"

"I don't know," I huffed. "The medicine I took is making me act weird or something."

"Ah," Eamon said.

I don't think he bought it. I don't know what was up with me tonight. Maybe it was because it was only Eamon and I here. But we've been alone together a bunch of times, so what made this time any different? I didn't know. It bugged me more than it probably should have and Eamon probably thought I was acting crazy rather than strange.

"Just go to sleep," I said.

"All right. Goodnight, Captain."

Eamon moved to another bench to lay himself down.

"Goodnight."

24

– ANGELA –

I SIPPED MY TEA and sat back on my chair, waiting for the Vultures to wake. When they stirred, I added a couple more sugar cubes to my cup and sipped from it again. Before I set it down, a group of swords pointed in my general direction.

"What the hell did you do to us, Angela?" Theron asked, gritting his teeth. "Where's the crew of *The Raging Storm*?"

I set the cup down. "I gave you all sleeping powder in order for the crew to escape. What do you think happened?"

Theron shot up to his feet and tossed his chair back. It hit the wall before falling to the floor.

I frowned. "That's an expensive chair, you know."

"I don't give a damn; the crew of *The Raging Storm* have escaped and you're going to pay."

"Oh?" I eyed him curiously. "What, are you going to kill me? A defenseless old lady? That is low, even for you, Theron. Why don't you sit back down and we chat like the good old days?"

"I have no time to chat," Theron argued. He started for the door, but paused when he almost stepped upon the trip wire I'd set up. I had set up wires all about the room.

"You should be more careful, my dear old friend," I said. "If even a hair touches those wires, you will meet an unfortunate end. I'm the only one who knows how to loosen the traps. If you try to do so, you'll surely make a mistake and lose a toe or two. So, if I were you, I would sit back down and, after our talk, I'll let you go. How about that?"

Theron grumbled something under his breath, but he cleared his throat and gave me a smile. Ugh, he still had that awful golden tooth. I was tempted to rip it out of his mouth and throw it in between his eyes. Now that would make my day.

"Alright, I comply." Theron put away his sword and so did the rest of his crew. "What do you want to talk about, Angie?"

"For one, don't ever call me that again," I warned, striking a finger at him. "And two, I would like to know what the hell you want with the Elphida and why you want to use Cordelia to get to it."

"The captain and I are trying to help each other out, simple as that," Theron said. "She wants to get cured and I, well, you know how I am with animals. I love to dissect them, study them, see how their anatomy works and such. The Elphida is such an unusual creature, I have to know and understand everything about it."

"Obsession isn't good," I said, taking another sip of my tea. "Especially when you can think of nothing else but it. However, no matter what I say, it won't change your mind. You'll still go after this obsession you've had for years, but use Cordelia and her crew. I suppose you're not going to let them go free after this is over, correct?"

"Do you take me as a monster, Angela?" Theron asked.

"I take you as someone who is so trapped in greed and pride that you've lost your way to redeem yourself even after so many years in jail. So, in a matter of speaking, yes."

Theron's eyes narrowed. "I'd watch your tongue."

"And I'd watch your next move," I warned. "You want everything to go your way because you've felt betrayed of what had happened so many years ago. Unfortunately, that cannot happen. You are so focused on trying to gain what you want that, in the end, you'll only face demise. Cordelia and her crew will defeat you, and you'll return to that crummy cell where you belong." I stuck my hand in my pocket and pulled out a pack of cigars. I lit one and clamped it in my mouth before blowing out some smoke.

"I've had enough," Theron said and pulled out his knife. "Release us. Now."

"I need a favor," I said and puffed out another smoke. "Bring me back one of those fruits. What were they called again? Eh, whatever, anyway, I need one so if you could just —"

"You are testing my patience —"

"Do you want me to release you or not?" I asked. "We can stay here for hours, maybe even days or weeks, until we die of starvation and dehydration. Your choice." I picked up my cup again and took a sip.

Theron grimaced, and so did the rest of his crew. He pulled the chair up and sat back down. "All right. Fine."

I frowned. "How do I know you're not lying to me so you all can leave?"

"Well, I suppose you'll just have to trust me."

I scoffed. "Yes, because you're the most trustworthy person I know." I set the cup back down and stood up. "If you dare hurt Cordelia and her crew, I will send word to every captain and crew of what you've done and make certain you all recieve the punishment that you deserve. You'll be put on trial and be sent back to jail where you belong."

"I surely wouldn't want to go back there," Theron said. "All I want is the Elphida. That's all. We don't need to keep piling up more problems. I'll get what you want. The captain will get what she wants. And you'll get what you want. That'll be that. Now, release the traps, Angela."

I stared at Theron and his crew with doubt before I sighed. "Fine."

I went over, unhooked the traps, and made sure that Theron didn't do anything stupid while I released them. Instead, he and his crew stood up noiselessly, and when I was finished, I opened the door.

"You're free to leave."

"Thank you, Angela," Theron said.

"I will say you're welcome when you get me that fruit," I noted.

"That's understandable," Theron agreed. "Do you have any extra Arise Boats we could use?"

"Yes," I said. "Do be careful with them."

"We will, goodbye."

I feigned a smile and shut the door behind them.

25

– MARK –

I WOKE UP from one of the best, if not the *best* nap, I've ever had, but I was also confused when I found myself in my cabin. Then I realized, *Oh great, I ate the muffin, didn't I?* But who could blame me? It was a delicious muffin. I hope I didn't cause anyone any trouble, though.

I got out of the cabin to see Edna. She smiled once she saw me.

"Hey, feeling all right?" Edna asked.

"Yeah, sorry that I accidentally ate the muffin," I said, scratching the back of my head.

Edna shrugged. "I don't blame you; it tasted delicious."

"Mmm." I nodded. "So ... the captain and Eamon are gone?"

"Yes, we're following them right now and sent word to the rest of our crew for assistance."

"Will they reach us in time?"

"I'm not sure, but if they come across Theron and the Vultures, they'll be able to take care of them."

"That'll be great," I replied, with a swell of confidence.

I looked toward the sky and saw birds flying overhead. One in particular carried a letter and swooped down towards us. The bird dropped the letter, and it fell into my hand.

I turned to the front. It said: *To Cora from Caleb.*

"Oh, isn't Caleb the captain's brother?" I asked.

"Yes," Edna answered. "We'll put it in her cabin so it's safe."

"Mmm," I agreed. "Wonder what Caleb wrote about. I bet he misses his sis."

"That's probably it," Edna said.

"Do you have any siblings, Edna?"

"Nah, only child. You?"

"I have a younger sister named Nora. She wants to become part of the crew when she grows up. She's only ten, but she's really smart for her age. I write letters to my family all the time and Nora always responds with drawings."

"That's sweet." Edna smiled.

"Yeah, oh, here's one of her drawings." I dug into my pocket and pulled out a drawing Nora made of Domus. It was a pretty detailed drawing for a ten-year-old. She even added every individual building. Around the island were different creatures, like the Black Sting. But she drew a huge smile on it to make it look happy.

"That's really good," Edna commented.

"Yeah, she's quite the artist," I said. "If she doesn't make it on the ship, her second job is to be an architect."

"Looks like she already has her future planned out," Edna chuckled. "When I was her age, I just wanted to steal all the sweets that my parents kept hiding from me."

I chuckled too. "Were you successful?"

"All the time." Edna winked.

"When I was ten, I got myself stuck in the well in my backyard," I shyly confessed. "I was stuck for hours since I was really chubby at the time, so the fire department had the hardest time getting me out. The news spread all over the island and at school everyone called me 'Well Boy'. It was so embarrassing."

"Aw, sorry to hear that," Edna said, though it sounded like she wanted to snicker.

"Eh." I shrugged. "It's in the past now, but I do think about it from time to time. I remembered thinking I might die in there and how embarrassing that would be. 'Chubby kid gets stuck in well and dies' — that's what the paper would say."

"I'm glad you got out," Edna said, her tone quickly changed to concern right there.

"Thanks." I smiled and my cheeks warmed up.

My smile dropped when we heard a horn blowing in the distance. We covered our ears and Fable came storming through one of the doors.

"What the hell!?" she exclaimed.

"Over there!" Flint called from the upper deck.

A large, black ship with red sails headed in our direction. The horn continued its harsh sound, taunting us, as the ship drew closer and closer. And as it drew closer, I spotted a wooden boar's head sculpted into the bow. Its huge tusks, made of metal, resembled knives. Its hollow eyes glared at me.

"Whose ship is that?" I asked, taking a step back for precaution.

"I don't know," Fable said as she walked over to us. "But I've seen it at the pier back at home."

"Then shouldn't we know who it belongs to?" Edna asked.

"Must be a new ship," Fable said, crossing her arms.

"Hmmm."

I frowned as I kept watch on the mysterious ship, though nervousness tingled my skin like tiny needles. Still, I stood grounded to the floorboard with my head held high in alert.

When the ship got close enough, its sails lowered, and Flint lowered our sails too. Both ships now perfectly aligned with each other. Although ours was just slightly bigger, the latter was more intimidating with its boar's head and blood-red sails.

A few crew members from the red ship approached the deck. I didn't recognize them, except for one that caused my stomach to churn. It was Gideon. Immediately I thought back to the way he yelled at the captain after the Black Sting's attack. I clutched my hand into a fist, but I chose not to say anything.

Gideon and his mates hopped onto our deck and, in a flash, Flint came rushing down the stairs.

"Hey!" he called out. "You can't just get onto another person's ship without permission."

"Pfft," Gideon scoffed while his mates snickered.

"What are you doing here, Gideon?" Fable demanded as she stomped a foot forward.

"Sailing, what else? What, do you believe that you own the sky or something?" Gideon asked with a loud snort. "Anyway, where's your precious captain?"

"None of your business," Fable spat. "Why don't you go on your way and leave us be?"

"Is she too ashamed to come out and face me?" Gideon inquired, sticking out his bottom lip in a mocking way.

"She's not even here!" I called out suddenly, and then covered my mouth right afterwards.

Fable shot me a glare while Gideon raised a curious eyebrow. The rest of his mates stared in wonderment as well. I inwardly cursed myself and sunk back a few steps.

"Oh? Where is she?" Gideon asked. "It's strange that a captain is not with her ship."

"Again, it's none of your business." Fable gritted her teeth.

Gideon wasn't having it and reached for the sword fastened at his belt.

"I'm only asking a question," Gideon remarked in an icy tone of voice.

He moved towards us while we moved back. We all reached for our swords while Gideon's crew reached for theirs. There were only four of us and nine of them, we couldn't take them all. I wasn't that much of a fighter, so I would be a liability in this situation I felt sweat starting to build on my face and my mouth felt dry. My heart hammered against my chest. My fingers fidgeted with my sword's hilt.

"We don't have time for this," Fable exclaimed. "And I don't think you do either, Gideon. What would fighting even get us?"

Gideon paused, but a smile crawled on his lips. "Hmph, you're right, we don't have time for this. Besides, there's no point in fighting traitors, anyway."

"What was that?!" Fable barked.

"You heard me," Gideon spat. "You failed to protect our home. That makes you all traitors. If the mayor wasn't so thin-skinned, he would've thrown you all in jail. Every one of you. You would all be in jail." He threw a finger at each of us as he spoke.

"Watch your tongue or I'll cut it off," Fable threatened. Her hand never left her sword's hilt, and she was ready to yank it out. I'd never heard so much venom in her voice; it almost made me jump.

Gideon broke into a haughty laugh and he clutched his stomach. His mates joined in to laugh as well, and the collision of laughter caused the hair on the back of my neck to rise.

"You're all pathetic," Gideon stated, then clicked his tongue as he said, "But you are right though: fighting you would be a waste of time. And since your captain isn't here, there's no need for us to be here either. Let's go, men."

His crew collectively nodded and only presented us with glares before they turned away. My nervousness turned to anger as blood boiled up inside me, but it was best not to evoke them any further. All we could do was watch as they exited our ship, and prepared to depart.

We watched as Gideon's ship sailed past us and my anger had ebbed. But Fable repeatedly slammed her foot into the floorboard. She then pulled out her sword from its sheath and struck the blade onto the deck.

"Hey, careful with that!" Flint remarked.

"I can't believe that guy!" Fable exclaimed, ignoring Flint's words. She inhaled sharply as she brought the sword back into her sheath, but her hand remained on its handle. "If I could, I would've —"

"We couldn't do anything, and we can't do anything now. Let's all calm down and focus on our mission, alright?" Flint said, and he observed the damage on the floorboard. He huffed and pinched his nose. "You really do need to be careful. We just got this fixed up."

"That's nothing." Fable rolled her eyes. "And, yeah, I know we need to focus on the mission. Why don't you get us going then, Flint? You are in charge of the ship when the captain's gone, after all."

"I was going to do that," Flint grumbled, but instead of arguing, went over to let loose the sails.

After he did that, Flint returned to the helm. He veered the ship to the right, and the rest of us watched as Gideon's ship became nothing but a speck of red and black in the distance.

"I'm heading back to nap," Fable muttered and marched through the door which she had barged out. She then slammed the door shut.

Edna leaned into my ear. "We probably shouldn't bother her."

"Yeah," I agreed, and glanced at the letter in my hand. "I should put this in the captain's cabin."

"You do that, I'll be practicing my sparring on some dummies." Edna waved me off and disappeared below deck.

I took another look at the sky: Gideon's ship was nowhere to be seen. Even so, a chill still crawled through me, fearing that they would come back. Then a spark of anger returned to replace that fear. How could Gideon be so disrespectful to the captain? Not to mention, he threatened us too. It left a sickening feeling inside that I couldn't describe, but I fought to ignore it as I went to the captain's cabin.

The cabin appeared dark as clouds passed over the stained-glass ceiling. I took a moment to stare at the ceiling in awe, it always amazed me whenever I saw it. The décor differed completely from the rest of the ship, and I've always been interested in architecture just like my little sister.

Heading up to the desk, I placed the letter on a pile of papers. The captain's desk was a mess, and I had the impulse to clean and organize everything, but I stopped myself as an image of the captain's angry face crossed my mind. I gulped and took a step back. If I even touched anything on her desk, I would be dead. Even though the captain wasn't around, I didn't dare touch anything.

Still, I wondered how the captain could manage with her desk like this. Perhaps when all this was over, she'd be able to clean it up, and maybe I could help her. Or perhaps Eamon could help her. She trusted him more, after all. But again, if I dared touch her stuff, she'd be furious.

I then brushed the thought away as I exited her cabin. There was no need for me to stay there any longer. Heading over to one of the ledges, I glanced back at the sky. There was nothing as far as I could see, but I decided to keep watch just in case.

My thoughts somehow went back to the muffins. I still felt bad about eating them. I could've ruined our plan, but it wasn't my fault it tasted so good. Next time we went to Angela's, I'm getting that recipe ... without that powder, of course.

I chuckled at that thought. I really did need to be careful the next time. Who knew what would've happened if the Vultures found us out? And then there was Gideon. He had no right to say those things to us, and I was sure he was going to attack when he put his hand on his sword. I shuddered at the thought. Hopefully, we didn't have to deal with him anytime soon.

26

– CALEB –

I HAD WRITTEN A LETTER with Dad's help. I hoped it got to Cora okay. I told her that I hoped that she would get better soon, and come back in time for my birthday. That was coming up, but I didn't feel too excited about it. I knew I should, but with Cora gone, I only stayed sad. Dad told me not to feel sad, and he took me to the park to cheer me up.

The park was one of the busiest places on the island. There were always people there, and kids like me playing with kites. Today, though, it wasn't as happy as it usually was. People weren't as talkative and, while the kids played, they kept watch at the sky as if another one of those monsters came. It made me feel a bit scared too, but, with Dad by my side, I wasn't too scared.

Dad and I sat at a bench, and I nibbled on some strawberry ice cream. It tasted so sweet, I wanted to ask for more, but knew Dad wouldn't be too happy. He always said it wasn't good to eat too much ice cream — or too much of any sort of junk food. But I couldn't help that it all tasted so good.

While I licked ice cream off my fingers, I noticed a girl playing with a ball. She looked around my age. Her hair was yellow and orange and tied by two flashy hair strings. She also wore a yellow dress with a big bow.

I patted my dad's knee. "Dad, Dad, can I play with that girl over there?"

"Of course, Caleb," Dad said.

Immediately, I hopped off the bench and ran over to the girl.

"Hiya!" I cheered, and the girl jumped.

"Ah!" she exclaimed and dropped her ball, which rolled a bit across the grass.

I picked up the ball. "My name's Caleb. What's your name?"

"Ashling," the girl said in a small voice.

"Ah ... Ahh ... shhhh ... liiin?" I tried to say, my mouth twisting about.

She smiled. "Ashling."

"Oh." I nodded, but I still wasn't too sure how to say it right. "Um ... can I play with you?"

"Sure," the girl said and opened her arms. "Toss me the ball."

I tossed her the ball, and she tossed it back to me. We did this a few times, but then she bumped me on the head by accident and I dropped to the ground. My butt hurt when I landed, and I rubbed my head. The ball didn't hurt much, but Dad came running over and picked me up.

"Caleb, are you okay?" Dad asked in a worried voice. He sounded so scared, like I had hurt myself even more.

"I'm fine, Dad. Can you put me down? I'm playing with my friend," I said.

"All right." Dad put me down, but he brushed away some of my hair to see where I got hit. "It doesn't look bad ..."

"I'm fine, Dad!" I repeated in a louder voice.

Dad huffed and brought me into a hug. "Good, good."

"Can I keep playing with my friend?" I asked.

"Yes, yes." Dad pulled away and patted my head, then went back over to the bench and sat down.

Dad worried a lot, but I thought a lot of people were worrying since the attack. Even the girl didn't look too happy, even though we were playing.

"You doing okay?" I asked her as we returned to our game. "You look a bit sad."

The girl shrugged. "I'm okay ..."

She said that, but I wasn't sure if that was true. I dropped the ball once I caught it and I went over to hug her. She jumped again, but then she hugged me back. We hugged for a bit and when we hugged, I smelled something sweet.

"You smell like apple pie," I said.

"Thanks," the girl said with a small giggle.

She didn't seem so sad anymore, and it made me giggle as well. I was glad I was able to make her giggle. We could all use a little laugh, and a hug too. Hugs made everyone happy. And when Cora comes back, I'll give her the biggest hug ever.

27

– MAYOR THOMASTHAN –

I WATCHED AS CALEB PLAYED with his new friend, and I was delighted to know that he was doing better than before. It always broke my heart seeing him so sad. He was still a young lad; he shouldn't be carrying sorrow. He was supposed to be enjoying life, and right now this was his childhood. The happiest time to be alive.

As I watched Caleb play, I spotted Rebecca, wearing a nice pastel dress, walking her tortoise. She also acknowledged me, and came over to occupy the empty seat next to me. Her eyes looked puffy, as if lacking sleep, doing little to hide the forlorn expression on her face.

"Oh, Mayor, how are you on this lovely day?" she asked me.

"Well enough," I answered. "And you?"

"As well as I can be." Rebecca reached into her pocket and got out a handkerchief. A teardrop had slid down her cheek, but she wiped it off.

My heart sunk. "Anything wrong? Is this about Gideon again?"

Rebecca exhaled deeply and fell back in the bench. Her head gestured towards the sky, and a couple ships drifted hundreds of feet above us.

"Yes," Rebecca strained. "He wrote a letter which said that ... he didn't want to be bothered by me anymore."

"That's awful. Why would he say that?"

"I always wrote to him while he's away ... I've wished for him to come back, but ... he doesn't want to." Rebecca sniffed and wiped her eyes. "I remember when he was little ... He clung to me always and wanted his father and I to play with him all the time. Now that he constantly leaves ... without saying goodbye even ... it makes me wonder what I've done wrong as a mother."

"Oh, Rebecca —"

"I know that he's a young man now and people change, but ... he doesn't have to be so distant, and cold and — oh, I'm sorry you have to hear me ramble, mayor."

"Don't apologize," I said. "It's good to talk about your feelings instead of keeping them bottled up. I'm sorry that Gideon wrote that nasty letter. Perhaps when he comes back, you'll have a talk with him face to face. Let him know how this is affecting you."

"Yes, I'd like to do that." Rebecca paused for a moment to gather herself and turned to Caleb. "Caleb seems to be well ..."

"He is."

Rebecca twisted her handkerchief about. "Cherish this while you can; children grow up so fast."

"I know," I agreed, thinking about Cordelia and how mature she had become despite her age.

Caleb was only five, but it felt like yesterday when he was a baby and I was holding him for the first time. Marisa cried tears of joy, but Cordelia, on the other hand, seemed indifferent. When she held Caleb for the first time, Caleb snatched her hair and yanked out a few strands. Cordelia was certainly not pleased, but Caleb was simply a baby back then. He didn't know any better.

Cordelia and Caleb didn't get along as well as I had hoped, and since Cordelia was always away ... I feared that their bond would only keep straining. I didn't want that, and I didn't know what to do to keep it from straining.

"Mayor?"

Rebecca called me back into reality and I glanced down to see Phillip resting his head on my lap. I patted his head, and he squawked in return.

"Would you like to come by my house for some tea later?" I asked.

Rebecca blinked, confused by how I changed the subject, but she soon understood why. I, too, felt tears swelling up in my eyes and I was sure Rebecca noticed.

She answered in a soft voice, "Of course."

28

– CORDELIA –

I T WAS TWILIGHT. The sun rested on the clouds and made them look like a field of orange and gold. Stars peeked out over the horizon, but they were so dim it was easy to miss them. I wasn't sure how far we were from the island, but we've been sailing for nearly two days, so I was sure we were getting there soon. However, my chest had started to hurt again, and I found myself taking labored breaths. I had to inhale and exhale slowly and close my eyes in order to stay calm. When I opened my eyes, Eamon sat next to me with a hand on my shoulder.

"Are you alright?" he asked me in a gentle voice. His green eyes showed concern as he leaned forward.

"My shoulder's hurting again, but I'll be fine." I couldn't lie to him and say that I was fine. I wasn't fine. It felt like my shoulder was on fire again and a strong pressure weighed down on my chest. Now the pressure crawled up my throat, as if a hand was ready to take a hold of it and squeeze.

"I'll be fine," I repeated and pulled my shoulder away from Eamon's touch even though I did appreciate it. He had a soft and kind touch, I had to admit that it was nice. He was nice, and I was glad he was in my company right now. I really was grateful.

I glanced back at him, his eyes still reflected concern, but there was a flicker of hope within them — hope that I would get better in due time.

"Is there anything I can do for you, Captain?" Eamon asked.

"If we had any tea, I would certainly love some," I joked.

Eamon chuckled. "When all this is over, I'll definitely make some for you."

I faintly smiled. "Thank you, Eamon."

"Of course."

The flicker in his eyes shone brighter by the sun's ceasing light, and I couldn't help but stare wordlessly. Eamon really was kind, and I considered doing something nice for him when all this was over. I didn't know what exactly, but I wanted to pay him back somehow for all he'd done for me.

Before I could open my mouth to say anything, a billowing sound screeched in the distance. It sounded similar to the Black Sting, but it couldn't be. There was no way. We both swerved around, desperate to find the source of the sound.

Soon enough, we found it. From the brightness of the setting sun came a giant, three-eyed squid. Its eight long tentacles spiraled about; its glassy eyes glazed with fury. The squid flew straight towards us at an incredible speed, like an arrow as it whipped through the air.

"Damn it, we don't have time for this." I gritted my teeth and loaded up bolts in my crossbow. "I'll take care of the squid. Just get us to the island, Eamon!"

"Yes, Captain!"

Eamon ran up to the helm and switched a lever, causing the wings of the boat to flap so quickly that they became nothing more than quick flashes of white as they ripped through the air and drove us forward.

I got into position at the back of the boat, aiming the crossbow between the squid's eyes. I fired, but the squid dodged the attack. I loaded another bolt and fired once more. This time, I hit its tentacles and the creature screeched in pain. The squid pulled itself back, giving us more time to flee, but the creature recovered quickly and gained on us.

I loaded yet another bolt and fired. The squid dodged. When I fired the next couple of times, I managed to strike its beak. The creature screeched and slapped its tentacles at the boat. The Arise Boat went flying upward, and Eamon and I hung tightly.

When we regained our balance, Eamon regained control of the boat and steered it in another direction. I decided to bring out my grappling hook. I'd had enough of this.

"We can't outrun it," I exclaimed. "I'm going in!"

"Wait, Captain —"

I shot at the creature and, when the hook latched onto it, I flung myself through the air. While swinging, I avoided the squid's tentacles striking towards me and, when one drew too close, I stabbed it with a knife. When I found an opening, I jumped up and struck another knife into the creature's head. The squid screeched and attempted to shake me off, but I kept the knife lodged in.

One of its tentacles wrapped itself around my leg and ripped me off, tossing me away like I was nothing. I lost my grip on the grappling hook and fell through the air.

"Captain!"

Eamon swerved the boat towards me and reached out his arm. I grabbed it and he pulled me into his arms.

"Thanks," I said, and turned to the squid.

It screeched once more and came hurdling forward.

"Take the helm," Eamon said abruptly and unsheathed his sword. "I got this."

"Eamon —!"

Eamon ran forward and, when the squid threw down its tentacle to attack, Eamon swiftly slashed off a large portion of the tentacle. The severed limb went flying overhead while blood sprayed onto the boat and Eamon. Eamon paid no heed as he dashed forward and raised his sword again, this time slashing off another tentacle.

The creature screeched and fled back, but Eamon wasn't finished. He brought out his crossbow, loaded it, and fired an arrow that struck the knife that was still lodged in the squid's head. The knife drove deeper into the squid's thick head and it shrieked so loudly I swore my ears would burst. The squid was ready to collapse. With its bleeding head and tentacles, it was losing stamina and so much blood, but it threw in one last attack and hurtled forward, knocking our ship back. Eamon and I held on once more as the boat veered sharply, but I managed to take control of the helm and steered the boat back to its correct position.

The squid attempted to attack us again, but its strength failed. We watched as it fell and disappeared through the clouds.

Eamon and I sighed with relief. We both dropped to our knees, clutching our beating hearts. The fight took a lot out of me when it usually didn't. Maybe it was because of my arm that was hurting again. Probably. I needed to sleep. I became light-headed and placed a hand over my head, brushing strands of hair from my face. My heart kept hammering, and it took a bit for it to slow.

"Eamon ... would you mind taking the helm again?" I asked him between panted breaths.

"Certainly, Captain," Eamon said.

"Thank you," I breathed and dragged myself to one of the benches. Even my legs grew weary.

Damn it, it was if all the weight from my chest had now transferred to every part of my being. I couldn't take it anymore; I needed to sleep right now. I hoped that no other creature came by; I didn't believe I could handle it. I didn't believe I could fight anymore. Damn it, I hated being this way. I hated it so much as the weight became more dire, as if tons of rocks constantly slammed into me.

I sat on the bench and glanced about. There didn't appear to be anything out here as far as I could see. Good. Perfect.

"I'm going to close my eyes. It'll just be a few minutes, that's all," I said as I lay down on the bench. I faced the darkening sky. The stars shined more fully, but some clouds passed by to block them.

"You can rest as long as you want, Captain," Eamon said.

I lifted my head to him. Eamon stood tall at the helm, facing away. Somehow, as I lay there, he appeared far away while the stars drew closer. The stars became nothing more but quick flashes as my vision messed with me. A spark of nausea overwhelmed me and I shut my eyes, waiting for it to end. With the combination of the pressure and headache, I yearned to yell out of frustration of it all. However, I stayed quiet as I breathed in and out. In and out. I had to keep myself calm and not get so stressed out. It was hard. It was so hard, though. I needed to sleep. That was all I needed right now.

"I shouldn't sleep long though," I added, although with my voice slurred, I wasn't sure that Eamon heard me correctly.

I didn't care as drowsiness took hold of me just like that. I thought that Eamon said something, but I couldn't hear him anymore. The last thing I became aware of was the chilly wind passing by.

29

– MARK –

THE REMAINING CREW AND I joined in a circle to eat some dinner. Angela had given us some sandwiches and fruit, so we ate them as we chatted about random things — topics like plans for when this was all over, and what kind of vacation we would want to go on. Fable, though, barely spoke at all. She ate in silence, and sometimes I forgot she was with us.

"I think a trip to the Pink Isles would be nice," I said, "I heard that the waterfalls are actually pink, and the water tastes juicy."

"Interesting," Edna noted. "I've always wanted to go to Starna. They have a monthly festival that celebrates the constellation that appear the brightest that month. I want to go when it celebrates my birthday month constellation."

"Oh, what is it?" I asked, intrigued.

"It's Noctin, the owl constellation."

"So, would they be selling a bunch of owl souvenirs there?" I asked.

"Yes, and there would be a parade, food, a concert, all sorts of things," Edna said with excitement in her voice. Her eyes even lit up as she spoke. "What constellations do you guys fall under?"

"Lepu, the rabbit constellation," I said.

"Anguil, the snake," Fable said.

"Apis, the boar," Flint said.

"Ah," I said. "Does anyone know what the captain's or Eamon's are?"

"Eamon's under Cani, the dog," Fable answered. "As for the captain ... I believe she's under Vulpin, the fox."

"I see," I said. "Well, I guess that means we need to go to all the festivals that fall under our birth months."

"Let's do it!" Edna agreed, clapping her hands together.

"I'm down," Flint said.

"Sure, why not?" Fable loosely shrugged, answering with a flat tone.

"Then it's decided," I said with the snap of my fingers. "I believe this is the month of Apis, so we're gonna celebrate your constellation, Flint."

"Alright." Flint smirked. "When do the celebrations take place?"

"At the end of the month," Enda answered. "So, in twelve days."

"Okay, so that gives us enough time to finish the mission and go to Starna," I stated.

"We'll see about that," Fable said, still maintaining her flat tone. "Let's keep our expectations low. We're still on a dangerous mission, after all."

I faltered and dropped my head. "Right ..."

Flint sighed, tossing back his head. "Fable, do you have to be a downer? Let's all chill for a bit; we need it after all that's happened."

"The captain is still in a crisis, you realize that, right?" Fable stated, narrowing her eyes.

"Of course, but we all know the captain, she'll be fine," Flint said.

"That's right," Edna agreed.

"What about the Vultures?" Fable asked. "They likely stole another Arise Boat and are after the captain ... or us."

Her voice lowered at her last words. I shuddered in return.

Flint chewed on his lip before he responded, "If they come after us, we can handle them. If they go after the captain, they won't catch up. The captain is further ahead."

Fable's face contorted with a blend of unease and frustration. "I know ... but if they do —"

"Hey," Flint cut in and rested a hand on Fable's shoulder, "it'll be all right. Let's just keep eating."

Fable frowned, but decided to drop the subject. Our conversations also dropped as we ate. Unable to talk with cheerfulness anymore, we ate slowly and in a stillness that unnerved me. We all thought the same thing: we were worried about the captain and Eamon, and then there was us. What would happen if the Vultures targeted us instead? Sure, we could fend for ourselves, but still.

That uneasiness crept up to me, and didn't seem to go away. It felt like a parasite that had crawled its way through my skin. I attempted to open my mouth to say something — anything that would fend off this ghastly atmosphere that had descended on us — but nothing came up. We just kept eating, and that was that.

"Alright, I'm done," Flint announced, his loud voice breaking the thick atmosphere. "Anyone else? I'll take your plates."

"Yes," I said and handed Flint my plate. "Thanks, Flint."

"No problem." Flint collected the rest of our plates. He smiled to us and started for the kitchen, however —

WHAAAMPH!

The ship suddenly shoved backward.

Flint dropped the plates and, with a sharp crash, shards went everywhere. We toppled from our chairs, and Flint disregarded the broken plates, running up to the helm to steady the ship.

"What the hell!?" Fable yelled.

"Over there!" Edna pointed a finger to our left.

We looked and saw a ship approaching us from a group of clouds. It wasn't just any ship; it was Gideon's. The ship's blood-red sails burnt into the sky, waving at us in mockery. Cannons stood situated on the ship's upper and lower decks, ready to fire at us again. Seeing those cannons caused me to freeze. My feet pinned themselves to the floorboard, unable to move the smallest muscle. A bead of sweat trembled down my cheek, but I couldn't even find the strength to wipe it away.

"They're going to kill us, they're going to kill us." I croaked out a whimper of distress.

Fable grabbed my collar, forcing me to look at her. "Pull yourself together, Mark. We're not going down without a fight," she exclaimed.

For a second, I was certain that she was about to slap me, but she released her hold and I fidgeted my collar. "R–right," I gulped.

"Go check what the damage is on the ship," Fable stated and nudged me forward.

I nodded and headed beneath the ship.

While I ran, Flint managed to steady the ship and swerved it around. When I got to the bottom, I found two holes on either side of the cargo hold. Fortunately, the holes weren't too big, so the ship didn't undergo much damage. This was the strongest vessel on Domus, after all, but even the strongest wouldn't always hold up. It was the sails we needed to worry about. If all of them were taken down, we wouldn't be able to maneuver the ship.

We had our own cannons situated on the level above, but we rarely used them since it took a while to prepare.

However, now it was the time to use them. I ran back up one level and saw Edna and Fable preparing one of the cannons.

"What's the damage?" Fable asked me.

"It's not too bad. Nothing was ruined except two walls," I informed.

"Alright," Fable said. "Flint is steering the ship into the clouds. We're going to surprise them like they did with us. Now, help us with this cannon."

"Right."

As we got the cannon into position, we saw another cannon ball spiraling towards us. Fortunately, Flint managed to swerve the ship away. The projectile flew right by us, and we all collectively sighed.

"That was too close," I muttered.

"Flint's got this. Don't focus on them," Fable ordered.

"Right."

We added the ball into the cannon and aimed it towards Gideon's ship. We were passing into the clouds now, but before the clouds moved in, we fired. The cannon ball spiraled through the air and struck one of their sails. The sail went tumbling over the ship, and that was the last thing we saw before clouds obscured our vision.

"That should slow them down a bit," Edna said.

"Don't get too excited," Fable remarked with a stern frown. "You two stay down here and put another ball in. I'll signal you when you should shoot. I'm heading up."

"Right," Edna and I agreed.

Fable passed us another look before she disappeared. Her footsteps stomped hard on the floorboard above us before they faded away. I faced the window again, but still saw only the clouds. They were thinning out, and we caught the silhouette of Gideon's boat moving closer to us. My heart pounded so loud in my chest that I nearly lost focus until Edna touched my shoulder.

"Hey, you okay?" she asked me, her voice gentle and sweet as it usually was.

"Yeah ... yeah ... a bit nervous, that's all," I answered with a heavy gulp.

"I'm also nervous too," Edna admitted, but a small smile tugged at her lips. "We got this though."

"Yeah, we do." I smiled back.

"Alright!" Fable's voice called out, her voice booming from up above. "In a count of three, you're going to fire. One ... two ..."

We waited for Fable to call three, but she didn't. We exchanged perplexed looks before Edna called out, "Fable?"

She didn't answer us, and fear rattled up as an unwanted chill prickled me.

"Fable!" I called as well, but again she didn't answer.

"Mark, look." Edna directed me to the window, and every fiber of my being went numb right there.

White clouds were replaced by dense black smoke. Not too far from us was Gideon's ship, engulfed in flames. Fire burned every corner, every part of the ship, and ate away at the wood like a ferocious and hungry animal. The masts toppled over, and sails disintegrated. The boar's head sculpture at the bow reduced to ash in mere seconds.

The worst thing was seeing their crew. They were on fire. rushing in a frenzy, screaming at the top of their lungs. Some vanished within the hell storm. Some of them even jumped off. We watched them falling to their deaths. Embraced by the flames, they fell through the sky in quick streams of red and gold, like falling pieces of the sun. Soon enough, the ship collapsed within itself, and went tumbling down. The only thing left were the screams of its crew as they met their demise.

My heart flew to my throat. Edna covered her mouth, then heaved over as she produced a grotesque gurgling sound, but she swallowed back the vomit and shuddered. I guided her away from the window and took a look at her face. She was completely pale, and a bit of vomit crawled down her lip. Edna wiped it off, but coughed right afterwards. I patted her back in assurance, but didn't know if I was of any help. My hand shook as I patted her; I could barely pull myself together either.

"We need to go," Edna started to leave, but I grabbed her elbow.

"Wait, you're —"

"I'm fine," Edna cut me off as color gradually returned to her features. She coughed again, but gathered herself and rushed to the upper deck. I tightened my lips as the fear intensified, but, with a sharp breath, I hurried to the deck as well.

When we reached the deck, we found Fable struck frozen. I'd never seen so much trepidation in her eyes before. Her mouth fell agape as she stared at the partially empty sky. The white clouds appeared again, as if nothing had occurred. Even the screams had vanished, leaving us in a sort of stillness that lingered on for far too long.

"What happened?" I asked.

"I–I don't know," Fable stammered. "The clouds cleared and suddenly the ship caught on fire. Something else must've hit it."

"Something else? Like what?" I asked, but the sound of wings cutting through the air forced us to look up ahead. I stared as two smaller boats came our way. Both were Arise Boats, and the Vultures sat high and mighty on them as they leered down at us.

Then there was Theron. He gave us a cruel smile, but it was his eyes that frightened me the most. There was so much glee in them, so much joy, so much twisted pleasure that it made my stomach coil.

"Damn it," Fable cursed under her breath.

The Arise Boats descended, and the crew of *The Green Vultures* stepped onto our deck. We all backed off, and I took Edna's arm as a precaution. Edna passed me a look of utter desperation, but I couldn't do anything else to comfort her. I didn't believe any of us could do anything at the moment. We could only watch as the Vultures stalked up to us like predators ready to pounce.

When Theron approached, the glee in his eyes vanished, replaced by bewilderment. He tilted his head, and rubbed a hand flanked with rings across his chin.

"Why do you all look displeased? We just saved your lives," Theron remarked, pursing his lips.

"What the hell did you do?" Fable asked in a tone filled with malice. The fear in her eyes had disappeared, but my fear still seized me like the parasite that it was.

"Like I just said: we saved your lives," Theron repeated. "Did you want those men to kill you?"

"You just murdered them," Fable stressed.

"We had a plan to avoid them!" Flint countered, tossing himself from the helm and and rushing to our side.

"As I recall, you were using cannons too," Elliot scoffed.

"It was only to slow them down so we could get away," Fable remarked.

"But sooner or later they would catch up to you again," Elliot noted. "Admit it: you all would be dead by now if it weren't for us. A 'thank you' would be in order."

This time Fable scoffed. "'Thank you'? Sure, I would love to thank the people who threatened our lives and stalked us down."

"You ran from us," Elliot stated with a frown. "That was fairly harsh for you all to do that."

"So, what?" Fable threw a step forward, her hand reaching for her sword. "You want to fight? We're ready."

Theron released a haughty chortle. "Of course, you are, of course. However, there's a little problem." With the snap of his fingers, Elliot pulled out a black crossbow in which the arrow glowed a striking red. I squeezed Edna's arm, but she didn't budge or even make the smallest sound.

"We could ignite your ship in flames as easily as we did with that other ship," Theron threatened in a callous tone of voice.

This time Flint stepped forward. "What the hell is that, and where did you get it?"

"It's called 'Instant Fire Arrows' — a little invention of mine," Theron answered with a grin as he showed off his golden tooth. "I've only made a couple of these, but I'm willing to do it again if you're unable to cooperate."

Fable clutched her hand into a fist. "Why did you destroy that ship if you want to destroy ours?"

"Because we made a deal," Theron remarked. "We get the fruit for your captain, and, in exchange, I get the Elphida. However, since you're willing to break that deal and run, I'm willing to blow this ship up. But, since I don't like dirtying my hands, I'm offering one more chance to cooperate with me. So, what will it be?"

We all glared at the Vultures, although my gaze faltered as fear overcame my anger. However, I managed to keep standing.

We stood there stiff until Fable spoke up. "If you strike the boat, that means you'll be caught in the flames, too."

"That would be true," Theron remarked without hesitation. He still had a smile on his face. It sickened me.

"You're willing to risk your own lives?" Flint asked, taken aback.

"Yes," Theron answered. "We do take deals quite seriously."

"That's crazy," Edna breathed out, covering her mouth. "You got to be kidding."

"We're not," Theron said with nonchalance. "And since you are against killing, I would say that letting us go down with you all would definitely not suffice."

Fable cursed something under her breath as she clutched her fists. She inhaled sharply and shifted her gaze away from the Vultures. "Alright, we'll comply ... What do you want from us?"

"We just want to get to Aer, that's all," Theron said. "We'll do you no harm unless ..." Theron motioned for Elliot to move forward, and the arrow was pointed to the floorboard, "you decide to disobey that wish."

"We'll comply," Fable repeated, but her voice wavered as she spoke. She swallowed hard and turned to Flint. "Continue onto Aer, Flint."

Hesitation flashed in Flint's eyes, and his mouth dropped. But when he forced himself to look at the crossbow in Elliot's hands, he nodded with reluctance and marched back to the helm.

"Good. Very good," Theron commented, clasping his hands together.

My heart thrashed rapidly in my chest. I yearned to yell and say something, but no words could come out. I could only watch as the Vultures grinned and chuckled in a fit of mockery. Once again, we were their hostages.

•   •   •

We watched anxiously as Theron and the Vultures ate our food. They weren't loud or anything, they were polite about it — just like how they were previous times. Still, I dreaded every single solitary moment. With each passing minute, I swore my heart increased its speed. Even when the Vultures offered us food, we declined. We had already eaten anyway.

We sat close by, watching to ensure they didn't do anything rash. However, they did nothing but eat as if they were part of the crew. Despite that, that sickening feeling I had before returned, and it just grew worse and worse every time I looked at them. We just saw these people murder a bunch of others. I could still smell the smoke. It was stuffy and made me nauseous; I wasn't sure I could even think straight right now.

"Ah, my friends," Theron called for us. "Would you be interested in a story?"

I didn't believe we had the option to say no, so we only nodded with reluctance and meandered our way closer to the Vultures.

"Excellent." Theron clapped his hands together, his golden tooth glowed amongst the moonlight. "This is about a dream I had just the other night. I've dreamt that I was an old tortoise. Strange, right? Well, it gets stranger. I was wandering through a forest where I saw a group of fireflies in the air.

"They led me deeper into the forest until I came across a cave. The fireflies disappeared into the cave, and so I continued to follow them inside. Within the cave was a pool of water. It glowed this brilliant silver, as if it was an exact replication of the moon. I peered within the water's reflection and ..."

I couldn't hear anymore. My head was spinning and everything sounded fuzzy. I excused myself to the washroom and shut the door behind me once I got there. I also locked the door as a precaution.

I stared at myself in the mirror, but only for a moment before I hurled my stomach into the sink. My throat burned and I coughed out more as I wondered how long this was going to take. Fortunately, it didn't last long, and I turned on the water right afterwards to wash away the remnants of my dinner.

When I finished, I sat down on the floor and held my head. The fuzziness in my head had disappeared, but there was a lingering feeling that it'd return. I still felt sick in my stomach. I dreaded vomiting again. Damn it, I wanted to go home. I just wanted to go home. That was all I wanted right now. I wanted to be in my own bedroom, curled within the warm sheets and blankets. That was all. That was all.

Knock. Knock.

I jumped up in sudden alertness and nearly hit my head on the wall. Great apprehension paralyzed me as I faced the door.

"Mark, it's me, Edna," Edna's gentle voice called from the other side.

"Oh ..." I managed to say, placing a hand over my beating heart. With a sigh of relief, I opened the door.

Edna's face was pale as she presented me a concerned look. She closed the door behind her so we could talk quietly.

"Hey, you doing all right?" she asked.

"No." I had to be blunt about it.

"I figured ..." Edna huffed and bit her lip. "All we can do is stay low and not do anything rash. We can do this, Mark."

"Yeah, I just ..." I paused as another sickening feeling welled up inside. "I just feel really don't feel well right now."

"Why don't you go back to the cabin and lay down?" Edna suggested. "It's getting late, anyway."

"Right, right ... I'll do that." I sighed and Edna patted my shoulder.

"You'll be all right," she assured with a small smile.

"Thank you, Edna."

30

– EDNA –

I LET MARK BE, BUT STOOD BY THE BATHROOM DOOR. I wanted to go back in and comfort him, but Mark looked like he wanted to be alone. I couldn't blame him. I felt sick knowing that those people were here ... and seeing what they did, it disturbed me. I went to the kitchen to get myself some water, but even when I drank down the cold, refreshing liquid, it did nothing for my nerves. I filled another glass anyways, and carried it back to the upper deck.

The Vultures were still gathered in a circle with Fable and Flint. My comrades passed me sympathetic looks, while the Vultures stared on with curious gazes.

"What happened to Mark?" Theron asked.

"He's not feeling well," I said and sat back down. "He just needs some rest." I took a slow sip of water and set the glass on my lap.

"I see, such a shame," Theron said. "He seems to be a nice lad. I would've enjoyed more of his company."

"Perhaps later," I said.

"Mmmm." Theron nodded. "Anyhow, it's getting quite late, but before we head to bed, why don't I share one more story?"

Fable frowned and stood up. "I believed we've had enough stories."

"Come now, one more wouldn't hurt," Theron insisted, gesturing Fable to sit down with a small wave of his hand.

Fable's frown deepened, and she glanced over at Elliot. The crossbow sat right beside him with the arrow still burning red. Fable's expression of indifference changed to one of silent unease, and she slumped back down.

"Fine. One more story," she muttered.

"Good, good." Theron rubbed his hands with anticipation. "This story is quite short, so don't fret, my friends."

Fable's eyes narrowed at the last part, but she refused to rebut him, and so did Flint and I.

Theron cleared his throat and leaned forward, passing us cordial looks as he spoke. "Well, this is more of a riddle than a story .... Long ago, there was a man walking in a tall field of flowers. Have you ever heard of the huinis flower? They're bright orange flowers with a white center that only grow on the Twin Isles of Cornu. The flowers are said to give you visions of the past or future once consumed, and so the man ate one of the flowers. When he did so, he dropped to his knees and cried. Why did he cry? Was it something that he regretted? Or something in his future that scared him? Who knows? But whatever he saw, he vowed not to go to the island again, and warned others not to as well."

Fable raised an eyebrow. "Then how do you know that the flowers showed those visions if he never said?"

"Good question," Theron said. "This is simply a tale, after all. Some say it's ludicrous, but then again, Aer exists, and so do many more strange, strange islands. So, I want to ask, if you had the chance to eat one of those flowers, what would you want to see? The past or the future? Let's start with you." Theron directed to me, and I paused for a moment as I shifted my attention to the floorboard.

"Maybe ... the past," I answered.

"And why is that?" Theron asked. "Is there something you want to see again? A loved one who passed? A moment from your childhood that you want to cherish again?"

I thought for a bit and then said, "I suppose I want to see a friend who had moved away a long time ago."

"Ah." Theron nodded. "The loss of a friend; that's always quite tragic. As you all know, Mayor Thomasthan and I were great, great friends, but not every friendship lasts forever, unfortunately. Do you still keep in touch with your friend? Edna, was it?"

I faltered, but said, "Not really ..."

Theron shook his head and clicked his tongue. "That's too bad. I understand how hard that must be for you. Truly, I do." His eyes gleamed with sympathy.

But I didn't buy it, and neither did Flint nor Fable. Especially Fable, who scoffed and rolled her eyes.

"How about you?" Theron turned to Flint. "What would you want to see? The past or the future?"

Flint scratched the back of his head and his lips toyed with the toothpick that flicked up and down. "I guess the future ..."

"Ah, what would you want to see there?" Theron inquired, leaning forward.

Flint shrugged and plucked the toothpick from his mouth. "I suppose just seeing how things changed ... like if home would be any different ten years in the future or something. I'm not sure, really."

"Change ... hmmm." Theron himself pondered as he rubbed his chin. "Yes, I'd be curious to know what changes would occur in the future too. After all, not everything can stay the same." He then turned to Fable, who kept her focus on the stars that loomed over us. "What about you?"

"I don't know," Fable bluntly said.

"Come now, I'm sure you've always been curious," Theron coaxed.

Fable tossed her head to the side, still avoiding any direct eye contact. She took a stand of hair and twisted it about her finger before releasing it. The strand coiled as it sprung back, and she did the same with another strand.

"I choose neither," Fable confirmed. "The past is over, so there's no need to go back to it. Besides, there's nothing that I really miss from it. As for the future ... I just don't have the desire to see or focus on it. It seems pointless when you have no control over it. What I want to focus on is the now."

"Ah, so you're one who wants to live in the moment," Theron said. "Yes, I can see how that would be a preference. The past is indeed over, and the future is, well, the future. What would be the point of seeing it when we have the present to worry about?" Theron then directed his attention to each of us as he noted, "So there's friendship ... change ... and being mindful. Fascinating. Thank you all for sharing this to me. You really do learn a lot from someone when you ask them one simple question. It really is fascinating."

"Now are you done with your story?" Fable asked in a dry voice.

"Yes, yes." Theron nodded. "Though I wonder what your other crew members would say, especially your captain. I bet that she would want to see her future, what she'll bring to your island ... Well, if they'll accept you all back, that is."

Fable shot up to her feet, her face contorted with anger as her lips twitched and eyebrows furrowed, but her voice remained calm as she said, "I believe we're done here."

A crooked smile spread from Theron. "Of course, my apologies. Didn't mean to strike a nerve."

Fable's nose flared. She appeared ready to attack him, but she held back when her focus went to the crossbow. Elliot still had his hand rested on it, his fingers caressing the metal spine of the arrow, and tapped the tip of the arrowhead. I've just now noticed that the crossbow had been aimed at Fable the entire time, and a chill jolted through me.

"Was there something else you wanted?" I found myself asking, bringing all of the attention to me.

Theron blinked at me, bewildered for half a second before shaking his head. "Not at all, you're all free to go. Goodnight."

I gradually rose to my feet, keeping my eyes on the Vultures, who stayed where they were. Fable passed them a swift glare before she marched off. Flint walked away with a slower stride, but kept his shoulders and back stiff.

As I was about to head below deck, Theron called out, "Edna, my friend, could I have a moment, actually?"

I flinched and became aware of how loud my heart rung in my ears. "Yes?"

"Could you get me some tea, please?"

"Oh." I blinked, dumbstruck. "What kind of tea?"

"Mmmm ..." Theron pondered and then said, "Mint would be lovely."

"Alright, um ..." I tossed an edgy glance to the Vultures. "Anyone else?"

The Vultures merely shook their heads, and that was the extent of it. I believed the only Vulture I've heard speak was Elliot, and even he fell quiet. It was if they were all just statues ... staring at me.

"I see ..." I trailed, struggling to steady my voice. "I'll be right back." Having said that, I excused myself to the kitchen.

When I got there, I splashed cold water on my face and gave myself a moment to relax. After doing that, I boiled water in a teakettle and rummaged through the cabinets to get tea. I picked out the box of mint tea, realizing that we were almost out. The captain's favorite tea was mint, after all. She had it almost all the time. A small smile tugged my mouth when I remembered my talk with her not too long ago. I rarely talked to the captain much, since she could be quite intimidating, so it was nice to have a normal conversation with her. I hoped she was doing well.

When the water was ready, and I put in the tea, I realized that I forgot to ask if Theron wanted any sugar. I supposed he would've said something if that was the case. I always needed sugar in my tea; it doesn't taste right without it. Bearing a small frown, I poured the tea into the cup and waited for it to cool before bringing it up.

When I reached the deck, a sense of dread returned when I saw the Vultures in the same, stationary positions as before. They really were like statues. They hadn't even moved an inch when I was gone for those few minutes. I didn't even believe they were talking before I returned. They were utterly quiet, and that stillness loomed over me.

With delicate footing that barely produced a sound as I walked, I approached the Vultures and Theron. The latter's eyes sparked with gratitude as I gave him the cup.

"Thank you so much," he said and took a sip. "Ah, delicious."

A bead of sweat tumbled down my temple when I realized that the Vultures were still leering. I swore they had moved closer, but I didn't hear any noise come from them. The only sound I heard was Theron drinking his tea. He drank it slowly and cautiously, as if the cup would break if he wasn't too careful. When he finished, he gave out a sigh and handed me back the cup.

"Might I talk to you about something?" Theron asked.

I swallowed a mouthful of cold air. "Sure."

"When you spoke about missing a friend ... I understood that completely, I truly did," Theron said, his voice dipping. Even his eyes expressed a sort of melancholy that almost caused me to do a double take. "I can't help but think ... what difference it would make if Theodore and I resolved our quarrels and remained partners. Do you think, if you stayed in touch with your friend, there would've been a difference to your life?"

I pondered his question, then eventually said, "I don't think so."

"Ah." Theron nodded, his voice still low, practically a whisper. "Might I ask, why did your friend move away?"

"I don't remember, actually," I said. "It was a long time ago."

"I see ..." Theron rubbed his chin and leaned forward. "That's a shame ... but I hope that someday you two cross paths again."

"Thank you," I mumbled and glanced back at the Vultures.

Within the darkness, the blood-red arrowhead stuck out, and I instinctively slid my foot back. Theron's eyebrows knitted together at my reaction and he swerved to Elliot. His eyes bulged, and he brought the cup down, but it didn't break when it touched floorboard.

"Elliot, put that thing away!" Theron demanded, jabbing a finger at the crossbow. "I don't want you to scare our friend. We're only having a talk, that's all."

With mild aversion, Elliot pushed back the crossbow, and the arrow disappeared from view. Relief settled on me and I swallowed some more air.

"I deeply apologize for his behavior." Theron's voice returned to a softer tone and clasped his hands together in a remorseful way. "You seem like such a sweet girl. Edna, was it? I keep forgetting your name."

"Yes, that's it," I mumbled.

"Ah, lovely." Theron clapped his hands again. "It sounds similar to Edanya — it's an island far down in the south. Have you been there?"

"I haven't."

"Oh, it's beautiful," Theron said, gesturing his head to the sky. "The island is nothing but a massive garden with all kinds of plants and wildlife. Though, I believe my own garden back home surpasses all. Ah, I look forward to returning there ..."

He trailed off with a wistful expression drawn on his face. Still gazing up at the sky, he sat there in a daze for several moments. Before long, however, Elliot cleared his throat to bring his leader back from his stupor.

"Ah, my apologies," Theron said with a light chuckle. "Sometimes when you think of home, your mind just wanders off … I'm sure you miss home too, don't you?"

"Yes," I admitted, shuffling my feet.

"Don't worry, I assure you that this will all be over soon." He passed me a smile, but I couldn't tell if it was genuine or not. However, I couldn't help but think back to how he reacted while recounting his own home, and, for that moment, he looked like a simple man wishing for something simple.

I stood by, still shuffling my feet as I found myself asking, "Is there anything else I could do for you?"

"No, no, that's it." Theron dismissed with the wave of his hand. "Thank you again for the tea, and I once again apologize for Elliot's behavior." He shot Elliot a fleeting glare, but his features softened upon facing me again.

"Goodnight, my dear friend," Theron added and handed me back the cup.

"Goodnight," I echoed in an inaudible way as my focus fell on the cup. With one more wary look at the Vultures, I disappeared from the deck and returned to the kitchen.

After I placed the cup in the sink, I splashed cold water onto my face several times until my skin numbed. I stared at my damp face in the mirror, thankful that nothing bad had happened — at least not yet.

31

– MARK –

I LAY IN MY CABIN, UNABLE TO SLEEP. I stared up at the ceiling with a blank stare. One part of me wanted the ceiling to crumble on me, while the other wanted the floor to swallow me up. I still felt sick inside, but not so much that I needed to throw up again. I couldn't get the image of the burning ship out of my head. I didn't know why, but somehow it seemed worse than seeing the Black Sting attacking Domus. Perhaps it was because we were able to take down the Black Sting not long after it attacked the island. Here, on the other hand, the danger was still present, and we were entirely vulnerable.

I stared at my door unblinking, worried that either the Vultures would barge right in, or the door would go up in flames in a snap. My heart beat quickly in my chest again, and I feared it was going to beat so fast that it'd burst. I huddled my body to collect warmth, because all of a sudden it felt cold. Extremely cold.

I peeked out the window; it was the middle of the night now. The only source of light was the moon's creeping in. I was left in partial darkness, but the door was clear to my eyes. I was just waiting for some sound to emanate from it, but nothing came. It was quiet. Extremely quiet. I didn't know whether to feel grateful or fearful. Either way, that sickening feeling inside wasn't leaving, and my head felt fuzzy once more.

I shut my eyes, hoping that these feelings would go away, but they didn't.

Damn it, just go away. Go away. Go away.

Knock. Knock.

"Ah!" I nearly toppled out of bed from the sound.

"Mark, it's Fable. Come to the upper deck."

But it's the middle of the night. What the hell? Before I could question her, Fable's footsteps marched away. I grabbed a pair of boots, threw them on, and ran up the stairs to the deck.

I met up with Fable, Edna, and Flint, who stood in the middle with concern looks written on their faces. Edna rubbed her arms as she huddled herself, and I came to her side. Flint tapped his foot into the floorboard and Fable slapped a hand to her hip.

"What is it?" I asked.

Flint cleared his throat. "The Vultures are gone. They must've left some time ago while we were all sleeping."

"They're gone?" I repeated slowly, my mouth hung with disbelief.

"Yeah." Flint nodded. "I decided to do some patrolling, and I found their boats gone."

"What if some of them are hiding here?" Fable asked with a critical eye to her left and then right.

"Doubt it, I checked all over the place," Flint said. "They're gone."

"Then why the hell did they bother staying here, then?" Fable demanded as she threw out her arms. "Was it to just to mess with us?"

"Most likely," Flint huffed. "Well ... all we can do now is to head to Aer."

"There's no point, they're going to get there before us," Fable argued.

"We're still heading there anyway, and so are the others," Flint said, and he went to the masts to free the sails. "The captain and Eamon will handle it. Why don't you three return to bed? I'll do the best I can to reach Aer. We shouldn't be far off now."

We nodded in agreement, though that sickening feeling inside me didn't subside. Fable stepped forward and announced, "I'll check the ship to make sure they didn't leave any traps for us."

"Alright," Flint agreed, despite that he already inspected the ship. But it was always safe to check twice, just to be sure.

While Edna and I headed back to our cabins, she nudged my shoulder and said, "What if we don't have much to worry about?"

"What do you mean?" I asked.

"All the Vultures want is the Elphida, so there was no point of them harming us," Edna said, chewing on her lip. "What I'm saying is that we shouldn't worry too much about the captain and Eamon. They just need the fruit, and the Vultures will have the Elphida. When that's done, the Vultures won't bother us anymore."

"How can you be sure of that?" I asked, surprised at the remark. "Yeah, they didn't harm us, but they were willing to if we didn't comply with them. They've threatened our lives several times. They could've gone with a better approach."

"I know, I know," Edna said. "But, somehow, I have a gut feeling that everything will be fine in the end, and knowing that we weren't harmed seems to prove it."

"I suppose ..." I trailed off, but that sickening feeling was still there. Not to mention that burning ship. Damn, it just wouldn't go away. "All I want is this to be over," I said.

"I know, we all do."

Edna patted my shoulder and gave me a smile. I smiled back, but it was only faint. I didn't think Edna even noticed it.

32

– EAMON –

I WATCHED THE CAPTAIN SLEEP for a while as we continued to sail through the night sky. I placed my jacket over her since it was starting to get cold. Once I gave her the jacket, the captain smiled and I smiled too. She looked peaceful at the moment, but patches of gray stole the rouge from her cheeks. I tried not to think about it, but the thought lingered and only left me shaken. I couldn't lose the captain.

I closed my eyes to compose myself; I needed to push the thought out. I strived to think of something else to clear my head. But what? My mind drifted elsewhere ... I began thinking of the first time the captain and I met. It was at the Academy during the second semester. We were sparring together and the captain easily beat me. She was incredible, though. She had this ... air of confidence to her that was admirable. Truly, it was.

• • •

Once I entered the gym, I was nearly blinded by the bright white lights that surrounded the room. Within its spacious area stood a circlet of stands that faced a platform where two students were already sparring. They wore helmets and gear for protection as they fought with wooden swords. Their grunts and exclamations were drowned out by the cheers of their classmates sitting in the stands. I recognized some of my classmates — one being Fable, who was too busy reading a book to really care about the match. She must've been dragged there by one of her friends.

The only teacher present was Coach Harrison, who stood by at the stands, checking his watch every so often before his eyes returned to the students. Not long after, one kid knocked over the other and the winner was praised with louder cheers.

"Great job, James!" one classmate yelled.

"You did great!" another cheered.

Coach Harrison climbed the platform and slapped a hand against James's back. "Our winner for the fourth time in a row is James O'Mallus. Anyone still want to go against him?"

Students glanced at one another until Fable spotted my presence at the doors.

"Eamon should go!" Fable remarked, her voice rung loud and clear.

"Uh —"

I couldn't formulate a sentence as Coach Harrison was already dragging me to the platform. He shoved a wooden sword in my hand and slapped my back.

"All right, kid. Y'know the rules, right?"

"Yeah." I nodded. *I wouldn't be here if I didn' t ...*

"Good."

Coach Harrison jumped off the platform and stood next to the stands. I turned to James, who already slipped into a fighting stance. He gave me a coy smirk, as if he already knew who the winner would be.

"Right, ready ... go!"

James immediately advanced. His sword lunged forward, but I managed to deflect it. I was better at blocking than attacking, while James was the opposite. He was ruthless as he came at me, but I was able to dodge or deflect every attack.

I finally found an opening and struck at his side. James was instantly stunned, his eyes nearly bulged out of their sockets. He acted as if he had never been hit by anything before. I didn't hit him too hard, but James thought otherwise as he dropped to the ground and exclaimed, "No!" a bit too dramatically.

"All right, all right." Coach Harrison came forward with an annoyed expression drawn on his pudgy face. "Don't be a baby. Get to the nurse if you're hurt that badly."

James shot me a look before he stumbled off the platform and out of the gym. Almost everyone watched him go while the others stared at me with awe. Fable had this smirk on her face that made me assume she wanted to fight me next, but someone else beat her to it.

Cordelia Thomasthan stepped onto the platform and everyone became quiet. I swore I heard someone whisper, "You're so dead" to my left.

Cordelia was well known throughout the Academy — not just because she was the mayor's daughter, but because of her skills. It was practically cheating that she decided to spar. But why me?

"Are you ready?" Cordelia asked.

Her tone was cold and impatient. It literally sent a shiver through me, but I couldn't let my guard down. I simply nodded, and we got into position. On the count of three, we charged.

Unlike James, Cordelia came forward with a sort of grace, as if she had commenced a dance rather than a fight, and that I was her partner rather than her opponent. Her left arm swung the sword while her right one was folded behind her. Her gray eyes sparkled by the lights above us reminding me of the likes of an incoming storm. She sure was one as she took great advantage in countering my attacks and striking forward. She did this gracefully though: light on her feet, as if she was that dancer.

Our spar didn't last too long due to my lack of attention. Cordelia struck the back of her hilt to my abdomen, and my bottom collided to the floor. I didn't expect to win anyway, but it was a good spar. I glanced up at Cordelia, who reached out a hand to me. I took it and got to my feet.

We met eye to eye once more and, in her eyes, in that incoming storm, I saw a spark of contentment. She didn't say anything, but I could tell in those eyes that she had enjoyed our match.

"So, uh ..." I started and turned to everyone on the stands. I almost forgot that dozens and dozens of eyes were on us. While we had sparred, it had felt like we were alone. But now, we were done and realizing that we've been stared at the whole time. Embarrassment crawled up my skin and I found myself quickly getting off that platform. I had known that I wasn't going to win anyway, so I shouldn't have felt that way. I was actually glad I had been able to spar with her, and I hoped we get a chance to come together again.

•   •   •

I heard the captain shuffling in her sleep, and I turned to her. She lifted her head and glanced about before her eyes fell on me.

"How long have I been out?"

"A couple hours," I responded.

"Ah."

The captain sat up on the bench and stretched an arm. It seemed like she slept fine, but it was best if she slept more to keep her strength up. She needed it when we reached the island.

"Might I ask something, Captain?"

"What is it?"

"I was thinking," I started as I turned my attention to the sky. "Back at the Academy where we first sparred, why did you spar with me and not anyone else? Not even James?"

"I beat James's ass so many times it got boring," Captain remarked. "I wanted to spar with someone new and someone who could beat that guy. He was a good fighter though, might actually add him to our crew."

"Really?" I asked.

"Yeah, he was one of the top students in the Academy, seems fitting."

"That's true," I agreed.

I checked my compass. We were still heading in the right direction. I wasn't sure how long it would be until we reached the island, but so far, we were in the clear. It didn't appear that there was anything else to hinder us, but I didn't want to jinx it. I placed the compass back in my pocket and returned my attention to the captain.

"So, Captain, I —" I paused, seeing that the captain had fallen back to sleep. That was quick, though it was best not to disturb her now.

We continued onward, and my mind wandered elsewhere. However, it wasn't long before distant screeches broke my concentration. The screeches jolted me like a shock wave, and, when I turned, my blood ran ice cold.

A great horde of giant squids sprouted from the horizon, charging towards us at an incredible speed. I couldn't say how many there were. Three dozen? Four dozen? Possibly five dozen or more? There were too many to take all at once, and it had taken forever to take down that one from before. We had to flee. We had to flee now.

I jumped back to the helm and steered the ship downward. I lowered the lever, and the wings flapped as fast as they could muster while the horde of squids chased us down. I searched in desperation for somewhere we could go, but there were no islands in sight, just the vacant sky. Damn it, we needed to hide somewhere, anywhere. The Arise Boat wasn't going to keep up like this for long. It definitely wasn't, but I prayed with all my might that it would. *Come on. Come on. Come on!*

My focus then flew to the captain. She was still sound asleep. It struck me as a surprise that she could sleep through all this. Even when she had rolled off the bench and lay on the floor, she stayed asleep. For a split second, I wanted to wake her up, but I disregarded the thought. She was exhausted and needed rest, and the next time she awoke we would be safe. We would be safe. I kept telling myself that. We were going to find somewhere safe. We were.

I swerved the boat into a field of clouds, hoping to lose track of the horde. Once I got us inside, white mist filled my vision, barely giving me a sense of where I was. Still, I directed the boat further and further into the dense fog.

As I drove the boat onward, adrenaline rippled through every fiber of my being, and my eyes searched every direction in the hope that the squids didn't ambush us. Fortunately, I couldn't hear any of them. Their screeches had faded and the only sound I heard was the slapping wings of our ship. My guard didn't falter, however. I kept a keen eye at my surroundings, especially when the boat broke from the fog and we emerged back into open sky.

The sun appeared almost crimson, eerie but strangely beautiful. I couldn't stop looking, but a profound sense of dread crept up, prickling at my nerves and tugging at my heart as I stared on. The sky, a deep, deep red with hints of gold and orange here and there, reminded me of how the sky looked when the Black Sting had attacked the island. Suddenly a spark of gold stood out, even against the blazing red sun.

It was Aer.

Like a broken piece of glass floating in the sky, the island glimmered from the sun's red light, akin to the dying spark of a flame. But there was something peaceful about it — something warm and welcoming, and I couldn't help but smile. I smiled with gratification and, without a moment's hesitation, directed the boat towards it. This was it. We had found it. We had found it.

"Captain!" I called out. "We found the island, we —" My voice faltered upon seeing the captain. With all that had happened, with all the joy in my voice, she hadn't awakened.

I slowed down the boat and rushed to the captain's side. Taking her shoulder, I gave it a small nudge, but then my body froze upon a cruel discovery. The soft colors that animated her face had vanished, replaced by a stark gray tone that barely made her recognizable.

"Captain?" My voice hitched as I called for her, but she didn't stir.

I shook her again.

"Captain, wake up," I called once more, but she wouldn't wake. "Captain, please, we're near Aer. We're almost there!"

I shook again and again, but she wouldn't wake. I felt for her pulse: it was faint. Very faint. Damn it.

I shook her again, but no matter what I did, nothing changed. She remained motionless. And even I lost sense of myself.

"Cap—"

Screeeeeech!

From above, a giant squid came charging at us. Its tentacles struck down like falling arrows, and its mouth widened as it produced its desperate cry.

I cursed under my breath and gained back the strength to stand and rush to the helm. I pulled down the lever, and the wings ripped through the air in haste.

I occasionally turned back to the captain to see if she would wake, but she wouldn't. I wanted to call for her again in hope it would do something, anything. I needed her to wake up. I needed her to. But my voice was lost as the squid's screeches drowned them out. I could sense it getting closer, but I refused to avert my eyes and look.

Sweat trailed down my face and my hands grew clammy upon the helm. They almost lost their grip and I had to force myself to hold on. We were almost there. We were almost there!

Screeeeech!

The horrific sound rang in my ears and I nearly yelled in return. We weren't going to make it in time unless I did something. I made a dash to my crossbow on the ground and fired a shot at its body. The squid cried out and jammed its head into the boat, sending us flying, almost spiraling while being flung skyward. I lost grip of the crossbow and I skidded back into a bench. The boat twisted to another angle, and the captain rolled near the edge.

"Captain!"

Flinging myself across the crooked boat, I snatched the captain's arm before she fell. At the same time, I latched my leg around the bench. My arm strained while I pulled the captain from the edge. The strain traveled to my neck, which pulsed and burned. But with a shout, I brought the captain to a safer spot. But I refused to let go of her.

The wings of the boat still flapped, now drifting due to a wind pushing it, but its movement was limited. Remaining at a stilted angle, the boat now lingered over the island. A long, golden river flowed beneath us, beckoning us to jump right in. We didn't have much of a choice as the squid prepared itself for another attack.

The creature released yet another screech as it came at us, but, before it got any closer, I knocked the boat over. The sky spiraled with gold, orange, and red clashing together. A ringing sung in my head. Still, I maintained my hold around the captain as I brought her into my embrace.

In a rapid pivot, my back slapped into the river first, and the water broke our short fall. Water rushed into my nose and mouth, and I barely had time to react. Rising to the surface, the current carried us along, but I stretched out my arm to snatch the bank. My hand clawed into dirt, and, with a throaty grunt I guided the captain onto land.

A moment later, I climbed out of the water and rolled onto my back. I began to cough rapidly, struggling to clear my throat and take a breather. I yearned to rest, but the squid's outbursts thwarted that.

The squid charged downward, drawing closer and closer. With a sudden burst of adrenaline, I heaved myself up, brought the captain in my arms, and dashed into the golden fields.

Long stalks of grass, flying as high as fifteen feet, covered and wrapped us in what I could only describe as a fuzzy warmth with a resemblance to feathers. The stalks tickled my nose, but I clamped a hand over it to prevent myself from sneezing.

While carrying forward, I slowed my footing to silence our tracks, and I stole glances up above to spot the squid stalking about. Its screeches slipped into guttural drones while it glided, but it refused to leave. I held the captain close to me while watching the squid with a wary eye. Aside from the squid's whines, the only other sound was my heart thrashing in my chest. My limbs ached, but with my remaining strength I carried the captain.

I couldn't outrun it. We could only wait for it to go away. We could only wait. Just wait. But the waiting hindered my patience and heightened my trepidation. The captain's skin continued to lack warmth, with a coldness overlaying it, causing my own skin to shiver. My nerves became tangled and my legs moved on their own as I wandered as quietly as I could across the field. I avoided glancing up in case we were spotted, but I needed to know if the squid was still around. I didn't hear anything anymore.

Wait. I didn't hear anything.

I halted in my tracks and listened closely. Aside from my thumping heart and labored breathing, there wasn't a sound. Even the wind had ceased whistling. My eyes surveyed every direction they could, but the squid was nowhere to be seen. But, just to make sure, I moved cautiously to where the grass had grown only to my knees. A small sound of surprise escaped my throat.

The giant squid lay sprawled on the ground close by. Still, but clearly alive. Its chest area rose and fell steadily while its eyes rested. The squid had fallen asleep somehow, its tentacles wrapped around its body like a blanket, and its head nestled beside a tree. A few leaves drifted onto it. Even some birds came to inspect it before flying off.

Curious, but perplexed, I placed the captain down and made my way over to the squid. I needed to know what had occurred; it made little sense. The squid had just been chasing us, and now it was completely out. I didn't even recall hearing it land.

As I drew near the sleeping squid, a large shadow loomed over me, and I halted in my tracks. My first instinct was to turn to the captain, but the grass kept her well-hidden, at least for the moment. I then turned to my right, and my breath got caught in my throat.

A peculiar-looking creature stood before me. Wide, bronze antlers sat partially hidden within a large, golden mane that could surpass even the sun. The creature's body was covered in white feathers, and its eight long legs supported its ridged body. Three glassy violet eyes stared back at me, blinking with a curious gaze while tilting its head.

It was the Elphida.

33

– EAMON –

I STARED IN AWE at the creature before me. It studied me with its large purple eyes and, for a moment; I forgot how to move. It was if every part of my body had stopped cooperating. I could only just blink at it, wondering if I was stuck in some sort of dream.

After what seemed like forever, the Elphida nodded its head and gestured to the area where I had left the captain. It then moved in that direction with all eight legs taking delicate, but brisk steps. I broke out of my stupor and went ahead to return to the captain.

She still rested amongst the tall grass, and the grass caressed her darkened skin. Something inside me ached upon seeing how dark she had turned, as if covered in ash and smoke. I lifted her gently, collecting her in my arms, but shuddered from how cold she felt. Nonetheless, I carried her out of the field and brought her to the creature.

The Elphida sniffed all over her, particularly her shoulder. Releasing an odd mix of a snort and whine, it raised its front two legs and galloped away up a hill. On top of the hill stood a single golden willow tree that bore golden fruit.

A great sense of relief swept over me and I felt a burst of stamina. Chasing after the Elphida, I nearly broke into yells of excitement, but exhaustion kept from doing so.

The tree loomed over in a great column of branches that twisted and turned and spiraled, tangling in all sorts of directions. Its branches bore fruit that had been kissed by the first rays of the sun's red light. My mouth watered and my stomach grumbled once I saw them, but I dismissed my hunger. The Elphida jumped up and picked out a single fruit. It dropped the fruit near my feet and I bent down to pick it up. In haste, I returned to the captain and patted her cheek.

"Captain, I have the fruit. Please wake up so you can eat it," I said, still gathering my breath.

But the captain didn't wake. Nervousness rattled through me, and I patted her cheek once more. Her skin only grew colder and colder, and the ringing returned to hum in my ears.

"Captain, please," I begged, finding myself shaking again and unable to stop it. "Captain."

Still no response.

No. No. No.

I turned to the Elphida, but the creature stood motionless beside the tree; blinking, not making the slightest movement or noise. I couldn't recall hearing anything right then. Even the wind became quiet. Then it already returned above. like a whistle squealing inside and I couldn't make it stop. I couldn't do anything at the moment, and it unnerved me. I had to do something. I had to.

I pressed my fingers to the captain's hand to ensure there was still a pulse. There was, but the faintness of it intensified my fears.

"Captain," I stressed, giving her another nudge on the shoulder, but she still didn't wake.

Running out of options and time, my attention went to the fruit, and I bit off a piece. I had to help her swallow it.

Carefully, I tilted the captain's head up to allow the fruit to fall in. The piece was small enough for her to swallow, although I worried about her choking on it. Fortunately, that wasn't the case, but she remained quiet and still.

I waited about a minute before I saw the grayness fade from the captain's skin. Natural color once again settled on her features and her eyelids twitched before they bulged open.

She shot up as a gasp erupted from her throat, followed by a coughing fit. I patted her and she eased herself back.

"Wha— Ea–Eamon?" she stammered between coughs.

"Are you alright, Captain?" I asked.

The captain cleared her throat, and her coughing ended. "I ..." she touched her shoulder, "guess ..." The captain blinked several times in realization. "I don't feel a sting anymore."

I smiled widely and couldn't help but throw my arms around her, taking the captain by surprise.

"What do you think you're doing?" the captain asked.

The hardness of her voice convinced me to let go. "I–I'm sorry, Captain. I'm just glad you're better."

"Are we ...?" The captain glanced drowsily about, then her eyes fell to the Elphida. They widened, and she stood up suddenly. "It–it's real!"

"Yes, it saved us from one of those giant squids," I said. "I think it has sleeping powers or something."

The captain scoffed. "That's ridiculous."

"It saved us, though."

"Mmmm."

The captain turned back to the creature. It approached us with an air of grace, and stopped a mere foot from us. It leaned its head forward, staring at the captain with its wide purple eyes. The captain seemed to be caught in its gaze.

"Thank you ... I suppose." She turned to me, her gray eyes sparkled by the sun's dying light. "And ... thank you, Eamon."

"You're welcome."

The captain smiled. She didn't smile that much, but when she did, everything around her appeared brighter. Her eyes sparkled and her hair was played with by the wind. With the grayness now gone, she looked like her old self again. There were circles under her eyes, though, since she hadn't slept well for some time. I hadn't been sleeping well either, and right now I could use a nap. A long nap, actually.

I closed my eyes for only a moment, allowing the soft breeze to brush past me. When I opened my eyes, the Elphida had sat down right beside us. It emitted a sound I couldn't exactly describe. It was an odd mixture of a bird's chirp and a whistle, but somehow there was something soothing about it. I reached my hand forward and touched the Elphida's head. It felt as if I'd dipped my hand in a pile of the softest blankets. The Elphida whistled and turned to the captain, as if gesturing her for a pat.

"I think it wants you to pet it," I said with a chuckle.

"Really?" Cordelia raised her eyebrow.

"It's the least you can do for it.; It did save your life." I pointed out.

The captain stared at me and then to the Elphida. The creature stared back at her, its wide purple eyes staring back like a puppy stares back at its owner. Finally, the captain gave in and she shrugged.

"Alright, whatever." A small smile played on her face as she patted the creature's head.

"Humph, I still can't believe this guy really exists," the captain remarked as she kept petting the Elphida.

"Yeah, I suppose there's a lot in this world we still don't know about."

"Right ..."

The captain got up to her feet and stretched her arms to the sky. The morning sun bathed her in a rich red and golden light. I was so glad to see her better.

"So, where's our boat?" the captain suddenly asked.

"Oh, uh …" I paused and looked around. "It got destroyed when we were under attack. But our crew should be here soon."

"Destroyed?" The captain repeated, gaping at me.

"Yes," I said, "but none of us got hurt." Though, our dive into the river did cause my back to ache. But I refused to tell the captain that. My back didn't hurt much anyway.

The captain frowned slightly and returned to her sitting position, her head still pointed toward the sky.

"So … I guess we can just relax for a bit and wait," I said.

"We can't really relax when those Vultures are on our tails," the captain muttered.

"Mmm."

I nodded and turned to the Elphida. The creature couldn't stop looking at us. Its eyes appeared so wide and filled with curiosity. It was if we were the strange creatures here. It then produced a whistle before galloping up the hill with the golden willow. The Elphida twisted its head, emitting another whistle, as if prompting us to follow. The Captain and I did so, and we sat beneath the tree once we reached the hill. The Elphida jumped up and snatched one of the fruits from a branch. With another whistle, the Elphida nudged for me to take the fruit.

"Oh, thanks," I said before receiving it.

I took a bite, and immediately my taste buds jumped up with joy. The taste was a combination of sweet and tangy, like I'd bitten into a red apple dipped in honey. A warm feeling blossomed inside me, as if all the stress of these past few days had slipped away.

"This is amazing … " I breathed and took in another bite. I wondered how such a thing could exist. It felt as if we were living in some sort of dream. If this was a dream, I didn't want to wake up from it.

34

– EAMON –

S EVERAL HOURS PASSED, and the sun dangled above the cream-colored clouds. The captain and I lounged on the hill as we waited for our crew ... and the Vultures. Tension hung in the air as we waited, but the Elphida's presence eased it somewhat.

The creature sat between the captain and I, its large eyes directed at the sky. On occasion, though, it gave us passing glances — a sign that it desired a pet. With a small smile, I obliged, and I had to coax the captain into doing so too. She did so, but got tired of it, so she that she scooted a few feet away, turning her back towards us. I had to chuckle, but did so inaudibly so that the captain didn't throw me a glare.

After a while, the Elphida got up on its strange legs and rounded the perimeter of the tree. It collected more fruit for us, but I believed we had our fill. I lost count of how much I ate, but each one boosted my energy. Any sort of tiredness I'd had ceased to be. Now I sat awake and alert, awaiting the inevitable encounter of the Vultures. But as I lounged under the protection of the tree, knowing that the captain was all right, I didn't want to deal with anything. I simply wanted to enjoy the moment, as I knew it would come to an end, eventually.

I fell back onto the soft grass, glancing up at the sky and watching as the puffy clouds drifted by. I spotted one that vaguely looked like a ferret, making me wonder how Amabel was doing back on the ship. More importantly, I wondered how everyone else was doing back home. Despite how delicious the fruit was, I missed my mom's cooking. She made the best roasted duck; I could imagine the smell and taste of it already.

I smiled at the thought and asked, "Hey, Captain, what are you looking forward to when we get back home?"

"A long bath would suffice," the captain answered dryly.

I took a whiff of my coat and my nose scrunched up. "Yeah, I could go for one too. I'm also looking forward to a nice warm meal."

"Mmmm ..." the captain trailed off.

"So," I said, deciding to change the subject, "has your brother's birthday passed?"

The captain fell quiet for a moment, her back still towards me. "Yeah, it did."

"Are you going to get him anything?

The captain shrugged. "I'll buy him a toy ship or something."

"That'll be nice. He'll be happy to see you back."

"Mmmm." The captain paused and then said, "I suppose ... it would be nice to celebrate that brat's birthday."

"You really shouldn't call him that," I said.

The captain finally faced me. Her lips settled to a frown. "I can call him whatever I want."

Ignoring her grimace, I smiled. "I'm glad you're doing better, Captain."

That stern frown that the captain usually carried faded, now replaced with a smile. I would describe it as timid, yet simple — actually, a rarity of hers, but a welcome one at that.

We both smiled to each other and, with the sun's light bathing the captain's face, I had to admit: she looked stunning. She appeared so contented at that moment, and, at that moment, I felt contented too.

Whoosh!

Thump!

It only took a split second for the captain's expression to plummet. Eyes that once sparkled in the sun's light now glazed with immense horror. Her mouth fell agape when she turned, and so did mine. My heart tumbled to the pit of my stomach.

The Elphida lay motionless on the ground, amidst a growing puddle of blood. The blood glistened like rubies from the sun's light, while its wide purple eyes dimmed to a glassy slate. A silver arrow stood upright from its neck, buried deep in its throat. I felt as if I had been struck in the throat as well.

"No," I croaked out.

The captain shot to her feet and so did I. We rushed to the creature's side, but it was too late. The Elphida was dead.

A distant clapping shattered the silence, and we saw Theron and his Vultures stroll up the hill with disgusting, smug looks on their faces. Theron strode ahead of his crew with a bronze crossbow strapped to his back. He carried himself with pride, while the Vultures behind him trailed along like a group of shadows as they mimicked their master's arrogant posture.

"Thank you for leading us to the Elphida," Theron praised us with a mocking gesture. "Even though you deserted us, you both did your task accordingly. You got your cure, and I get the Elphida. Thank you so very much. Now, we must take you back to your families."

The captain glared at them and curled her hand around her sword's hilt. "You're lying."

Theron shook his head and clicked his tongue. "Captain, Captain ... I don't have time to quarrel. We both have what we want. Why don't we finally end this and call it a day? I promised Angela that I would bring her a fruit too, and I don't feel like dealing with her anymore. Now come, let's all go home."

"Drop your weapon first," the captain demanded, baring her teeth.

"Of course, of course. Silly me." Theron put down the crossbow and walked closer to inspect the dead creature. His slimy flingers ran over one of the creature's antlers, and that smug look turned to great glee. "Mmm, what a beautiful, beautiful thing. It'll look wonderful in my library. What do you think?" he asked as he turned to his crew.

"I think the library would be perfect," Elliot agreed. He came to Theron's side and bent down to examine the Elphida's dimmed eyes.

"We could turn one of the eyes into some kind of ornament," Elliot added.

"Yes, I agree." Theron nodded.

"You're all monsters," the captain spat, gripping her sword to the point that her knuckles paled.

Theron chuckled and so did the Vultures. "I'm simply doing what I like to do, nothing more. That doesn't make me a monster."

"It does," the captain said without hesitation.

"That hurts, Captain, very much so," Theron remarked as he placed a hand over his chest. "As I said, this is what I like to do. It's my passion in life. We all have our passions."

"You're still sick."

"Please, as if you didn't know that this was going to happen," Theron remarked. "We've made a deal: you'll get the fruit, and I'll get the Elphida. Simple as that. Now, since that's done, we can all go home. Men." Theron snapped his fingers and some of the Vultures picked up the dead Elphida and carried it toward one of the two Arise Boats they had taken. The boats sat hidden in the tall blades of grass below the hill.

"Please be extra careful with it!" Theron called out to them, and then he turned back to us. "Come along now. It's quite the journey home."

"We're waiting for our crew to meet up with us," the captain remarked. "Our deal is done after all, so we don't need to be in each other's presence anymore."

"Ah, that's right." Theron nodded. "But I figured that, since we're already here, you might as well come with us." Theron motioned to some of his men, and a couple of them pushed us forward.

"Hey!" the captain exclaimed. "What the hell did I just say?"

"Please, Captain, this is simply a friendly gesture for all your help," Theron insisted, showing off that golden tooth again.

The captain scoffed. "We don't need anything else from you. Grab your fruit and leave."

Theron sighed. "Oh, Captain, you're so stubborn. But very well, I'll abide to your wish. After all, we're all tired and simply want to go home now."

After Theron snatched a fruit for Angela, he brushed past us and beckoned for his men to come along. It was as simple as that, but there was something off about it. The captain and I stood our ground in case any suspicious activity would arise, but nothing did. The Vultures left us alone, just like that.

I leaned toward the captain's ear. "Should we do something?"

"No." The captain shook her head, her face grim. "There's no point, it's over now."

"Right ..." I swallowed hard on that resolution.

It was hard to watch as the Vultures carried the dead Elphida and place it on their boat. It was even harder to walk away like that, knowing that we couldn't do anything about it. It was done. It was over. Now we had to wait for our crew to pick us up, and hope that we never deal with Theron and his crew again.

However, before any of the Vultures neared the boats, a strange rumbling sound began. The sound came from the ground, almost if an earthquake had stirred. The tall grass trembled; even the tree on the hill shook. I nearly lost my footing, but the captain caught my arm.

"What the hell?" some of the Vultures asked.

"Move!" Theron barked as he pushed one of his mates forward.

But just when he did, the ground split open between us and the boats. Then, more and more fissures formed as the ground kept trembling and we all struggled to maintain balance. What disturbed us the most, however, was the strange, colossal sound that erupted from the bowels beneath us.

Rrrrrrooooaaaaagggghhhh!

It sounded as if some creature had been trapped deep within the earth and was trying to get out. Or ... perhaps the island itself was the creature. No, there was no way.

"Get on the boats, quickly!" Theron shouted to his crew.

We all ran, but some of them tripped. Before they could get up, the roots of the tree sprouted out from the ground and wrapped themselves around three of the men, squeezing them until they turned purple. The men gasped for air and tried to squirm their way out. But it was too late. They were dragged into the ground without making another sound.

"What the hell?" Elliot demanded.

"Go, go!" Theron shouted to the rest of the crew.

We finally got onto the boats. Elliot had taken the helm of the boat the captain and I were on. Just when we were about to go, the tree's roots wrapped themselves around the vessel.

"Damn it!"

The captain unsheathed her sword and hacked off the branches, allowing us to break free. However, the other boat wasn't so lucky. We watched as it was dragged back onto the island by the roots, shattering it into pieces. Two of the members tried to run, but they were caught in the roots' grasp and, instead of being suffocated, they were hauled into the fissures while their screams echoed alongside the island's colossal roar.

The Elphida was left alone on the ground. That didn't prevent the branches from chasing after us. The roots shot skyward. Elliot pulled down the lever, allowing the wings to tear through the wind current and soar through the darkening sky. The sun had left the horizon and the only light left was the fearsome golden glow of the island that raged like a star about to explode. When it seemed like we were fleeing away from it, we weren't. The island came at us, as if it truly had a mind of its own.

"What the hell!?" Theron barked.

"Is—is the island alive? What is this?" one of the crew members asked.

"Impossible!" another exclaimed.

Rrrrrrrraoagh! The island appeared to roar as it drew closer and closer to us.

"Faster, Elliot!" Theron yelled through the island's colossal screams.

"This is the fastest it can go!" Elliot exclaimed.

"Let me see that!" Theron pushed Elliot out of the way and snatched the helm.

His face contorted, twisted with great anger and desperation. It differed from his regular appearance. His calm and collected demeanor vanished, replaced by that of a true monster. Even his eyes sparked with a sort of ire that embodied mercilessness.

Theron threw down the lever with profound force, and the wings increased their speed. But it wasn't enough. The island was gaining up on us quickly, as if the sun itself chased us. I didn't know what to do, and neither did the captain as we watched in shock and horror at the monstrosity coming our way.

The roots and branches of all the trees had extended outward, like snakes yearning to feast on prey. The fissures it had created broke out more and more. The island was destroying itself, ready to combust at any moment.

"I think it's going to explode!" I exclaimed.

"How the hell is this even possible?" the captain demanded.

"Damn it, damn it!" Theron cursed.

He frantically played with the lever, hoping the boat could go faster, but it failed to do so. The boat was at its limit and the island was nearly at its peak. The island glowed so, so brightly that I was sure it would blind me.

I turned away and discovered Elliot pulling out a crossbow. What struck me off-guard was how the arrow glowed red. That wasn't a regular arrow. What was that?

"What the hell is that going to do?" the captain barked at him.

"Just watch!" Elliot exclaimed, and he shot the arrow at the island.

But it didn't do anything. Instead, the arrow burst into flames once it neared the island.

"Damn," Elliot cursed under his breath, stomping his foot. His eyes darted from left to right before his focus trained on the captain and I.

With a look that I could only describe as insanity, Elliot loaded another arrow, and aimed the crossbow at the captain.

"It appears that we're at our end. Let's first start with you."

"No!" I exclaimed and pushed Elliot down before he could fire.

We grappled over the crossbow until Elliot struck my jaw with the heel of his hand.

"Ah!" I grunted as my head knocked back into a bench.

"Eamon!" the captain called, but the remaining Vultures aimed their swords at her.

"We have no time for this." The captain snuck a hand into her pocket, but I didn't know what she was retrieving. "Let go of him!" she yelled with rage burning in her eyes.

"Or what?" Elliot asked. "We're all dying here. Might as well use our remaining minutes doing what we should've done in the first place."

Elliot threw a punch at my face. I cringed at the stinging pain on my cheek. My eyes blurred, but, before I could register anything else, the captain lunged forward and jabbed a knife into Elliot's neck.

"Ugh!" Elliot yelped as blood sprayed from his neck. A moment later, he fell, dead.

Theron remained too focused on the boat to notice that his first mate was now dead. The remaining crew members stared at the captain in shock. They even dropped their swords.

"Anyone else?" the captain asked.

But before she gained a response, the boat shook as one of the island's roots had wrapped itself around the vessel, crushing it. Before we could react, the island exploded in great flashes of gold that shot through the sky in a rain of shooting stars.

The boat collapsed, and we fell through the twilight. Fortunately, we managed to clutch onto broken pieces of the island that floated in the air. The captain and I were barely several feet away from each other as we hung for dear life. Our legs dangled in the open sky, while our arms struggled to support our bodies.

The fragments were barely large enough for us to settle onto. About half the size of our bodies, they cracked at the smallest touch. If we were able to climb onto them and sit, I didn't think they would be able to support our weight for long. So, we just hung there, clutching to shards of gold that floated nimbly in the sky. There was nothing left of the island but these remnants. There was nothing else in the sky either. The sun had left us, and the stars were nowhere to be seen. These shards of broken gold replaced them, glowing against the incoming dark. Everything had fallen still and quiet, but then ...

"Ugh ..."

Below us Theron hung onto a broken fragment as well. He struggled to keep his body upright, and grunted as he attempted to stay steady.

When he saw us, he chuckled, showing off that ugly golden tooth. "It looks like this is it then, eh?"

We both didn't say anything and just listened to the man's laugh.

"This reminds me of my book ... Wreath of Violet Roses, the beautifully tragic story about the last man and woman in the sky," Theron remarked. "It ends with the lovers falling to their deaths, because they couldn't bear living all alone in the world even though they still had each other. Despite that, they hold each other's hands and dive to their demise, leaving only a wreath of violet roses behind to show that their love is eternal. So, I wonder ... will you two fall as well?"

"Shut up!" The captain snapped. Her hands clawed into her fragment. "I'm so sick and tired of you. You're the cause of all of this."

"Really?" Theron chided. That golden tooth shimmered. "Who was the one who put her island in trouble?"

"Shut up!"

"Who's the one who caused casualties?"

"Shut up!"

"Who —"

"SHUT UP!" Cordelia screamed to the top of her lungs.

Her voice echoed throughout the sky. I noticed there were tears in her eyes, but she didn't dare cry. She couldn't, but I knew she wanted to.

Theron laughed, laughed as if he had won, but he hadn't. He hadn't won, because the fragment he was holding onto crumbled and he fell.

Theron tumbled into the dark abyss. His laughter echoed in the air. It was cold and filled with mockery. The sort of laugh that tried to sound triumphant, but ultimately failed as the man fell to his death. The last thing we saw of him was that golden tooth. It shimmered in the darkness before it, too, vanished.

"Captain ..."

I turned to her and she finally let loose her tears. I've never seen her so hurt before. I wished I could comfort her, but she was so far from me. So far. Even worse, my arms were reaching their limit. I couldn't hold on much longer.

I clung to the fragment with all my might, and my legs kicked vainly in the air. I looked down again, hoping that there were other fragments we could land on, I saw nothing but the darkness below. My heart quickened in my chest, but I chose to ignore it as I tried to stay calm. I breathed in and out slowly as I turned back to the captain.

"Captain," I repeated and managed to grab her attention.

She looked at me with so much hurt and defeat in her eyes. It pained me so much to see her like this.

"Remember what I said before, back at the cave?" I inquired

The captain only gave me a small nod.

"What happened at the island was not your fault; you had no control over the incident. You're only human and you can only do so much. But what you have done is great, and you will do more great things. You will, Cordelia."

"Eamon." Cordelia's eyes widened with surprise and they sparkled from the light of the broken island. Against the darkness, they shone like fireflies, and it felt like we were back in that cave. I felt at peace. Despite where we were right now, I felt peace knowing that I was with her now.

"You are strong," I praised. "You're the strongest person I know, and I don't want you to lose sight of it. You're a great captain and ..." I paused. My arms were slipping. The strain was becoming too much. However, I looked at Cordelia like we were having a normal conversation. Just a normal conversation, like nothing was wrong. It was only us two now, just us in the sky that was now a deep, deep blue. In the distance, I could see traces of reds, purples, and, of course, gold. I've seen the sky so many times, but it was the first that I really took in the beauty of it all.

"And," I added as I took in a breath. "I want you to take care. Please."

I smiled at Cordelia, and a small smile crossed her lips.

But it wasn't long before it fell as my fragment shattered.

I fell through the air and watched as the broken shards of gold drifted, and blinked out like fireflies. The last thing I heard was Cordelia calling my name. The last thing I thought was wondering if she ever had genuine feelings for me like I did for her.

35

– MARK –

W E SAW SHARDS OF GOLD scattered across the dark sky, stretching out as far as the eye could see. At first, we thought they were some sort of fireflies, but when we drew closer, it turned out that they were broken pieces of land. It was if some explosion had occurred and destroyed an island, but we couldn't figure out what had caused this. Not even the largest creature in the sky could destroy an island. So what had happened?

"This is strange ..." I mumbled mainly to myself, but Edna heard me, tugging at her sleeve while surveying the area.

"It is," she agreed. "This can't be an island. There's no way ..."

"I think it is ..." I said. "We saw the Vultures take down Gideon's ship with that arrow ... Maybe they did the same here?"

"But an entire island? That can't be possible; there's no way. No way." Edna shook her head, tugging at her sleeve some more.

"I don't want to believe it either," I said. "But what else could it be? This isn't natural."

"We should turn around," Edna insisted.

"Wait!" Fable called out in a sudden burst, running across the deck. "Over there! Look!"

Edna and I followed Fable to another side of the ship. We peered across the wreckage, and, with gasps of surprise and horror, we spotted the captain within the midst of it all. She was barely conscious, clinging and clawing to the piece she gripped, attempting to pull herself up but to no avail.

"It's the captain! Flint, get the ropes!" Fable ordered.

"On it!"

Within seconds, Flint left his position at the helm and came dashing to us with a pile of ropes.

Fable tied the ropes to the baulster, tightening them to ensure the security. "All right, who's going in?"

"I'll go," I insisted.

"Are you sure?" Edna asked.

"Yes."

"We don't have time for chit-chat," Fable reminded and bound the rope to my waist, fastening it to a firm knot. "Get going, we have your back."

"Thanks," I said and climbed onto the ledge.

I stole a quick look back at my companions. Edna pressed her hands together while Fable coaxed me to go forward. I nodded and faced the broken path of gold. The captain hung on not too far away, but I paced myself carefully as I jumped onto one shard and then another. Fortunately, the pieces were big enough for me to jump on and catch a breath, but the rock that the captain occupied could only fit her.

"Captain!" I exclaimed, once I landed on the rock right next to her.

The captain lifted her head, her eyes bloodshot and swollen. She had been crying. *What the hell happened?*

"Take my hand!"

I held out my hand, but the captain took several moments to stare at me, as if she didn't recognize me.

"Captain, it's me, Mark. Take my hand, please," I begged her.

But again, she just stared at me.

"Captain," I stressed.

Fortunately, the captain slowly rose to her feet, but she acted as if she was standing for the first time. I've never seen her so vulnerable.

My muscles tensed, but I managed to pull through. We had to move. I felt the fragment quiver from my weight. We needed to move *now*.

"Come on, you can do this," I reassured her and guided the captain across the field of rocks.

The captain almost tripped a few times, and I did too, but our crew watched and helped us back on the ship. While I returned to the deck with careful precision, the captain slumped onto the floorboard and huddled herself in a corner. She bowed her head and her bangs covered her eyes, but she didn't bother to swipe them away.

"Captain?" I asked and moved towards her, but Fable took my elbow.

"Give her space," Fable said.

I bit my lip, but obliged and stepped back. So did everyone else. We watched the captain worryingly for a long moment before she steadied herself to her feet. She didn't bother looking at any of us. Instead, her attention went to the wreckage behind her.

"I'm going to take a nap. No one bother me," she announced in a strained voice.

The captain carried herself unsteadily to her cabin and, when I went up to help, she brushed me away. When the captain got to her cabin, which took longer than it usually did, she slammed the door shut, leaving us confused and worried.

•   •   •

Hours passed, and the rest of our crew met up with us. Immediately, they asked what happened, and we told them what we knew. They told us that pieces of gold could be seen from miles away, and that was what led them to us. There were probably thousands of pieces scattered across the sky. There were small pieces the size of hands; while others were the size of trees. We searched for clues of what could've happened and found something that caught our eyes.

"There!" I exclaimed.

On the largest piece we've seen so far lay a peculiar-looking creature. Its antlers lay partially hidden within a large, golden mane. Its body was covered in white feathers, and its eight long legs lay sprawled beneath it. The creature had three wide, but dimmed eyes that stared blankly into space. A silver arrow stood embedded into its neck, its shaft glimmering against the early morning light.

The creature was dead.

"Is that ...?" Fable paused, trying to gain a closer look. "The Elphida?"

"What happened?" Edna asked with a small gasp.

"It looks like the Vultures killed it," Fable said, baring her teeth. "Those sick bastards ..."

"So ... all of this land is ... or was Aer?" I inquired.

"It appears so," Fable crossed her arms, clicking her tongue. "Perhaps ... the Elphida's death caused the island to become this."

My eyes widened in disbelief. "How? That's ... that's insane. What exactly was the Elphida?"

"How should I know?" Fable tossed down her arms. "Whatever the case, the captain's skin is back to normal, she's been healed."

"But Eamon's missing," I said. "And so is Theron and his crew."

"When the captain wakes up, I'm sure she'll tell us everything," Fable said.

"Yeah ..." I sighed. "I'm sure she needs a lot of time to rest. It might be days until she finally speaks. She didn't look like herself we found her. I've never seen her like that before."

Fable fell silent while Edna noted in a small voice, "If we only saw the captain ... do you think ... Eamon ... he —"

"Don't say it," I urged. "Eamon is around here, somewhere. We have to keep looking."

"Right, forget I said anything." Edna hugged her stomach and dipped her head downward.

I placed a hand on her shoulder. "Don't worry about it."

"Let's continue our search," Fable declared.

We nodded, but my body had grown tense from Edna's words. Eamon was one of my best friends, and if he was gone, then ... No, I couldn't think about it. I couldn't. He was still out there. He was, and we were going to find him. There was no mistake.

●   ●   ●

Morning slipped into afternoon, and the afternoon slipped into evening. There was nothing but the scattered pieces of land as we journeyed along. I had been calling out Eamon's name for hours, but there wasn't a response anywhere. Regardless, I kept calling and calling until my throat grew raw. Tears stung my eyes and, when I was about to call once more, Edna rested a hand on my shoulder.

"We can't find him," Edna said.

"But ..." I hiccupped, "he has to be somewhere."

Edna gave me a sorrowful look. Her green eyes also glistened with tears and she shook her head. "I'm sorry."

I inhaled sharply and allowed tears to fall down my face. How could he be gone? Eamon was one of the strongest people I knew and ... he was gone. Just like that. He couldn't be gone. He couldn't.

"Eamon!" I yelled into the sky. "Where are you? Eamon? Eamon!"

"Mark!" Fable shouted. "Enough! We've been searching all day and Eamon isn't here. We're just wasting our time."

"But ..." I tried to speak, but couldn't find any words.

"We'll send in a search party once we return home," Fable said. "For now ... we need to go."

I stared wordlessly at Fable, unable to formulate any more words to her. Just like Edna, she too bore a sorrowful and regretful expression. I could only just nod to her in defeat, and I slumped onto the floor, covering my face.

"Flint!" Fable called. "We're heading back home!"

"Alright!" Flint called back.

The ship turned around, but I looked back, hoping to find Eamon standing somewhere on one of those pieces. But there was nothing but gold strewn across the dimmed twilight.

36

– CORDELIA –

I WOKE UP WITH THE SUN nearly blinding me. It took me a while to adjust before I finally decided to rise. I was about to pull over the sheets when I heard snoring at my side. To the left of the bed lay Caleb, wrapped in a ball, sleeping soundly on a pillow. His great mass of red hair partially covered his face. Drool leaked from his bottom lip and a small snore escaped his open mouth. I leaned over to ruffle his hair and Caleb's eyes blinked open.

"Cora?" Caleb mumbled and rubbed his eyes. "Are you okay?"

I blinked and looked at my shoulder. The wound was completely gone. There were no stinging sensations. No pressure on my chest. But there was an empty feeling inside …

"Yeah, I'm fine," I answered quietly.

"Good." Caleb smiled widely. He had a cute smile, I had to admit. I smiled too. But it was fainter.

"You were sleeping for a long time," Caleb said. "I was worried that you weren't gonna wake up."

"How long was I sleeping?"

"Almost a week."

A week! My eyes widened, and I flew out of bed and ran out the door. I rushed down the stairs and saw Father cooking breakfast in the kitchen.

"Ah, Cordelia, you're finally —"

"I *did not* sleep for a week!" I exclaimed, slapping my hands on the countertops.

Father sighed. "Unfortunately, you did, but you needed your rest."

"But a week!" I cried out.

"Cordelia, the most important thing is that you are safe at home now," Father said in a gentle voice. "I don't know the full details of what happened but ... what I do know is that a lot had happened, and I want you to relax, eat some breakfast, and spend time with your brother. He missed you very much, and so did everyone else here."

"Everyone else?" I asked. "No one's ... still angry at me for what happened?"

"Cordelia," Father sighed again and stopped his cooking. "No one was angry. We were all just concerned for you. We didn't want to lose you when you were attacked, and when you left. We wanted you to come back safe and sound, and now that we are, everyone can relax."

"What about Gideon?" I asked, throwing out my hands. "He was furious with me."

"Gideon gets furious with everyone," Father said. "Look, we all make mistakes and do things that we regret. But do remember that people care about you, and those who don't, well, they themselves aren't good people if they don't have sympathy." Father shrugged and continued to make breakfast. "I've been making your favorite pancakes every morning in case you woke up. Would you like some now?"

My arms fell to my side, and my shoulders slouched. "... Sure, I'd like that."

Father smiled and, when I sat down at the table, he handed me the plate and I found myself eating quickly. I hadn't eaten in days, so I couldn't help myself.

Father chuckled. "Careful, you don't want to choke on your food like Caleb does."

I realized how foolish I must have looked eating and started to take it more slowly. The pancakes were warm and smothered in butter, just the way I liked them. I remembered back to my childhood days when I would ask for pancakes every single morning.

Mom was the one who used to make them for me. I used to run down the stairs, screaming for pancakes while Mom laughed and baked the pancakes with a huge smile on her glowing face. I missed her so, and I remembered there being an empty feeling inside when she was gone. Now that empty feeling had returned. I settled the fork and knife down and fell back on the chair.

"Eamon's gone ..." I mumbled under my breath.

"What?" Father turned to me, confusion in his eyes.

I bit my lip and inhaled and exhaled softly before closing my eyes.

"Eamon ... he ..." I opened my eyes and stared down at the food. "He ... fell right in front of me ... and I couldn't do anything."

"Oh, Cordelia." Father sat down across from me. "I had heard that he ... disappeared ... and we've sent search parties to find him. Hopefully, something comes up."

"I suppose, but ..." I paused as I felt tears stinging my eyes. "He ... he talked to me as if it was the last time."

"Sweetie." Father got up and came over to hug me.

That was when I broke down. I hadn't cried so much since Mom died. It hurt. Everything hurt right there. It hurt worse than the Black Sting's poison. It hurt worse than any other pain imaginable. I couldn't stop crying. Even when I heard Caleb walking down the stairs, I couldn't stop.

"Cora?" Caleb asked.

But I couldn't answer him, I couldn't focus at all. I felt Caleb wrap his arms around me and gave me one of his tight hugs. Father and Caleb continued to hug me for several minutes more as I sat there crying like a baby, but I didn't care. I didn't care. Another important person in my life was gone. Eamon was gone.

•　　•　　•

The streets were quiet, and it had started to rain. Only a few residents were out and about, busying themselves with errands before heading back to their homes. I considered heading back, but I just wanted to be alone for a while.

The rain fell harder as the clouds completely covered the sun. Grayness coated the sky, a blanket of ash overhead. Little candles came to life on the windowsills of the houses, causing the glass to glow orange and gold. I saw little children's heads peeking through those windows before they hid once they were spotted.

The houses were also quiet, as they should be. There were no disturbances, nothing to disrupt the peace of the town or the island. But when I turned to see the few houses that had been destroyed from the attack that morning, that feeling of peace dwindled.

I came up to those houses — or at least what was left of them. I stood before their ruins and found flowers strewn amongst the rubble. A couple of flowers grew nearby, so I plucked them from the ground and placed them with the rest. Then I kneeled and whispered a small prayer, and, while I did so, footsteps approached me from behind. I turned to see one of those little kids from one of the windows.

"Shouldn't you be inside? It's raining," I told her.

"My Auntie used to live there," the girl said. "She doesn't anymore, but I like to visit her. Did you know my Auntie?"

"No, I don't believe so," I said.

"You fought that giant monster before, right?" the girl asked.

"Yes."

The girl's eyes lit up. "Ah! You were so cool! My classmates talked 'bout how cool you were and now I can tell them I met you! Now I'll be the coolest kid in class!"

I smiled slightly. "I bet you will be."

"Can you tell me how you did it?"

"How I did what?"

"Kill the monster! Did you use your arrows to strike it down? Or used your sword to stab it a bunch!"

The girl's enthusiasm about this seemed a bit strange, but, then again, I was as young as her when I wanted to start out.

"I fought the Black Sting, but I didn't deliver the final blow," I said. "My chief mate, Eamon did."

"Ooh!" the girl exclaimed. "Where is he? I wanna meet him!"

A pang in my chest erupted, and I inhaled slowly to stay calm. I glanced back at the flowers now smothered by the rain, and turned back to the girl who stood there soundlessly. Patient even.

"He's away right now," I answered.

The girl tilted her head, innocence in her eyes. "When will he be back?"

"Later," I said, but the word came out strained. I cleared my throat as if I had something caught in there. "I don't know when he'll be back."

"Oh," the girl pouted. "Well ... I'm glad you're back, a lot of us missed you."

"Really?"

"Yeah!" the girl's excitement resurfaced as she jumped up, but then the rain started to come down harder and the girl shrieked. "Ah! It's raining so much!"

"I'll walk you back to your house, c'mon."

I took the girl's hand, and she led me back to her house. The girl knocked excitedly on the door and her mother answered. She was a tall woman with wavy blond and chestnut hair tied in a loose ponytail. Her blue eyes widened with a mixture of concern and anger when she saw her daughter.

"Young lady, what were you doing outside?"

"Captain Cordelia's back and I wanted to see her!" the girl exclaimed as she pointed to me.

The girl's mother smiled to me. "It's wonderful that you're back, Captain. Would you like to join us for lunch? I just made cheese quiche."

The girl gasped. "My favorite!"

I smiled. "Thank you, but I can't right now."

"I understand. Maybe another time?" the mother asked.

"I'll see." I wasn't sure if I could give her a definite answer. But knowing that I was still welcomed here ... it gave me some peace.

•   •   •

Later, when I felt somewhat better, I gathered my crew, Father, and even Caleb, to the sunroom at home. An assortment of colorful flowers sat on the windowsills, and plants hung down from the high ceiling. It looked as if a forest was growing up there. We sat on wooden lounge chairs that faced the three tall windows where remnants of rain trailed down the glass. The sunroom was lit by lanterns cased in glass, casting the area in a lively glow. But the conversation that we delved into didn't carry warmth.

Father made tea and pastries for all of us, and, as we indulged in the food, I told them everything that had happened up to this point. They listened attentively — even Caleb paid attention, which was rare.

"So ... Theron and his crew are really gone?" Father asked first when I was done. He fell back in his chair, looking on with a mixture of relief and melancholy.

"Yes," I answered.

Father's mouth twisted about before he finally spoke again. "Theron and I go way, way back. We were partners ... friends once ... but he changed." He sighed and closed his eyes. "I have to confess that I knew of the Elphida's existence as well. Theron and I went searching for Aer one time. I agreed to come along because I wanted to see the creature with my own eyes. We never found it but ... I knew it existed."

"You knew ..." I repeated.

Before I could say anything further, Father continued.

"As for the island exploding. Well, this is an ... interesting thing." Father cleared his throat and said, "The islands that we're on ... they're alive, but dormant."

"Alive?" my crew and I asked, eyes widening in disbelief.

We exchanged looks and sat there in complete shock. Caleb, on the other hand, nearly rolled off of his chair.

"That's so crazy!" he exclaimed, throwing out his arms.

I shushed him and Caleb settled back onto his chair. He stared on with widened eyes as Father spoke.

"Yes, it's ... strange, but long ago all the islands used to be one. It was a giant creature that completely filled the sky. But since it was the only creature, it became lonely, and so it broke itself into hundreds of smaller pieces. But the energy to do that turned out to be too much and caused all of the new creatures to fall asleep. There, civilization was able to thrive. However, if there's a great disturbance to the island, the island wakes up and destroys itself. That's what happened to Aer ... Theron killed the Elphida, the only inhabitant of the island, and so it attacked."

"Why didn't this island wake when the Black Sting attacked?" Fable asked.

"The danger wasn't strong enough to cause the island to wake," Father answered. "Same goes with the other islands that were attacked. There might even be some islands that aren't alive at all. But as far as the Elphida goes ... it was a powerful creature that belonged on Aer. It was its home and

259

killing it sent the island in a panic. And so it did whatever it took to destroy the danger before it exploded."

"Should Theron have known of this?" I asked. "And shouldn't we too?"

"Yes, Theron should've known," Father said. "But he was so locked in greed and pride he couldn't think logically. As for not knowing about the islands ... islands waking and attacking is an extremely rare occurrence that sounds too absurd if I tried to explain —"

"After what I encountered, absurd things don't really faze me anymore," I deadpanned.

"Yes, well ... I just thought I didn't need to tell you," Father said, and he dropped his head. "I'm sorry, now that I think of it, I should've told you sooner..."

I sighed and sat back in my chair, crossing my arms. I was irked that Father never told me about it, but I understood why. Now that I know, it did add more reason for me to protect the islands ...

Caleb piped up suddenly, "Are there any more Elphidas, Dad?"

"It might be possible." Father shrugged, but it was clear he didn't know.

"Mmm." Caleb tilted his head to the side.

"Well," Father huffed and stood up, "does anyone want any more tea? Or treats?"

Caleb raised his hand. "I want another cookie!"

"You already had six," Father pointed out.

"No, I didn't ..." Caleb drawled, trying to blink innocently, but everyone knew he was lying.

Nonetheless, I did miss Caleb's little banters, even though he was annoying.

"I'd like some more tea," Mark said, raising his hand a little.

"Might as well make more for everyone," I said.

"All right, I'll be right back. Caleb, would you like to help me?" Father asked.

"Yes!" Caleb cheered and followed Father out of the room.

I sighed. I was actually getting a bit of a headache, not just because of Caleb's obnoxious voice, but due to all this info thrown at us. It was overwhelming and I had just encountered a strange creature with eight legs and a feathered body. It proved to me I haven't explored the world entirely.

"Captain?" Mark asked. "Are you alright?"

"Yeah," I answered. "A lot has happened this month."

"Definitely," Mark chuckled. "We're taking a long break now, so we're gonna go easy until we're given our next job."

"Yeah, we could all use a break."

Mark smiled and so did the rest of my crew. It was good to see them all smiling and I couldn't help but smile too.

I rarely smiled in front of my crew, but right now I didn't care. We've been through so much we needed time to relax and just be ordinary for a change.

37

– CORDELIA –

"CORA! CORA!" CALEB EXCLAIMED as he ran across the deck of *The Raging Storm* and jumped in my arms. "Thanks for bringing me here!"

"Yeah, yeah," I sighed. "Just don't do anything stupid, you got that?"

"Yes, Captain!" Caleb giggled and saluted me.

I put him down and he ran back to the other side of the deck. The sun was setting now: pink, purple, gold, and orange mixed together as the sun dipped over the horizon. A cool breeze swept by, but it was a pleasant breeze that I felt content with. Everything here right now was serene, and, for once in a long time, I was able to breathe. I still felt that empty feeling from before, but ... sooner or later I'd be able to let go. I did the same for my mom, and I'd do the same with Eamon. They wouldn't want me to mourn them forever; they would want me to be happy ... to be strong. And I would continue to be strong for them.

"Are we ready to go?" Flint called from overhead.

"Yes!" I answered back.

Flint nodded, and he set the ship into motion. I watched as the houses and people disappeared as we passed through the clouds. We sailed above a sea of clouds, and soon it became nighttime. Stars scattered the sky and I saw a shooting star fly overhead.

"Woah!" Caleb gasped. He jumped up as if he wanted to catch one of the hundreds of stars above him. "This is so cool! I want to live here!"

I rolled my eyes while Mark, who was walking by, patted Caleb's head. "Maybe one day you'll have your own ship and get to sail whenever you want."

"Yeah! I wanna do that!" Caleb remarked, clapping his hands together. "I'll be Captain Caleb! The Red-Haired Pirate!"

"Pirates are criminals, Caleb," I tried to explain, but Caleb laughed and pretended to fight with an imaginary sword.

"I'll help animals and use the gold I find as pebbles to toss in the water!" Caleb remarked.

"I don't think you understand what a pirate is," I said.

"Yeah, I do! I do!" Caleb couldn't stop laughing.

Mark chuckled. "Just let the kid have some fun, Captain."

I rolled my eyes. "Why did I agree to bring him here again?"

"Because your father wanted to?"

"Ugh, good thing this is only for the night," I muttered.

"Ah, I should've brought my sister along," Mark considered. "Caleb should have a little playmate so he's not bugging you."

"You consider on bringing another kid on my ship? Don't even think about it. I can't even deal with one," I said bitterly.

Mark chuckled nervously and stepped back. "Sorry, sorry, just a suggestion."

I glanced at Caleb, who pretended he was peering through a telescope. He gasped and exclaimed.

"There's a giant three-headed dragon!"

"Sure, there is." I rolled my eyes.

"Hey, with all the things we've seen of late, you never know." Mark shrugged.

"Whether or not there really are dragons, I don't want to deal with any creatures for a while."

"Yeah," Mark agreed. "When there are no conflicts to deal with, it's really nice being up here. It's quiet. There's a nice breeze. The sky is always beautiful. At night, the fireflies are always out."

I nodded and spotted a few fireflies flying by like little flashes of gold and ivory dancing about. Caleb danced with a couple before he caught one in his hand.

"Ah, Cora, Cora!" Caleb squealed with delight and ran over to me. "Look! Look!" He opened his palm, but the firefly dashed away. "Aw, I wanted to keep it."

"You can't keep fireflies, Caleb," I told him.

"Why not?" he pouted.

"Because fireflies aren't pets. Besides, you might accidentally squish one."

"Awwww." Caleb stuck out his bottom lip.

"You can still play with them, just be careful."

"Mmmkay!" Caleb saluted me and ran back to play with the fireflies. A few of them got caught in his giant mane of hair. Caleb laughed and brushed them off. "You don't belong there!"

"He's a cute kid," Mark noted.

"Sometimes." I shrugged. "He was cute when he was a baby, but that was because he never had anything obnoxious to say."

"You're strict, Captain."

"I know." I smiled to myself. Since my smugness was coming back, it meant I was feeling better. Good. I hated the fact that I was so weak beforehand. It felt like I couldn't do anything. Like I was giving up. Fortunately, I was able to overcome it. Even though I hadn't fully recovered from the incident, I was still standing.

"Ah! Look!" Caleb suddenly pointed to the sky.

We all looked up. A pod of whales appeared from the clouds and drifted hundreds of feet above us.

"It's at least ten Blubbys!" Caleb jumped up and waved his arms around, as if he could jump up and fly to them. "Cora! Cora! Are you seeing this?"

"Yes, I see them," I answered.

"It's so cool! So cool! Ah can I have one?" Caleb asked.

"None of them can even fit inside our house," I remarked.

"Then we need to get a big, big, pool, the largest pool ever!"

"No," I bluntly said. "We're not getting any whales. Besides, you couldn't even take care of the fish Dad got you."

"It was an old fish."

"You tried to hug it."

"I thought it wanted a hug."

I huffed. "Fishes don't want hugs."

I turned to Mark, and he was clutching his stomach, trying not to laugh too hard, but he was about to fall over.

"Oh, stop laughing," I remarked through gritted teeth.

Mark wiped a tear. "I'm sorry, Captain. But your brother is so funny."

"If you want him, you can take him," I deadpanned.

"Eh?" Caleb asked, tilting his head. "But I don't wanna leave you, Cora."

"Your sister was only making a joke," Mark assured him.

But Caleb was ready to burst into tears. "You've been leaving us too many times!" Caleb cried out. "I don't want you to go away forever!"

"Caleb," I sighed. "We're not getting separated. It was only a joke."

"Really?"

"Yes."

"Really, really?"

"Yes, now stop it."

"Yay!" Caleb went up to hug me.

I groaned in defeat. This kid was definitely something, but he was my brother, so I did have to deal with it ... forever ... ugh.

"Oh, Captain, look!"

This time it was Mark who pointed upward. The whales were now flying in a circle around the boat. They began singing a low, but melodic tune that reminded me of the song they sang when Eamon and I saw them last.

Their melody sounded melancholic, as if they knew what had happened, and were giving their condolences. It caused my entire crew to stop what they were doing to listen.

Caleb stopped dancing, watching with awe. His eyes grew so wide I was sure they were going to pop out of their sockets. His jaw dropped so low I wouldn't be surprised if he strained it. He appeared to be in a trance.

Caleb really liked it up here, but ... I couldn't take him with me all the time. It was dangerous, and I didn't want to lose anyone else that I cared about. Perhaps when he was older and more mature, he'd sail his own ship and have his own crew, but right now I wanted him at home where I knew he was safe and sound.

I watched as Caleb reached out his arms, hoping to touch a flipper or a belly, but the whales were too far away to even be close to the sails. Still, Caleb tried with all his might to reach for the whales, and throughout that entire time he had a big smile on his face. He never looked happier, and I was happy to see him like this. I didn't want to admit that I liked his company sometimes, but we were family, after all, and we had to tolerate each other so, might as well try to enjoy it.

These rare moments of happiness together would be few, however. I had a job to protect the islands, and it was a tough one. Knowing now that the islands could attack and self-destruct if they were in grave danger put me on edge. I could understand why Father didn't tell me, but it was ... rather unsettling.

If something bigger than the Black Sting came to attack us, my crew and I needed to be ready. I wasn't going to let my guard down as I did before. What happened at the island may not have been entirely my fault, but I did have a duty to protect everyone here. I don't want to feel like a failure and sit back and do nothing, so I would continue to do my job for the islands, the people, and for my brother.

"Ah, the whales are going away!" Caleb cried. He jumped up once more, but caught nothing but the air. "Bye, bye, Blubbys!" He waved to them as they disappeared from the clouds. He twirled to me and rocked on the balls of his feet.

"I want to see them again soon!" he announced while pumping his fists in the air.

"That may be difficult," I said. "We're lucky we were able to catch the whales; they hide from humans a lot."

"Why do they hide?" Caleb tilted his head.

"They're a bit scared of us," I answered. I couldn't tell him the truth.

"Why would they be scared?"

"I don't know, but if you behave like a good kid, they might sing to you again," I assured him, even though it was definitely a lie. I just wanted to end the conversation and get Caleb to quiet down.

"Oh, okay!" Caleb said. "I'll behave!"

"Good." I patted his head and nudged him forward. "Why don't you try to catch some more fireflies?"

"Okay!" Caleb clapped his hands and ran over to play with the fireflies.

"Don't squish them!" I called to him, but I it was certain that soon, he would come dashing back with his hands covered in tiny body parts. I cringed at the image and turned back to the sky.

Another shooting star flew by.

"Captain." Fable's voice brought me from my thoughts. She saluted me once she approached.

"What is it?"

"There's a matter that I need to discuss to you about," Fable said in a grim tone. "It's about Gideon."

"Gideon?" My eyebrows knitted together, and I noticed that Mark's face paled. "Did something happen?"

Fable opened her mouth, but then noted Mark's reaction. Mark scampered away as if he saw something frightful, and that seemed to change Fable's own demeanor. However, she ran a hand through her hair and continued, "When you and ... Eamon were gone, Gideon and a few others tried to kill us. But ... the Vultures they ... murdered them instead."

My mental balance became uncertain for a second, but I swiftly composed myself. "Did you tell my father or anyone about this?"

"No." Fable shook her head. "People only think Gideon went missing ..."

"Missing ..." I repeated in a whisper. "You said that he tried to kill you guys, why would he ...?"

"He thought we weren't capable of protecting the island, that we were traitors, so he took his anger out on us."

My concern slipped into a silent rage, and I inhaled slowly to steady myself. "Did you recognize anyone else with him?"

"No, I didn't," Fable said. "So ... should we tell them —"

"It's too late to tell them anything else. They're missing, so that's that." I cut her off.

Fable stared at me wordlessly, but, in the end, she bowed her head and said, "Very well, Captain."

I turned my back on Fable and faced the sky. I wasn't sure if I made the right choice, but Fable had already told others that Gideon was missing. Besides, who was going to miss that monster, anyway? Father was right about him: He was going to kill my crew, so how could I not be glad that he was gone?

"Is there anything else you want to report to me?" I asked as I glanced back at Fable.

"No."

"Alright." Before Fable walked off, I stopped her. "One moment, Fable ... I have a favor to ask of you."

"What is it?"

"Since Eamon is absent, as far as we know, would you consider being my temporary chief mate for the time being?"

Fable's eyes widened with surprise. "Of course, Captain, thank you. I will do my best." She saluted me and I smiled.

"Very good."

I turned back to Caleb, who was still trying to catch fireflies. Edna and Mark had also joined in to help. Caleb jumped and danced and acted out how any six-year-old would act in front of flashing bright lights. He was happy; that was all that really mattered. I went up to him and bent down to his level.

"Are you having fun?" I asked.

"Yes!" Caleb said. "Do you wanna catch some fireflies with me?"

"Uh …" I paused, but then shrugged. "Sure, whatever."

"Great! First one to catch eleventy-one wins!"

"Don't you mean eleven?"

"No! Eleventy-one!" Caleb held up some fingers.

"You're holding up six fingers."

"No, I'm not, eleventy one!" Caleb stomped his foot. He was about to throw a tantrum and I didn't want to deal with that.

"Alright, alright, eleventy-one," I huffed with defeat. Why were kids so dumb?

"Great!" Caleb jumped up. "Ready and go, go, go!"

Caleb reached his hand up to snatch a firefly, but he missed. I just stood around, glancing at the fireflies that drifted by me. *Might as well play Caleb's game so he doesn't go crazy.* I sighed and cupped my hands open. Immediately, a firefly drifted into my hands.

"Eh? How did you do that?" Caleb asked.

"I didn't do anything," I admitted. "I just held my hands out."

Caleb cupped his cheeks and whispered, "You must be made of magic."

"Sure, Caleb, sure." I just went with Caleb's weird fantasy, but considering that I had gone through some weird events, what was fantasy anymore?

•　　　•　　　•

We continued to catch fireflies until it was Caleb's bedtime. I sent him inside one of our extra cabins and tucked him in. He fell asleep quickly, although it was no surprise since he had been running around and squealing so much.

I watched him sleep for a bit, listening to his quiet snoring. He really was cuter when he was asleep. He had curled up in a ball with his red mane all over his head. Caleb really needed a brush, seriously.

I glanced out of the window to see the ship slowly drifting by the clouds. The window was open, so a cool breeze swept in. Caleb shuddered from the cold, but went back to sleep. I closed the window so it wouldn't disturb him, but he didn't seem to mind too much. He was deep in slumber, anyway. I wished I could fall asleep that quickly. Lucky brat.

A smile crossed my lips at the thought. He was a brat. He could be the most annoying little thing ever, but he was still my brother. I patted his head and my hand got lost in that fiery mane. I was tempted to just get out a brush and comb that monstrous hair of his, but I didn't want to deal with him if he woke up.

I returned to the deck to find that my entire crew had gone off to sleep. It was me alone. Just me. It was fine. I preferred to be alone. Here, with my thoughts.

I decided to climb up the mast and sit on top of it. I've never done it before and, since no one was looking, then what the hell? I climbed up the mast and sat on the tallest point on the ship.

The fireflies had disappeared. Now there was only the moon to accompany me. It sat there on top of a group of gray clouds, staring at me like a wide, white eye. It shone so brightly that it could almost compete against the sun's rays. But, unlike the sun, the moon was more beautiful. It didn't turn into a ghastly red or anything. The moon just sat there, showering its silver rays on my now sleeping ship.

ABOUT THE AUTHOR

Lauren Massuda wanted to be a writer ever since her grade school principal read her poem to the entire school. She was 12 at the time, and the memory sticks to her to this day. Lauren graduated from Goucher with a B.A in English and a Creative Writing concentration. She also participated in UCLA's Professional TV Writing Program and turned one of her scripts into a 120-page screenplay. She hopes that one day, her script could be transferred to the silver screen, but she's content with the fact that she can share her debut novel to the world.

YOU MIGHT ALSO ENJOY

GRIMAULKIN
BOOK ONE OF THE "GRIMAULKIN" SERIES
by L. A. Jacob

Treading the straight and narrow is not natural to one who summons demons.

JUST A BIT OF MAGIC
by Barb Bissonette

Every morning, Jenny Smith stares into her magic mirror, searching for glimpses of two girls. Today, she is joyful with anticipation, knowing that this is the day they will materialize in her village.

SOMETIMES AFTER DARK
by J Dark

Explore the past, future, and triumphs of the human soul.

Available from Water Dragon Publishing in
hardcover, trade paperback, digital, and audio editions
waterdragonpublishing.com

Made in the USA
Columbia, SC
04 April 2022

58461895R00169